# Bob: The Right Hand of God

## A novel by Pat Bertram

*Bob: The Right Hand of God*

© 2020 Pat Bertram
Print ISBN 978-1-949267-58-7
ebook ISBN 978-1-949267-59-4

Other books by Pat Bertram:

*Grief: The Inside Story*
*Grief: The Great Yearning*
*Unfinished*
*Madame ZeeZee's Nightmare*
*More Deaths Than One*
*Daughter Am I*
*Light Bringer*
*A Spark of Heavenly Fire*

**STAIRWAY PRESS—APACHE JUNCTION**

Cover Design by Guy D. Corp, www.GrafixCorp.com

# STAIRWAY⫤PRESS

**www.StairwayPress.com**
1000 West Apache Trail
Suite 126
Apache Junction, AZ 85120 USA

Another one for Jeff

# Chapter 1

CHET THOMLIN SCOWLED at the television. He clicked the remote and clicked again, trying to lose himself in the glow of violence and canned laughter and sexual innuendo, but he couldn't get thoughts of Isabel out of his head. He'd asked, told, pleaded, *demanded* that she leave everything alone. She agreed. Yet he could hear her in his kitchen, rearranging the cabinets again.

He had no other choice but to tell her to go. Maybe this time she'd pay attention.

*Yeah, right. And maybe the world is coming to an end.*

Hearing footsteps draw near, he winced. He should have bought a television for his bedroom months ago when he first realized she wasn't going to leave, but it had seemed too much like giving her permission to stay. And now he was trapped.

Isabel came and perched on the arm of his easy chair.

"What are you watching?"

He focused his gaze on the screen. A young woman, whose studied perfection made her look as though she were dipped in plastic, was denouncing the latest White House scandal.

"Makes me sick." Chet clicked off the television. "When one of us little people breaks the law, it's a crime. When the big, important people break the law, it's a scandal."

Isabel made a grab for the remote, but he held it out of reach.

"I wanted to watch that."

"We have to talk, Mom."

"I asked you not to call me that. Do I look like a mom to you?"

He had to admit she didn't. She'd been waxed, creamed, botoxed, and still managed to look fresh and natural. And beautiful. Her artfully streaked blonde hair framed a perfect oval face and periwinkle-blue eyes.

He stiffened his spine.

"I need my space, Isabel. I keep telling you that, but you don't listen."

Her eyes widened in a show of innocence.

"I never encroach on your space. I know what it's like to have an overbearing mother." She ruffled his hair. "I've tried to be your friend, which is more than my mother did. She smothered me, needing everything done her way. You're lucky to have me for a mother."

"It's time for you to go home. You came for a week's visit six months ago—" A ghastly thought struck him. "You didn't sell the house, did you?"

"No, though with prices in Castle Rock the way they are, I could get a fortune for it. Since you won't come back home to live, maybe I should sell it, buy a house here in Denver big enough for you to have your own suite of rooms. Or we could get side-by-side condos."

He took a deep breath and let it out slowly. He didn't want to be cruel, but at times that was the only way to get through to her.

"I like my apartment. I just want to be alone in it."

She gave him a vague look, and he wondered if she was on something. He sniffed. Not pot. Could be diet pills.

"You only live forty-five minutes away, you can visit whenever you want. And I'll come for dinner once a week like always. I'll even cook."

"Don't do me any favors. I just hope someday you have a child of your own so you will know what I have suffered. Are we done talking? Give me the remote. I want to watch the news."

He handed her the remote and sagged back in the chair.

Isabel turned on the television.

The plastic woman said brightly, "This afternoon a jury convicted Ricky Warneke of murdering and mutilating three women."

The screen went black.

"Something must be wrong with the cable," Isabel said. "I'll call them tomorrow."

After thirty seconds of whistles, hums, and buzzes, the picture came back on. Instead of the anchorperson, the head of a gnomish man with a round, bespectacled face, a bald pate, and a receding chin filled the screen.

"I am Bob, the Right Hand of God. As part of the galactic renewal program, God has accepted an offer from a development company on the planet Xerxes to turn Earth into a theme park. Not even God can stop progress, but to tell the truth, He's glad of the change. He's never been satisfied with Earth. For one thing, there are too many humans on it. He's decided to eliminate anyone who isn't nice, and because He's God, He knows who you are; you can't talk your way out of it as you humans normally do. For another thing—"

Isabel clicked off the television and stood up.

"We must have missed the news."

Clutching the remote, she stalked to the guestroom and shut the door.

Chet continued to stare at the darkened screen. He would have liked to see more of Bob—looked like it could have been an interesting science fiction movie—but dealing with Isabel exhausted him. He didn't have the energy to get up and manually turn the television back on.

Chet took the water and food bowls out of the dishwasher he'd installed in the back room of his pet store and dealt them out on the long wooden table. The cinderblock room did triple duty as an office, stockroom, and work area, which made moving around difficult, but he didn't mind. It meant the animals up front could have bigger quarters, and they needed the space more than he did.

The orange marmalade cat jumped onto the table.

"I don't know how to get her to leave," Chet said.

3

The cat perked up its ears, but never took its eyes off the bowls. "She's my mother. I can't just throw her out."

He hefted the bag of dry cat food, then paused, arrested by the image of himself pushing Isabel out the door of his apartment. He erased the tempting idea from his mind. When he was a child, she'd worked two jobs to support him, and he owed her. But maybe he could talk her into taking a vacation; retirement seemed to bore her, and a trip would give her something to do.

The cat butted his hand with its head.

Chet laughed.

"All right, little partner. I'll get back to work."

He filled two bowls with cat food, four with dog food, one with chicken feed, and one with a special formula for potbellied pigs. After filling the rest of the bowls with water, he loaded them on a stainless steel service cart and trundled the cart out to the sales floor, the orange cat following close on his heels.

The sight of the cages, terrariums, and aquariums stabbed his conscience. He tried to create a pleasant environment for the animals in his charge by using full-spectrum lights, lush tropical plants, and heat turned up a notch too high for his comfort. Still, the poor creatures lived in pens, and they had done nothing to deserve imprisonment except fall victim to the capriciousness of their former owners. The snakes, lizards, and tortoises had grown too big. The seeing-eye dog had gone blind. Last year's Easter chicks had become unfluffy chickens. The cute little puppies had grown large and ugly. The supposedly spayed cat had gotten pregnant. The tropical birds grew too raucous. The potbellied pig didn't like to be held. The Colorado River toad lost its appeal when its owner got sick after licking it to get high.

A few, like the European barn owl with the broken beak and the Australian frilled lizard with the bad leg had belonged to zoos until they became infirm.

Only the orange cat chose to be there. The feline had been waiting at the shop when Chet came to work two months ago and had slipped inside when Chet opened the door. After inspecting every inch of the place, the tom lifted a leg in each corner, gave one final stare at the animals in the cages, then plopped down on the stack of cat beds and took a nap. The orange cat had lived at the store ever since.

As Chet distributed the bowls, then fed the fish, birds, and small reptiles, he thought about the refuge he hoped to own one day. Though he loved his store, *Used Pets*, he wanted more for his lodgers than incarceration. He let them out of their cages when he could, but it didn't often prove feasible with customers bumbling around, and of course, there was the problem with some of the creatures wanting to chew on the rest of the creatures. If he could get the down payment for a place with plenty of acreage, like a farm or a ranch, he could apply for grants and solicit donations. That money would allow him to create special habitats where discarded pets of all kinds and old or unwanted animals from zoos and circuses could roam free. Everyone, even the fur and feather people, deserved liberty.

A chime intruded into Chet's thoughts. A second passed before he recognized the sound as the bell over the door heralding a visitor. He seldom heard the peal so clearly; usually the clamor of the birds and animals drowned out the fainter noise.

John Pellizari, the wiry forty-three-year-old butcher who owned the shop two doors down, dumped a large parcel on the service cart. The heavy white paper wrapping did nothing to contain the reek of meat scraps, fat, entrails, and dead mice.

Chet wrinkled his nose.

"My daily reminder of why I'm a vegetarian."

John laughed.

"You and me both. Sally wants you to come this Sunday and spend Easter with us. It's supposed to be warm, so we're going to have our first cookout of the season. Garbanzo burgers with Bermuda onions and a big salad—your favorite."

"Sounds great, but I don't know if I can."

"Why not? Oh. Your mother. She still at your place?"

Chet nodded.

"I'd invite her, too, but the last time we had her over she made

Sally cry."

Sally, John's wife, had the bubbly personality of a perennial cheerleader, but Isabel had found the younger woman's weak spot: the twenty extra pounds she retained after the birth of her sixth child. Chet had been appalled at the pointed remarks Isabel had shot at her. He still didn't know why his mother had been so unpleasant to Sally—until then, she had saved her barbs for his girlfriends.

John gave him a sympathetic look.

"You're never going to find a woman to marry with her hanging around. You turned thirty-five last month; you should be starting a family of your own."

"I know, but I don't want a wife. Don't they say that guys end up marrying somebody like their mothers? I couldn't stand that."

"There's always divorce."

"Now that's romantic. 'Honey, will you marry me? I promise to love you until you turn into my mother, then I'll divorce you and live happily ever after.'"

John chuckled. "Works for me."

"Don't let Sally hear you say that. And anyway, what if we had kids? I would be tied to my mother-clone forever and ever and *ever*."

"I feel your pain. Let me know about Sunday, okay?"

"Definitely. And thank you for..." He nodded at the parcel.

John started to leave, hesitated, and turned back.

"Does it feel a little strange to you today?"

"Strange how?"

"I don't know. Just a creepy feeling I have, like a storm's coming." He twitched his shoulders. "Probably nothing. Maybe I let that Bob thing get to me."

"What Bob thing?" Chet asked.

"Some guy pulled an April Fool's prank last night. Hacked into the television signal. Claimed he was The Right Hand of God. Silly, but I've been feeling creepy all day."

"I thought it was a movie."

"Nope. A friend of mine at Channel Ten told me they lost the signal for about five minutes."

Chet shivered.

"Now I've got the creeps. Thanks a lot."

After John left, a man in jogging shorts entered.

"I saw a flyer down at my health club about jogging with a pal. I need the exercise, but I hate running alone. Thought I'd sign up for your program."

Chet gave the man a short form to fill out—name, address, phone and credit card numbers—then introduced him to the dogs.

The man flinched when they came to an especially unattractive and ungainly animal with grizzled fur and red eyes.

"What kind of dog is that? I've never seen anything like it."

"He's his own dog. He looks vicious, but he's gentle, a bit of a clown, and loves to run."

The man pointed to the German shepherd.

"What about him?"

"He's gentle, too, and a good runner, but he's blind."

"Oh." The man bounced on the balls of his feet for a minute, looking from one to the other. "Okay if I borrow both of them?"

"No problem."

The two dogs quivered with excitement as Chet let them out of their cages and fastened their leashes. He opened the door, and they were out in a flash, towing the jogger along behind.

Chet smiled. Finding good homes for used dogs and other pets was a challenge, but he'd come up with a few marketing strategies that worked. Jog-With-a-Pal, for example. Several people had become so fond of their jogging companions that they offered them a home. Same with the Pet-a-Pal and Hug-a-Pet programs he'd initiated at the senior centers in the area.

The rank odor of meat reminded him he hadn't finished feeding his charges. He took the butcher's parcel into the back and portioned it out as quickly as he could. Snakes, lizards, and other carnivores had to eat, but still...yuck.

At least John brought dead stuff; Chet didn't know if he could bear feeding the creatures live food.

The chiming of the bell over the door reverberated through the quiet store. All day, the animals, especially the birds, had been uncharacteristically silent. Chet thought John was right about something strange going on. But what? Not a storm. Usually the extra electricity in the air preceding a storm made the creatures animated, not lethargic. Unless, perhaps, the storm was gathering strength, like a tidal wave sucking water away from the shore before crashing down upon it.

Deciding he had too active an imagination, Chet went to wait on his customers—a woman and a little boy in search of a puppy.

"I'm sorry. I don't sell puppies."

While managing a pet store in the mall, he learned the horrors of puppy mills, and now that he had his own store, he refused to support those businesses.

"Kitty!"

The boy toddled over to the orange cat and squatted down to study it.

The cat stared back, its emerald eyes narrowed to slits.

"Does it have a name?" the woman asked.

"I'm sure it does."

"Well? What is it?"

"I don't know. He never told me."

Her brows drew together.

"How much do you want for it?"

"He's not for sale; he's my business partner. But I have a litter of kittens that will be weaned in another week."

"I really wanted a puppy."

"Would you please take one step to your right, Ma'am?"

"What?"

Chet gestured to the knee-high frilled lizard that had released itself from the cage and, on its hind legs, was running laps from wall to wall.

Stifling a shriek, the woman scooped up the boy and scurried outside.

Chet reached into a pocket for the small bag of lemon drops he always carried and popped one in his mouth while he watched the little dragon. The zoo had kept it in a cage too small to allow it freedom of movement, and a muscle in a hind leg had atrophied, but now that it got plenty of exercise, the leg seemed to have healed.

When the lizard finished its laps and scampered back to its cage, Chet looked down at the orange cat.

"Would you watch the store for me? I'd like to run next door to see if Rosemary has any stale flowers for the tortoises."

The cat licked a paw then washed behind an ear.

"I'll take that as a yes."

Rosemary Gibbs greeted Chet with a broad smile. He knew she liked him, and he felt comfortable with her, but they had never dated. And as long as his mother was staying with him, they never would. It wouldn't be fair to Rosemary.

She handed him a bouquet of tulips, irises, and daffodils that had begun to turn brown around the edges.

"I've been saving these for you."

"Wow. Perfect. Thank you."

She giggled, sounding younger than her thirty years.

"I've never known anyone to be so pleased at getting a bunch of old flowers."

"It doesn't matter how they look. It's how they taste."

"That's what everyone says." She drew in a breath and exhaled with a flurry of words. "Will you go out with me tonight?"

"I'm sorry, I can't."

"When your mother leaves, will you?"

"How did you know...oh, John. He told you about my mother, didn't he?"

"I asked him why you didn't have a girlfriend. I mean, you're a good guy, and you're sort of cute." She blushed. "You must think I'm a total idiot."

"I think you're smart and very pretty."

And her eyes seemed to look on the world with amusement. Why shouldn't he go out with her? He didn't have to be a monk just because his mother wouldn't leave.

No, he had to wait; he couldn't bear his mother trampling over another budding romance.

He raised a hand in farewell.

"I'd better go check on the store. Talk to you later."

A kid in his late teens or early twenties with drooping trousers that exposed his dingy blue boxer short waited by the front counter, a wire cage at his feet. Approximately eighteen inches high, the enclosure appeared to be filled with scarlet, blue and yellow feathers.

A low-pitched squeak came from the mass of feathers, and Chet realized a live scarlet macaw had been scrunched into the cage. He clenched his hands and glared at the kid.

*I'd like to stuff you into a space half your size and see how you like it.*

The kid grinned, displaying large teeth and a tongue ring. "Some...dude told me you buy used pets. How much will you give me for this...um...this parrot?"

"A hundred."

"A hundred dollars? You trying to cheat me? It's worth at least a thousand."

The bird looked half-dead from mistreatment and starvation. When raised in a loving atmosphere, a macaw was an affectionate creature, but when mistreated, it could be vicious. Even if the bird survived, it would probably be unsalable.

*You little shit.*

"A hundred and twenty. Take it or leave it."

"You can't do that."

"I'm not the one trying to peddle an almost dead bird."

Chet started to walk away.

"Okay, okay, but I want cash."

Chet strode to the cash register and pulled out six twenties. The kid grabbed the money and bolted from the store, almost tripping on his pant legs.

The orange cat circled the cage. The macaw let out another feeble squeak.

Chet lifted the cage and gently set it on the counter.

"You'll be free in just a minute, little one."

He went into the back room for a dish of nuts and seeds, a peeled banana, and a bowl of water. He set them in front of the cage, then opened the door and stepped back.

The bird did not move.

Maybe he should try to pull it out? No. One thing the creature didn't need was more rough handling. It would come out when ready.

While he waited for the macaw to extricate itself, he popped another lemon drop into his mouth. The candy dissolved into tart nothingness, and still the macaw didn't move.

Without warning, the exotic birds in their oversized cages flapped their wings, squawking and screaming. The dogs yipped. The snakes coiled and uncoiled. The fish churned their waters.

And from a distance came the sound of gunfire.

# Chapter 2

*GUNFIRE?* COULDN'T BE. This was Denver, not a war zone. Must be kids playing with firecrackers. Chet Thomlin stepped outside his store, turned toward the bursts of sound, then stopped and stared at the sky.

A dense gray shape, perhaps a mile wide, moved rapidly in his direction. Bits of the gray seemed to be breaking off the mass and plummeting to Earth.

*So that's what people were shooting. But what was it?*

Rosemary came to stand beside him, her eyes round.

"Is that a spaceship?"

Chet laughed.

"Yeah. From the planet Xerxes. Come to turn Earth into a theme park."

Her brown eyes grew even wider.

"Really? How do you know?"

"Bad joke. Something I heard on television last night."

The pops and blasts of gunfire grew louder, and the gray mass flew closer.

"My God," Chet breathed. A mothership from the planet Xerxes might be unbelievable, but this…this was impossible.

"Oh," Rosemary said, disappointment tingeing her voice. "Birds."

"Not just any birds. Passenger pigeons."

"Can't be. They're extinct."

"Yet here they are. So beautiful..."

The bluish gray bodies with the soft rose throats and breasts looked exactly like the drawings he'd seen.

"Oh, ick." Rosemary held out an arm. A blotch of white bird dung stained her pale green shirt. "I'm going back to the shop."

"Good idea," Chet said absently, recalling accounts he'd read of so much dung falling that it lay two inches deep on the ground. A biological storm, the birds and their acidic droppings destroyed crops, forests, even dwellings. If humans hadn't killed them off, they might have become extinct anyway when the ever-growing flocks annihilated their own habitats.

The birds flew directly overhead, blocking the sun. In the sudden gloom, Chet shivered, but he had no desire to go inside for a jacket. Over the increasing gunfire, he could hear the flapping of millions of wings, like the chugging of an engine.

Humans had last heard that sound more than a century ago. Where had the birds been hiding? And why were they so far from their old migratory paths? They had never been sighted west of the Rockies.

Until now.

A line from a poem he'd studied in high school flashed through his mind.

*Out of the everywhere into the here.*

He found himself smiling, pleased with the image.

Guns going off nearby jarred him back to reality. On the other side of the street, men and even a few women and children were shooting at the pigeons with rifles and handguns. They didn't seem to be aiming, just firing blindly at the flock. Hundreds of birds fell. Cars screeched to a halt with windshields shattered by the rain of bodies. Horns blared. Dogs barked as they darted between cars to retrieve the kill.

A fifteen-inch-long pigeon thudded to the sidewalk in front of Chet, its lovely body broken and bloody, its orange eyes dull.

Feeling sick to his stomach, he screamed, "Stop it! Leave them

13

alone!"

But the din swallowed his words.

The flock was a relatively small one.

In 1873, a continuous stream of passenger pigeons flew over Saginaw, Michigan from 7:30 in the morning till 4:00 in the afternoon, but this flock streamed over Denver for less than an hour. Within two hours it was out of sight, roosting in a mountain forest, perhaps.

Skirting fallen birds, het walked home from work. So much carnage. For what? Fun? He wished he could secede from the human race; he didn't want to be associated with a species that could take enjoyment from such wanton destruction.

When he reached his apartment building, a six-story rectangle of yellow brick, he noticed the empty space where his mother usually parked.

Hope lightened his step. Her absence would go a long way toward balancing the defeats of the day. Not only had he done nothing to stop the killing; he had been unable to entice the scarlet macaw out of the cage.

He unlocked his apartment door. Isabel came to greet him, a mischievous look in her eyes like a child who has done something wrong but doesn't care.

"You're still here," Chet said flatly.

The light died out of her eyes.

"I thought you'd be pleased."

"Where's your car?"

"At the service station for a trip check. I want to make sure I get home safely."

"You only live forty-five minutes away. Why—never mind."

He brushed past her, intending to watch the news, but didn't see the remote on the coffee table or the couch. His mother must still have it. He didn't know why she insisted on controlling the device, but he was sick of her games.

"Isabel! What did you do with the remote?"

"You always come in and plop down in front of the television, and I thought tonight we'd go out to dinner."

"I'm not hungry."

Her eyes teared up.

"I just want us to be a family."

Chet turned away, unmoved. He'd seen her use that tactic too many times before.

"The remote?" he said.

"It's on my bedside table. I'll get it."

Re-entering the living room, she flounced onto the couch and turned on the television.

A pretty man was saying, with patented sincerity, "…warns you that wild birds carry diseases. Don't touch them with your bare hands, and don't eat them. The police have issued a reminder that it is illegal to shoot firearms within the city limits. They detained twelve men and two women on a related charge, but released them on their own recognizance. Ornithologists from the University of Colorado say that global warming caused massive numbers of doves to migrate. Because the doves' usual habitats—"

"Doves?" Chet paced, too agitated to sit still. "Global warming? Passenger pigeons flew overhead today, not doves. I saw them. Doves are smaller, not as brightly colored, and they have dark brown eyes."

"Why do you do that?" Isabel pursed her lips. "You always have to be contrary. Those birds were doves. It said so on the news. Oh, not again!"

Chet glanced at the television. The screen had gone dark, and it was buzzing and whistling. When the noises stopped and the picture came back on, the head of the gnomish man filled the screen.

"God is not pleased."

"Oh, sheesh. It's that same silly show."

Isabel directed the remote at the television and clicked.

The gnome still peered out at them.

"Contrary to what you have been told, you did see passenger pigeons. A test to—"

15

"What the hell?"

Isabel gripped the remote with both hands and clicked again.

"You humans today are so proud of how civilized you are but, like your predecessors, you slaughtered needlessly and with great glee."

Isabel slammed the remote against her palm.

"This stupid thing doesn't work."

"You're going to break it." Chet held out a hand. "Give it to me."

Isabel reached an arm back as if to lob the remote at the television.

Chet spoke through clenched teeth.

"Give. Me. The. Remote,"

The gnome rolled his eyes heavenward.

"The things I have to put up with. Give him the remote, Isabel."

Isabel froze, arm still in the air.

"Did you hear how he talked to me, Chet? Are you going to let him get away with that?"

"Isabel, would you please shut up and give Chet the remote."

She looked from the screen to Chet, then silently handed over the remote.

Chet felt a pressure in his ears as if he were flying too high in an airplane without oxygen, and nothing seemed quite real. Was he in a hypnotic trance? He must be. He thought he heard the television giving orders to his mother. And she obeyed.

"What a dodo," Isabel muttered.

The gnome smiled. "Thank you."

Isabel's nostrils flared.

"Hey, Jack-in-the-Box, that was an insult."

"Not to me it isn't. Not to God it isn't. The dodo was a sacred bird—kind, gentle, intelligent—so God protected it by putting it on an island where it would have no predators. Then you went and slaughtered it."

"What are you talking about? I wasn't even alive then."

Chet cradled his head in his hands. This couldn't be happening.

16

Maybe his mother had finally pushed him over the edge.

The gnome shrugged.

"What difference does that make? You are all alike. If your ancestors hadn't killed it, you would have, the way you killed the passenger pigeons today. To you humans, gentleness and docility equate to stupidity. You only revere aggression as intelligence. And my name is not Jack. I am Bob, the Right Hand of God."

The television clicked off.

Chet opened his mouth wide and forced a yawn. The pressure in his ears returned to normal, but the feeling of not being quite real remained.

First the passenger pigeons, then Bob. No wait—Bob was first.

*Did that mean the galactic renewal program was genuine?*

He tried to remember what he'd heard last night. Something about God not being satisfied with Earth because there were too many humans on it and how he was going to eliminate anyone who wasn't nice.

A chill crept through him.

"I don't think Bob or God likes us very much. I think we should be worried."

"You go ahead and think what you want. You always do anyway." Isabel rose. "The hell with Bob. I'm going to bed."

A voice, so faint it might have been the hum of electricity, seemed to issue from the television.

"I heard that," it said.

# Chapter 3

CHET WOKE FEELING out of sync with the world, as if it were spinning in one direction and he in another. Perhaps he'd feel more grounded at his store. The animals were real. And they needed him.

Stepping over a bloodstain on the sidewalk, he wondered what happened to the bodies of the pigeons murdered yesterday. Had people gathered them to eat? With meat prices so high, it must have seemed like manna from heaven.

He passed a bearded man in ragged jeans and a filthy coat pushing a grocery cart half full of dead birds. Vegetarianism was an ethical choice, he reminded himself, a choice some people didn't have the luxury of making.

And some people just didn't care. A man and a woman in matching silk warm-up outfits flitted about clutching shopping bags emblazoned with logos from Cherry Creek Mall. They checked behind bushes and called to each other when they found a pigeon, like children playing a party game.

Swallowing his distaste, Chet hurried past them and soon reached his storefront where Rosemary, John, and a stranger holding a large cardboard box stood deep in conversation. He stopped to listen.

The man with the box spoke in a high, excited voice.

"I tell you, it's true. I was trying to watch television last night, and the dang kids were making so much noise I couldn't hear the news. My eldest had that thump-thump-thumping music on full blast, the two youngest were fighting and arguing, and the wife was screaming at them to do their homework. I finally lost it and shouted, 'Shut up! Shut—' I didn't even finish my second shut up. This guy on television—called himself Bob—pointed a remote at us, and everything went still. The music stopped, the screaming, the fighting. My vocal cords froze. Couldn't utter a sound."

John waved a dismissive hand.

"It must have been the power of suggestion. The whole thing is an April Fool's joke. Someone hacked into the television signal or the satellite transmission. You'd think a person that smart could come up with a more original story than aliens."

"Could a hacker turn on a television?" Rosemary asked. "I had it off last night so I could read, but it came on all by itself and that actor started talking about the pigeons being a test, and that God wasn't pleased."

The stranger shook his head.

"Not an actor."

"Sure he is. I saw him in an old movie last week. You know, the one with that other guy and that actress. What's her name?"

"My television turns on by itself all the time," John said. "My next-door neighbor's garage door opener is on the same frequency. I better go open up." He pivoted, and a look of surprise came over his face. "Chet! I didn't see you standing there. Why didn't you say something?"

"I didn't want to interrupt."

"You the owner of the pet store?" the stranger asked.

Chet nodded.

The stranger gave him the box.

"I found this dove in my yard. It's still alive, but it acts dazed. Maybe you can help it. I've heard you're good with animals."

"I'm not a veterinarian, but I'll see what I can do."

The stranger trotted to a white Chevy Malibu and drove off.

Balancing the box on his hip with one hand, Chet dug in a pocket for his keys and unlocked the door.

Rosemary followed him inside.

"Did you hear what we talked about?"

"I heard."

He set the box on the counter a few feet away from the wire cage. The macaw still had not ventured out, but the food dishes were empty. Chet smiled, glad that the bird had finally eaten, then he glanced at Rosemary.

Her bleak expression erased his grin.

"I live on the fourteenth floor," she said. "There's no way a garage opener could have turned on my television. Do you know what's going on?"

"I haven't a clue."

"Me neither. She gave him a tremulous smile. "I don't like weird stuff. I hope things get back to normal soon."

After she left, Chet opened the box. The bird—a passenger pigeon, not a dove—seemed to be uninjured. He transferred it to a cage and supplied it with food and water. Popping a lemon drop in his mouth, he studied the legendary creature. Under the full-spectrum fluorescent lights, the back of its neck gleamed metallic bronze, green, and purple.

The bell chimed. A young man in a business suit but no tie charged through the doorway.

"I need to buy me a pet, man. You got, like, a really old or broken down one? I gotta prove to that Bob guy that I'm nice." He pointed to the orange cat, which was eyeing the pigeon. "I'll take that scruffy cat."

The cat's head jerked around, and it stared at the young man. Its peridot eyes turned to jade.

The young man took a step back.

"Whoa."

The cat raised its nose in the air and returned to its contemplation of the pigeon.

"What else you got? How about that ugly black and white dog?"

"That's a pygmy pot-bellied pig."

"Whatever, I'll take it."

Chet put the potbellied pig in a carrying case, went to the back for the bag of its specially formulated diet, then snagged a pamphlet on the care and feeding of pot-bellied pigs from under the counter and handed it to the customer.

The young man leafed through it.

"A pig. Cool. Then it won't bark."

An unfamiliar voice, scolding and chattering, brought Chet from the back room where he'd been cleaning up after the morning feed. The macaw hadn't moved, but the pigeon flapped around in its cage, vocalizing its displeasure.

A thrill rose in Chet's chest. He had a live, healthy passenger pigeon, not a stuffed one like the Smithsonian's Martha. He would never have gone out and trapped the bird—the stranger brought it to him. A gift. And anyway, the creature was extinct, a living fossil, so that gave him reason enough to keep it.

*Keep it?*

Chet couldn't believe what he'd been thinking. What was wrong with him? How could he, of all people, be falling into the human trap of wanting to keep a rare and beautiful thing for himself? If the bird were disabled or bred in captivity and unable to take care of itself in the wild, he might be able to justify keeping the pigeon, but there was nothing wrong with the bird except a frantic need to be free.

Sick at heart, he donned a pair of gauntlets and carried the cage outside. The pigeon pecked at the gloves while he opened the door of the cage. When he finished unhinging it, he stepped aside. Without a moment's hesitation, the bird flew out of the cage, soared over the building, and headed for the mountains.

Chet watched until it was long out of sight.

John's voice startled him.

"You okay?"

"I'm fine, now."

"Want to get some lunch? I haven't had a single customer all morning. People must be stuffing themselves on dove. I hope they don't get sick—those were strange-looking birds."

Even John thought they were doves? Chet didn't know if that was the influence of television or if passenger pigeons were out of the realm of possibility for someone as down-to-earth as the butcher.

"I could eat some lunch. Let me put the cage away first."

John held the door for him, then went inside and laid a small white parcel on the counter.

"Sorry there's not as much as usual.

"Any contribution helps. Thanks."

"Have you found out about Easter yet?"

Chet sighed.

"My mother is still at my place."

"What a bitch, what a bitch, what a bitch."

Chet and John stared at each other, then, laughing, turned to the macaw. It had pulled its head out from under its wing, stretched its tail out the door of the cage, and was chanting, "What a bitch, what a bitch, what a bitch."

"Did you teach it to say that?" John asked, still laughing.

"No. Just met it yesterday."

"Well, it sure seems to know your mother."

Chet took the stairs to his apartment on the fifth floor. He thought running the elevator for one person a waste of electricity, and he didn't mind the exercise, especially not tonight. It gave him time to rehearse what he was going to say to Isabel. He knew she hadn't gone home; he'd seen her silver Corolla in its usual parking spot.

The trouble was, he couldn't think of a single thing to tell her that he hadn't already said. Maybe he *would* have to push her out the door.

As soon as he stepped inside his apartment, Isabel came and planted her hands on her hips.

"Where have you been? They're talking about a terrorist attack. I've been calling and calling your cell phone all day, but you never answered. You're so selfish, just like your father. When he left, I had no one to share the responsibility with. You don't know how difficult that is, always worrying about you. Just because your son thinks he's grown up, that feeling doesn't go away. But how would you know? You're not a mother. All you do is think of yourself. What if something happened to you? What would I do?"

Keeping his tone mild, he said, "I didn't renew the cell phone contract."

"Then I won't be able to call you all the time."

"I know."

"Let's not worry about that now. We'll sign you up again tomorrow. Come on, I want to show you what they're talking about on the news. This is why I was so worried."

Chet advanced into the room and stood in front of the television.

The news anchor had a grave expression on his face, but his body seemed to vibrate with excitement.

"Homeland Security issued a bulletin stating that it's a federal crime to go on the airwaves and threaten the well being of the United States and its citizens. This behavior will not be tolerated."

A picture of the gnome's face appeared in the upper right-hand corner of the screen.

Deepening his voice, the anchor continued, "Homeland Security and the FBI are looking for this man, Bob, the self-proclaimed spokesperson for the terrorist organization G.O.D. If you have any information—"

"God is not amused," the picture of Bob said.

The anchor put a hand to his ear and looked off camera, his mouth forming the words, "Is anyone on the set?"

Chet backed up to the couch. Without taking his gaze off the screen, he sat.

*Could the anchor have told the truth?*

Commandeering the airwaves might be the work of terrorists, but would they have the technology to talk with viewers? To turn off human noise? To turn on televisions? And what about the passenger pigeons? Perhaps terrorists could have cloned one or two, but millions? And why? Were they planning on dunging us to death?

Inconceivable, but so was the alternative: that Bob told the truth.

"You humans have turned the earth into a toilet," the picture of Bob said. "An unflushed toilet. At first God found it interesting to watch the proliferation of new bacteria, but even a Supreme Being can only watch a septic tank for so long without wanting to puke. And believe me, you do not want God puking all over Earth.

"But you don't have to worry about that any more. The developers have signed the contracts. They have more money than God, and He is pleased that this time Earth will be created right. The first time He made it up as he went along, but now He knows better."

"You're telling me," Isabel said. "I mean, the appendix. What was that all about? Mine ruptured and I almost died."

Chet stared at his mother. He knew she lived in her own world, but he hadn't realized her total self-absorption. Couldn't she see that something very strange was going on? Maybe all the diet pills she took were making her irrational.

"And anyway," she said, "He can't be much of a God if the developers have more money than he does."

"It's just a saying, Mom."

"If He really was God, He wouldn't need money."

The picture of Bob's face zoomed out to fill the entire screen.

"He is not *the* God, the top God. He is an area supervisor God with more power than your puny brains can possibly fathom. But he is having a bit of a cash flow problem, which is why he's leasing Earth to the developers for a theme park."

Isabel laughed.

"B.O.B. Know what that means? Bottom of the barrel. Good archangels must be in short supply these days."

Bob gave a shake of his head.

"Isabel, be nice. Your life depends on it. I am Bob, the Right Hand of God. The galactic renewal program is at hand."

The screen went dark.

# Chapter 4

CHET POURED CINNAMON raisin granola into a yellow-flowered cereal bowl and drenched it with orange juice. From his place at the kitchen table, he could see the cloudless sky framed by the window, and he could hear the morning traffic five stories below.

The ordinariness of the day surprised him; he'd expected to wake up to a changed world.

*How silly was that!*

You'd think at his age he'd have learned not to believe anything on television, but somehow Bob and the galactic renewal program had slipped beneath his guard.

John was probably right about Bob perpetrating an April Fool's hoax. Hackers could have sophisticated equipment like voice activated computer technology and interactive television; if the past three days were any indication, they could do amazing things with them.

The television news team, putting the worst possible spin on the prank as they always did, called it terrorism. And in a way they were right. It sure had scared him.

*But what about the passenger pigeons?*

They weren't a hoax.

Oh, hell, what did he know? He'd only seen pictures of the pigeons, and besides, they were extinct. The birds that flew over Denver must have been doves flocked together in vast numbers looking for a more hospitable locale as the newscaster had said. Maybe they had even become so overpopulated that their physiology transmuted, like locusts. If any changes were coming to Earth, they had nothing to do with Bob and everything to do with the environment.

He spooned granola into his mouth and wondered if someday he'd be able to laugh at himself for being so credulous.

Isabel entered the kitchen and sniffed.

"How can you eat that stuff? Why don't you put milk on your cereal like everyone else?"

Chet ate another bite of granola. His mother made the same comment most mornings, so he saw no point in responding.

She fixed a cup of instant coffee, shoved it into the microwave, and slammed the door.

"What do I have to do to get some respect around here? You won't even talk to me. Maybe I'll leave. I've had enough of your abuse. At least in my own home I can do what I want."

She grabbed her coffee from the microwave and swept from the room.

Chet finished his breakfast, enjoying the unexpected respite from his mother's moods as much as the orange tang of his cereal, then set off for work.

As he walked, he looked for changes, but the houses, the trees, the street signs were the same ones he passed every day. The warm sun and the scent of lilacs filling the air clinched his belief that Bob was a hoax. The day was perfect, and perfectly ordinary.

At Used Pets, he unlocked the door, opened it, and inhaled the familiar odor, hot and musky. Though most people hated the smell of so many animals concentrated in one place, he found the aroma as pleasing as the scent of lilacs.

He listened to the screeches and squawks of the exotic birds for a moment, then turned on the light.

A quiet joy swept away all thoughts of the hoax.

The macaw had left the cage.

It perched on the counter in scarlet and royal blue splendor. The orange cat also perched on the counter, and the two creatures were staring at each other, the cat's normally green eyes reflecting the yellow of the macaw's.

Chet held himself immobile, not wanting to disturb the tableau.

After a minute, the cat leapt off the counter and the macaw dipped its head to peck at the few remaining seeds in its bowl, but another few seconds passed before Chet allowed himself to stir.

Chet did not see Isabel's car when he returned home, and she didn't meet him at the door to either welcome or berate him.

*Could she really have followed through on her threat to leave?*

"Mom? Isabel?"

Silence.

He peeked into the guestroom. No piles of ruffled pillows on the studio couch. No cosmetics or spills of dusting powder on his desk. No lingering scent of her heavy patchouli perfume.

When did she leave? Did she make it home okay? He made a move toward the phone, then stopped. If he called her, she might take it as a sign of weakness instead of simple courtesy and come rushing back. No, better to wait until she called. So what if she ranted at him for being an unfeeling son; it wouldn't be anything he hadn't heard a hundred times before.

He looked in the empty closet, and it slowly sunk in that she was truly gone. He had his life back. And his home office. He took shallow breaths, afraid that if he breathed too deeply it would ruin the wonderful feeling. It was such a tenuous thing, like a constant pain that vanished suddenly and any movement could make it flare up again.

Still breathing shallowly, he went to his bedroom, reached behind the stack of shoeboxes in the closet for the ceramic lemon cookie jar, and bore it to the kitchen. He set it in the middle of the table and whispered, "Daddy's home," as his father had said every evening when he entered the house after work. Daddy would lead Chet to the kitchen, take the top off the cookie jar where he kept his stash of lemon drops, and pull out a couple of pieces "just for the two of us." Daddy would smack his lips, and so would little Chet. They would smile at each other, then sit at the table sucking their lemon drops and recounting their day.

Michael, Chet's father, died of a heart attack when Chet was ten, though Isabel acted as if he had run off and left her for another woman. Chet knew how difficult it had been for her—he should, she told him often enough—and he felt guilty for being such a responsibility, but still he clung to the lemon jar against her wishes. It was the only thing he had to remember his father by; Isabel burned all pictures of Michael the day after the funeral. She also threw away the lemon jar, but Chet dug it out of the trash and hid it from her. He used to wonder if he'd created a drama out of nothing, but when she came to visit and spied the jar on the table, she tossed it in the wastebasket again. He rescued it and kept it in his closet ever since.

He checked the jar, noticed his supply of lemon drops was getting low, and made a mental note to place an order at an online store that sold old-fashioned candy. He bought the sweets in bulk and portioned them out himself, twelve drops to a sandwich bag. He allowed himself one bag a day; more than that and his teeth ached.

After eating a dinner of plain yogurt mixed with sunflower seeds and a touch of apricot preserves, he heaved his computer off the dresser top where he'd been storing the machine, lugged the device to his office, and set it on the desk. He turned on the computer, ordered the lemon drops, then pulled up his plans for the refuge.

Every day for the past six months he had felt a little less like himself because he had not been able to work on the plans. They were his dreams, his hopes, and if Isabel found out about them, she would ridicule him for being contrary and impractical.

*You really are a mama's boy. You can't get her out of your head for a minute.*

*Maybe so,* he answered himself, *but tomorrow I'm changing the locks.*

The next afternoon, clutching the wilted daisies and carnations Rosemary had just given him, Chet leaned against the doorjamb of the florist shop.

"Have you ever been to The Garden Spot?" he asked, trying to sound casual.

Rosemary shook her head.

"No, but I've heard the food is good."

"Would you like to go there for dinner tonight? With me?"

Her cheeks pinked.

"I'd love to."

"Great. Do you want to drive or should I?"

"How about if you pick me up at my condo about six-thirty?"

Chet closed his store a few minutes early so he'd have time to take a shower and get changed. Rosemary must have left work early, too. When he drove to her condo at exactly six-thirty, she answered the door wearing a teal dress with skinny straps instead of her usual jeans. Her long black hair was just-washed shiny, and she smelled of vanilla and tea roses.

Though it was Thursday, the restaurant buzzed with activity. If people believed the now waning television coverage of the purported terrorist threat, they didn't seem bothered by it.

"It's nice to see that everything's getting back to normal," Rosemary said, hanging her purse on the back of the chair. "I like normal."

"Then let's make a pact to talk only about normal things tonight."

She held out her right hand.

"You've got a deal."

Her hand in his felt strong and warm and full of promise.

He straightened his spine, then busied himself with the menu.

"I'm going to have the meat-free stroganoff and a salad."

"Me too." She set her menu aside. "I like the name of your store, Used Pets, but can you make a living selling old animals? Isn't it cheaper for people to get them at the animal shelter?"

He gave her a small smile.

"I do okay."

"How did you get interested in saving pets?"

"My father. We were out driving one day, can't remember why, and we almost ran over a dog lying in the middle of the road. My father stopped, bundled the filthy dog into the back seat of his almost-new car, and drove him to a vet. The dog had a small cut on his belly and he was starving, but other than that, he was okay. We brought him home, washed him, fed him."

He cleared his throat to cover a hitch in his voice. That had been a good day, but he couldn't think of it without remembering what came later: his father's death, and the dog's.

"He wasn't a pretty creature," he said quietly, "just a mutt with a lopsided grin, but he was sweet and loyal."

"It sounds like you really loved your dog. What was his name?"

"No name. My father told me we were merely the dog's caretakers. If we named him, it was like we were claiming ownership, and he said that no human had the right to own another creature." Chet took a deep breath. "After my father died, my mother dumped the dog at a shelter because she didn't want to be responsible for him, but she'd never fed or walked him. I did. When I found out what she did with him, I went to get him back, but he was already gone. I kept hounding the guy until he told me they sold the euthanized animals for pet food. I've forgiven my mother everything she's done to me, but I never forgave her for turning the poor dog into chow."

"Well, yeah. That would be pretty hard to forgive."

"I never forgave myself, either. I should have been a better caretaker. And I felt I let my father down."

"I doubt he saw it that way."

"You're probably right." He managed a grin. "But I got even with my mother. I did things she never forgave me for."

A sparkle came into her eyes.

"Like what?"

"She wanted me to be a stockbroker or a banker, something staid and stuffy and rich. I went to college, majored in business. At graduation, she said, 'I'm so glad that's over. I don't think I could have handled one more day. All that I sacrificed.' I put myself through college, though, working at a pet store in the mall. She about had a fit when I stayed on as manager, but she really hated it when I quit and opened up Used Pets. She was so furious she said she'd never have anything to do with me again. And she didn't. For a week and a half. Funny. I always thought never lasted longer than that."

His feeble attempt at humor drew a laugh from Rosemary.

Their server, a young man with thick-knuckled hands, brought glasses of water with lemon and a basket of whole-wheat rolls with pats of butter and packets of honey. He jotted down their order then clomped away.

Rosemary squeezed lemon juice into her water and took a sip.

"So that was your big rebellion? Opening a store?"

"I didn't open the shop to be contrary. I get along with the fur and feather people better than I do with humans, is all. I appreciate the simplicity and honesty of the animal world. Unlike humans, they never pretend to be anything other than they are. Humans do the same thing animals do, but they couch their savagery in pretty words."

She gave him a strange look.

"Do you realize you speak of people as humans, like you don't think you're one of us?"

Chet let his gaze slip from hers. He hadn't realized he was so transparent, but she was right: he didn't like being the same as everyone else. He thought of himself as a lone coyote—a creature who lived outside the pack. And he'd spent so much time with animals that he didn't feel completely human. But if he told her that, he'd probably scare her off.

"Occupational hazard," he said, keeping his tone light. "How did you get interested in flowers?"

"Because of my mother, mostly. All she ever wanted was to be married and have kids, but she loved color so much she could have been an artist. She constantly bought us paints and crayons and flower coloring books, the expensive kind. And every year she has a garden. Wins all sorts of ribbons at the Indiana State Fair. That's where I grew up. Indiana."

"And your father. What is he like?"

"Wonderful, too. Quiet, not as colorful or flamboyant as Mother, but just as encouraging. They were both thrilled when I told them I wanted to own a flower shop. They even lent me the money to get started. I've only been open a few months, but I've already paid back part of the loan. That pleased Dad so much he volunteered to lend me more so I can expand."

Chet nibbled on a roll and wondered what his life would have been like if his father hadn't died. He swallowed. What was the point? Nothing could change the past.

Focusing his attention on Rosemary, he said, "Tell me more about yourself."

"Wouldn't you rather talk about what you want to talk about?"

"I want to talk about you."

She beamed at him, and he felt a sudden wash of happiness and well-being. Life was fine and going to get better. He just knew it.

Chet slipped an arm out from behind Rosemary's neck and rolled out of bed. There hadn't been any fireworks or bells, but they had been good together. Comfortable without awkwardness. He'd thought perhaps this time he'd be able to fall asleep in the arms of a woman but, as always, here he was, wide awake.

Okay, he admitted it: he had a problem with women. No matter how much he liked them, he was unable to let down his guard enough to sleep with them after having sex. And maybe he did have a failure to commit, as his old girlfriends claimed. But what about their failures? They had allowed Isabel to run them off. Even the two who'd broached the subject of marriage didn't understand his problems. Nor did they stand by him.

Rosemary seemed different; she knew about his mother and still wanted to go out with him. She had enough padding to be attractive—no jutting bones or unsightly hollows. She had bright eyes and a nice smile. She was everything he wanted.

But he hadn't been able to fall asleep with her in his bed.

He paced the apartment in his underwear, avoiding the floorboards that squeaked so as not to awaken her.

With dawn came an edginess that seeped into his body.

*Something felt wrong. But what?*

The wrongness crawled just beneath his consciousness, like an itch under the skin, and he couldn't reach it.

Hearing Rosemary stir, he went to the bedroom and slid beneath the covers. She might be hurt if she woke up alone, and he didn't want to spoil the night for her.

He was about to pull her into his arms when he froze.

Oh, God. Isabel. She hadn't called.

His mother had an uncanny ability of sensing when he was having sex, and she always called. Always.

Except last night.

That's what was wrong, or at least part of it.

Everything with her was a big production, any change an excuse for a dramatic scene. Yet she had slunk off without a word.

Fumbling with the phone, he pressed speed dial one.

"The number you have reached is out of order or no longer in service. Please hang up and try again."

*No. That wasn't right. Couldn't be.*

Rosemary sat up and yawned.

"What's going on?"

"I think something happened to my mother."

"What makes you say that?"

She sounded merely curious, not affronted.

"You're not mad that I'm trying to call her when we're…you know."

"In bed together? No. Should I be?"

His heart swelled with love—or something like it.

"Don't laugh, but every time I have sex, my mother calls. I let the machine pick it up, but still, she does call. And she didn't."

Rosemary laughed.

"I'm not laughing at you," she said quickly. "It's just that all during college, whenever I was with a guy, that's when my father called. I swear he had spies."

Chet punched in all the digits of his mother's phone number and got the same recording. He hung up and shook his head.

"Can't get through."

"Do you want me to come with you to Castle Rock?"

"Not a good idea. Isabel isn't kind to my girlfriends."

Rosemary put up her fisted hands and jabbed the air.

"I can take her."

He pulled her close and whispered huskily, "I bet you could."

She kissed him then pushed him away.

"You better go. She might need help."

"Will I see you again?"

"Of course, at work." She paused, grinning impishly. "*And* tonight."

Despite his worry, a smile spread over his face.

"Great." He arose, pulled on his chinos, then stopped. "What am I doing? I have a naked woman in my bed and I'm getting dressed to go check on my mother. Something really is wrong with me."

"I think something is right with you. Your mother isn't very nice, but look how loyal and considerate you are to her. One day when you fall in love and get married, you'll treat your wife equally well. Or better. Who knows, that lucky woman might be me."

"Is this a proposal?"

She laughed.

"I hardly know you."

After dropping Rosemary off at her condo, Chet headed for Castle Rock. Though it was the beginning of rush hour, only a few cars besides his tan Honda Accord were on the highway, and he made good time.

He exited the highway, taking the road that led to Forest Highland Subdivision where he'd grown up. He knew every straightaway, every curve. Beyond this hill, the subdivision would be laid out before him in a valley, and he'd be able to catch a glimpse of his mother's home, a green-roofed single-story dwelling that looked like a child's Lincoln Log house.

He rounded the hill and slammed on the brakes.

## Bob, the Right Hand of God

The road ended six feet in front of him.
And the subdivision was gone.

# Chapter 5

CHET CLOSED HIS eyes and took a deep breath. No way could an entire subdivision disappear. He'd been out here two weeks ago to make sure the house had come through the winter okay. It existed then.

He gave a little laugh. And it existed now. Exhaustion had shut his brain down for a second. That's all.

He opened his eyes.

No subdivision.

He turned off the engine and climbed out of the car.

The subdivision had been a noisy place with dogs barking, children playing, traffic rumbling, chainsaws whining; now only the soft swish of a breeze remained. He knew he should feel something—anger, fear, grief—but he could not wrap his mind around the disappearance of hundreds of houses.

He stumbled across the field, searching for his mother's property and found no trace of human habitation. A plain of seedlings filled the entire valley. The trees had not been planted in rows, but haphazardly as if the seeds had been scattered by the wind.

Or strewn by a celestial hand.

Bob.

Then the galactic renewal program was not a hoax after all.

Feeling as if the world had been yanked out from under him, Chet sank to his knees. The rich loamy smell of the damp earth gagged him. Don't puke, he admonished himself. He flashed back to Bob saying, "And believe me, you don't want God puking all over Earth."

He let out a single burst of laughter that came close to being a sob, and struggled to his feet. Zigzagging around the miniature trees on his way back to the car, he felt like a giant towering over a forest, and he wondered if Bob or God or a jokester from the planet Xerxes was playing with him.

Chet turned on his computer, waited for it to boot up, then Googled "Bob, the Right Hand of God." The hard drive crackled and the fan whirred. Almost a minute passed without any results, then Bob's gnomish face filled the computer screen.

"What?"

Chet reared back, too startled to speak.

Bob's head seemed to loom out of the screen.

"Well? I don't have all day."

"Where's my mother?"

"Is *that* why you called me?"

"What did you do with her?"

"Oh, for crying out loud."

Bob's head disappeared and the computer shut down.

"What did you do with my mother?" Chet yelled, trying to start the computer again.

Neither the computer nor Bob responded.

Chet ran to the television, hoping to find Bob, but when he clicked the remote, the television didn't turn on. He dropped the remote on the coffee table and switched on a lamp to see if he still had electricity; nothing happened. After glancing out the window at the traffic signal on the corner and seeing that it too was unlit, he scooped up the receiver to call the electric company and report the outage, but the phone was dead.

He paced the living room, then stopped abruptly. He had seen something peculiar when he glanced outside, something that barely registered. He ran to the window and searched for foreign objects, but everything his gaze fell on was familiar—the budding lilac bushes and crab apple trees, the new apartments mixed with old houses, the downtown skyline, the mountains in the distance.

All at once he recognized the difference. Not something added. Something missing.

He angled his head to look down the street. As far as he could see, there were no cables, no utility poles.

Resting his forehead on the cool glass of the window, he tried to picture the world he knew vanishing bit by bit.

*Don't think about that. Think of something good. Think of Used Pets.*

*Oh, my God. The animals must be starving.*

He hadn't fed them yet.

He grabbed his keys, took the steps two at a time, and raced for his car. The environment would have to take care of itself today; he didn't have time to walk to the store.

The orange cat greeted him with a baleful look.

The scarlet macaw careened around the store screeching, "You're late. What a bitch."

To his surprise, Chet found himself chuckling with amusement. He tamped down a feeling of guilt, promising himself he'd worry about his mother later, and set about his morning chores. With no customer to interrupt him, he finished quickly. Then he went next door to talk to Rosemary.

How would she react when he told her about the subdivision being gone and perhaps his mother with it? Unless she asked, maybe it would be better to say nothing; if he tried to describe what he'd seen and felt, she'd think he'd gone insane. And maybe he had.

Without stopping, he extended a hand to open the door, but slammed his palm into it when it remained closed.

*What the...*

Using both hands, he tried to push it open; it didn't budge. He peered through the window. Blood pounded in his temples, and he gasped for air. Everything was gone—the flowers, the glass-doored refrigerators, the long counter where Rosemary waited on customers. Even the fake wood floor was gone; in its place stretched a green carpet. No, not a carpet. Grass.

On shaky legs he tottered to the butcher shop. It too was gutted, with grass where the old linoleum floor should have been.

This couldn't be right. Bob said God decided to eliminate everyone who wasn't nice, so why had he picked on Rosemary and John? Rosemary was one of the nicest people he'd ever met, and John was by far the most generous, giving not only his money but his time. He coached two of his son's little league teams, took his daughter's Brownie troop on cookouts, taught Sunday school at his church.

Chet brightened. Maybe Bob only had a grudge against the shops, not the people. He ran back to his store, locked the door, then hopped in his car and sped the few blocks to Rosemary's condo.

Buffalo grass swayed on the land where, mere hours before, the building had stood.

He wanted to cry, but he had no tears—just hot eyes, and an expanding lump of ice in his chest.

Chet knew what he would find when he reached John's house but still choked when he saw the acres and acres of buffalo grass. How many city blocks had converted to prairie? He couldn't even begin to guess.

He crawled back to his store, not trusting himself to drive as fast as the speed limit, and parked outside Used Pets.

The one bright spot—the only bright spot—was that so far Bob had left his store alone.

Opening the door, he heard not a peep, not a squawk, not a rustle. In the dim light, he could see the outlines of the cages, aquariums, and terrariums, and he thought the animals had quieted in response to the unnatural changes.

His eyes adjusted to the gloom.

"Bob!" he screamed. "What have you done with my animals?"

The phone rang. Chet snatched the receiver off the phone on the counter. A hollow silence greeted him.

Another ring. His cell phone. With one hand he scrabbled

around the shelf beneath the counter where he tossed it the last time he used it. Isabel had called and talked so long the battery went dead. And he had never recharged it. So how could it be ringing?

In the far recesses of his mind, he knew.

His fingers closed on the phone. Gingerly, as if handling a venomous snake, he pulled it out and flipped it open.

Chet studied Bob's face filling the tiny screen and thought how strange to know its every curve, every wrinkle, every pore, yet not have a clue what the rest of the man looked like.

"*Your* animals, Chet?"

Chet bowed his shoulders. Except for that moment with the passenger pigeon, he had never before claimed ownership. He knew the creatures didn't belong to him.

But they didn't belong to Bob, either.

He yanked himself upright.

"Where are they? I want them back."

"They are in a better place."

"Don't patronize me with euphemisms."

"I speak the truth. They *are* in a better place. God and the developers are rebuilding the rainforests and deserts, and He called the creatures home."

"They don't know how to take care of themselves."

"Have a little faith. God will gradually introduce them to the wild, teaching them the skills they need and watching over them until they become acclimatized."

Fury at Bob warred with pleasure at his charges living free, and all that emotion kicking around inside bruised his chest. A sputter of amusement momentarily calmed the turmoil as he imagined generations of scarlet macaws shrieking "what a bitch" into the wind, spreading the word about his mother.

*Oh, God.*

His mother. How could he have forgotten about her?

"What did you do with my mother? And Rosemary? And John? And all the others?"

"Are we back to that again? I thought we'd settled it. They've returned to the place they came from."

"What does that mean?"

"I don't know why God likes you. You don't seem very bright to me. Let me put this in terms you will understand. When you humans hit the delete key on one of your primitive little machines, the data disappears from sight, but it survives until it gets written over. If the hard drive had an infinite memory, there would be no reason for the data ever to be overwritten."

"So they're still alive?"

"Is that what you heard me say?"

Pain crept up Chet's neck and into his head.

"That first night you said God was going to eliminate everyone who isn't nice, so why did he take Rosemary and John?"

"The flower killer and the baby maker? That should be obvious even to one with your limited intellect."

"But John's children. They never did anything."

"No snowflake in an avalanche ever thinks it did anything."

Chet stared at the tiny image of Bob. Talking to the man was like breaking bricks with his skull. No wonder his head ached.

"That isn't an explanation."

"Little Sally had six children, like her mother," Bob said with exaggerated patience. "And John built dams that strangled rivers and kept them from running wild and free. Need I go on?"

"Little Sally and John are five and seven years old."

"It's a matter of time. You humans think time flows in a single direction, but past, present, and future are all one, and they don't flow at all. This is getting tedious."

Bob vanished.

"Wait, wait," Chet yelled. "What about the cats and kittens?"

Bob's voice coming through the phone was faint and thready.

"They're at my place."

Rubbing his chest with one hand, listening to the dull babble of his confused thoughts, Chet waited for the world to right itself and make sense again.

It didn't happen.

He made a slow prowl of his store, inspecting every enclosure where the animals had been and searching beneath the counter and in the backroom. When he realized he was hunting for ways to explain the unexplainable, he took one last look around, then stepped outside.

He blinked in the harsh light, and blinked again.

His car had disappeared and so had every other vehicle. Already green shoots were pushing their way up through cracks in the blacktop.

He leaned against the door to keep from falling; too much was happening, and he couldn't get a solid footing.

A thin man with huge hands poking from the sleeves of a cream-colored sweater lurched down the middle of the street, his glazed eyes looking neither to the right nor the left. A business-suited woman ran past him, the clacking of her high heels echoing in the stillness. Her angular face contorted with emotion, and her hair shone like copper in the sun.

Were the three of them the only people left in the world? Chet didn't think so, but he acknowledged that he based this conclusion more on hope than fact.

Sucking on a lemon drop, he watched the man and woman until they became blurred forms in the distance. Then, not knowing what else to do or where else to go, he headed for home.

Putting one foot in front of the other took a conscious effort. His eyes felt gritty, and his mouth tasted like brass. Sleep. That's what he needed. Lots of sleep.

When he woke tomorrow, maybe things would be different. Why not? They were different today.

# Chapter 6

IN THE MIDDLE of the night, Chet opened his eyes and remembered.

He remembered Isabel rearranging his cabinets and fighting him for control of the remote.

He remembered John inviting him to spend Easter with his family.

He remembered Rosemary cuddling into his embrace and how sweet she had smelled.

He remembered his store, the creatures in his charge, the macaw and the orange cat staring at each other.

Aching with the tears he could not shed, he closed his eyes and sank back into sleep.

A strange sound, like the cry of a hurt animal, awakened him, and he realized it had been torn from his throat. Pieces of a nightmare slithered through his brain, too quick to grasp. But he didn't need to recall the nightmare to know what it had been about.

*Bob.*

Who was he? An archangel as Isabel had called him? A minion of the devil? Or a cross between the two; perhaps a fallen angel like Beelzebub?

Beelzebob.

Chet's lips quirked in an involuntary smile at the thought, but he felt no amusement. Bob was not an entity to be taken lightly.

Chet dragged himself out of bed. Despite twenty hours of sleep, he felt weighed down by a weariness deeper than skin and bone. Though he had no desire to eat, he shuffled to the kitchen to fix breakfast. Whatever this day might bring, he knew he'd cope better with food in his belly.

The crunching of his orange granola resounded in the empty apartment. He hadn't realized how constant had been the hum of the refrigerator, the rumble of traffic outside the window, the drone of voices and the throb of music seeping through the thin walls.

He stopped mid-chew and listened.

The silence was tangible, a physical presence.

After chewing and swallowing the tasteless mouthful of cereal, he pushed the bowl aside. Maybe later he'd feel like eating, but now he had to...

His mind went blank for a moment, then a terrible understanding rocked him. Our work, our families, and our friends define us. When they are gone, what's left? What do we do?

Out of habit and with the irrational hope that yesterday had not happened, he pulled on a jacket over khaki pants and blue shirt, then went outside.

The sun shone darkly in a pallid sky.

Except for the lack of vehicles on the already weedy road and a block or two that had reverted to prairie, the neighborhood looked much the same today as it had yesterday. Without traffic fumes to dilute it, the scent of lilacs was overpowering, as if oceans of perfume had been dumped on the city.

The silence was as palpable out in the open as it had been inside his apartment.

He walked with his head down and didn't look up until he neared his store. Seeing a small figure waiting outside the door, he quickened his step. A grin stretched across his face, making his jaw ache.

"How did you get here?" he asked the marmalade cat.

The cat pricked up its ears.

Feeling as if time had rolled back two months to when the orange cat had first come to stay, Chet opened the door.

The last breath of hope died in his chest. The other animals had not returned.

"If I'm sad that the scarlet macaw and the frilled lizard and all the others are gone," he said, wandering through the store, "I guess that means I'm selfish. By wanting to keep them here under my control, I'm acting like a little god. Since the big God wants them, I should be happy. So how come I'm not?"

He hoisted himself onto the counter and sat with his hands clasped between his knees.

"Now what?"

The cat leapt to his side and nosed the pocket with the lemon drops.

"You're right. When in doubt, have a lemon drop." He reached for the bag, took out a couple of pieces of candy. "Just for the two of us," he said, popping one in his mouth and setting the other on the counter.

The cat licked it, rolled it, pounced on it.

The bite of lemon on Chet's tongue soothed him and gave him something to do, but he knew he could not spend the day sitting on the counter eating candy. If his teeth started to ache, he might not be able to find a dentist. And what if there were no more doctors? He'd better take care of himself. At least until Bob or God deleted him.

He stiffened, struck by a sudden thought.

*Why hadn't they already done so? What did they want with him?*

The cat cocked its head as if understanding what was running through Chet's mind.

Chet's gaze fell on the empty cages.

"I don't see any reason to hang around here. Should we go?"

The cat jumped off the counter and bounded to the door.

"Such indecision," Chet said, trying to lighten the mood, but the quip fell flat.

He trudged after the cat.

Outside, the cat padded in the direction of Chet's apartment.

Chet wondered how the cat knew where to go, then shrugged. Felines had uncanny abilities, this one more than most.

They'd traveled less than a block when Chet realized he had forgotten to lock the store. Oh, heck, what did it matter; the animals were gone. He took another step, stopped. Maybe it didn't matter, but the unlocked door would niggle at him, and he had enough to worry about without being poked at by trifles. Better go back.

He turned around. Clapped his hands over his eyes and shook his head. Nope. Not happening. No way.

He peeked through his fingers.

The sidewalk ended at the tip of his black canvas shoes. Every human thing—downtown skyscrapers, apartment buildings, offices, houses, shopping centers, roads, sidewalks, signs—had disappeared. Open prairie flowed all the way to the mountains.

He glanced behind him. The orange cat sat in the middle of the sidewalk, washing a hind leg, and beyond it, the remainder of the city stretched toward Kansas. Except for the absence of vehicles and paved roads, he could almost convince himself that nothing had changed.

Facing west again, he drew in a deep breath as if more air in his lungs would somehow put everything right.

He ran to where his store had been and slowly wheeled around.

All seemed silent, still.

His ears became attuned to the quiet, and he heard insects cricking and chirring and buzzing.

Then other sounds registered, sounds so faint several seconds passed before he comprehended what he was hearing: the relentless hunger of nature. The larger prairie creatures and the most minute devoured each other in a cacophony of crunching, tearing, ripping, gnashing, grinding.

At the realization he was sharing space with things that must be fed, he took a step backward and bumped into a tree, a gnarled oak that hadn't been there a moment ago. Leaning against the ancient tree, he heard the roots reaching out, creeping, grasping, wanting, needing. He jerked away from the tree and fell to hands and knees.

Blades of grass moaned under his weight, and the screams of wildflowers being murdered by more aggressive vegetation almost deafened him.

He opened his mouth to add his own shrieks to the clamor, but closed it again and cupped his ears when he became aware of a long sonorous undulation deep beneath the ground. The heartbeat of the earth.

Then all sounds ceased except that of a voice. Bob's voice.

"Try sight now."

The day grew brighter, and each color—the green of the grass, the blue of the sky, the red and yellow and purple of the tiny flowers interspersed in the grass—took on jewel tones so bright Chet could hardly bear to look at them.

Through half-closed lids, he saw the colors oscillate. The oscillation became waves that lapped against him, over him. He made swimming motions to stay afloat.

The waves disintegrated into tiny bits of light that moved farther and farther apart until he felt as if he were in the vast remoteness of space, his very body a galaxy of stars. He screamed but no sound came out, only a gaseous substance like a distant nebula. He tried to find something to stand on, to grab hold of to keep from falling into the infinity, but encountered nothing. The pinpricks of light were so far apart, all there is or ever will be was a blackness so deep it began to feel solid.

Gradually, like the most welcome dawn, color returned to the world, pale at first, then quietly deepening, until all was as it had been.

"You better leave them with their rudimentary senses," Bob said. "I don't think they can survive in the real world."

Chet struggled to his feet and looked around. No Bob.

"Why are you doing this to me?"

He cringed at the whimper in his voice.

Thrusting both fists above his head, he shouted, "Why are you doing this to me?"

A phone rang. He reached for the cell phone he didn't

remember pocketing and flipped it open.

"You?" Bob said. "Who cares about you? It's all about what's best for the tourists. The developers weren't sure tourists would be interested in seeing such primitive life forms, but apparently we cannot hurry evolution along without turning you humans into blithering blobs of protoplasm. And there is a certain fascination with primitivism among the highly advanced. Even beings of light, even purely spiritual beings get bored and need a vacation. I think they will be quite entertained by you humans."

Chet remained silent. He had no idea what to say. After a brief pause, Bob continued chatting.

"God is pleased with the progress we are making. There are no construction delays as there are with you humans. And the project is coming in under budget. It's hard to pad your expense account when God is your auditor."

Bob turned his head to the left and spoke to someone off-screen.

"I'll be right there."

The phone shut off.

Feeling as if his brain had come undone, Chet slogged through the prairie and joined the orange cat on the sidewalk. Side-by-side, they proceeded to Chet's apartment building, which seemed out of proportion. At first, Chet blamed the oddness on his addled senses, then he noted that the building was now only five stories high.

Too tired to think, he stumbled up the stairs to his apartment and fell into bed.

Chet struggled to breathe. A weight rested on his chest, suffocating him. He forced himself to waken. The weight remained. Opening his bleary eyes, he met the unblinking green gaze of the cat, who stood on his chest, studying him.

Chet groaned, thinking he'd have to go back to Used Pets for cat food. Remembering he had no store, he closed his eyes again and waited for sleep. The cat's weight lifted off his chest, but he could still feel the feline gaze boring into him.

He sat up and scratched his itchy jaw. He'd been too tired to shave this morning, and yesterday he'd been anxious to check on his mother. That meant the last time he'd shaved was Thursday night before he went to dinner with Rosemary.

Skittering away from the image of Rosemary smiling at him in the restaurant, he stroked his beard stubble to gauge the growth. About forty-eight hours worth. Good. At least he hadn't lost track of the days.

He smiled mirthlessly. So it had come to this: telling time by beard growth.

In the kitchen, he opened one of the cans of tuna Isabel had bought for herself and not eaten, scraped it into a bowl for the cat, then rummaged in his cabinets and warm refrigerator taking stock of his food supplies. He had enough nuts, seeds, granola, oatmeal, canned beans, and canned fruit to last a week or two but almost no fresh fruit or vegetables.

He seized the bowl of congealed granola left from breakfast, thinking to bolt it down so he could leave for the grocery store, but the cinnamon and orange smelled so exquisite he took a small spoonful of cereal and chewed it slowly.

The flavor exploded in his mouth. Never had anything tasted so delectable. The sweetness and tartness harmonized into a symphonic feast that made him moan with pleasure.

When he finished the last soggy bite, he dropped the bowl on the table and backed away. His enjoyment of the unappetizing mess wasn't natural. Neither was his heightened sense of taste and smell. Which meant that the morning's experiences were real, not a nightmare. What had Bob done to him? Fed him psychedelic drugs? Stuck a finger in his brain and stirred it like mush?

He grabbed his jacket and ran down the stairs. He burst through the door and kept on running. The brilliant blue of the sky and the shimmering green of the grass and leaves hurt his eyes. The blood rushing in his ears sounded as loud and as violent as a tornado.

"Leave me alone," he screamed.

Bob did not respond.

Chet ran west along the grassy swathe of what used to be Sixth Avenue, seeking the grocery store where he usually shopped. He had seen it yesterday, and he needed to stock up on all the basics, not just food but toothpaste, soap, shaving cream.

Chest heaving, he neared the edge of what was left of Denver. The grocery store was gone. The prairie had advanced a few more blocks, wiping it out. He was trying to remember where the closest stores were in the eastern section of the city when the smell of salt and fish caught his attention.

He stopped and stared. The prairie looked blue like the ocean. Colorado had once been part of a great inland sea. Was the development company bringing it back?

He trotted to the edge of the expanse. Not a watery sea but a sea of blue flowers. Blue bees, metallic-blue wasps, and delicate blue butterflies flickered among blue geraniums, spiky blue lupines, sky-blue poppies, delphinium, columbines, forget-me-nots, periwinkles, deep blue hydrangea.

Awe carried him into the blue.

He tilted his head back and watched a flock of bluebirds limned against the pale blue evening sky.

A chill creeping up his legs brought his gaze back to earth. He stood in water up to his knees.

Shivering, he waded to shore.

Although he lingered by the sea until long after the sun had slipped behind the indigo mountains, he did not see another blue flower.

# Chapter 7

DURING THE EARLY morning hours, Chet's euphoria at witnessing the blue reconstruction vanished, leaving him feeling listless and gray. A shower and shave, and a handful of nuts for breakfast, did not make him feel any more alive. Nor did going out to search for a supermarket.

The approaching dawn bleached color from the world, giving it the look of a black and white movie. Even the cat parading before him and what he could see of himself appeared as varying shades of gray.

Having no way of telling time, he did not know how long until the sun would rise. His stomach gave a sickening lurch when he realized that he did not know *if* the sun would rise.

But of course it would. Some laws of the universe must be immutable. If he didn't have certain truths to anchor him, he'd lose his mind, though chances were he'd already lost it and nothing he'd experienced in the past few days had actually occurred. He should be grieving for his friends and his mother, but he didn't feel that they were gone, so maybe they weren't.

A touch of gold brightened the sky.

"See?" he said to the cat. "I knew the sun would rise."

Before he finished speaking, the flare of satisfaction vanished. The light was coming from the north.

Blowing out a heavy sigh at this further manifestation of his insanity, he headed for the light. Could one lose his mind in so short a time? It had all started on Sunday, April first, when Bob appeared on television and made his ridiculous announcement. Monday the passenger pigeons flew over Denver. Tuesday the newscaster spoke of terrorists. Wednesday Isabel left. Thursday he went out with Rosemary. Friday he found the seedling forest and lost his friends. And yesterday Bob had scrambled his senses. That meant today was Sunday.

Easter Sunday.

Maybe Bob was re-enacting the resurrection for the benefit of those who had not yet been deleted, and there seemed to be many. More than a dozen men, women, and children trudged along the same grassy road as Chet, and when he came to an intersection, he caught glimpses of north-bound people on parallel roads.

Where had they been all this time? He hadn't seen another person since Friday when the man with the big hands and the woman with the coppery highlights in her hair had passed in front of his store. All these people must have been hiding out in their houses and apartments. He puffed up his chest and walked taller, thinking that at least he hadn't made a prisoner of himself.

Following the light, he came to Cheesman Park, which, fungus-like, had spread out in all directions, devouring buildings, roads, sidewalks in its path. Toward the middle of the park, on a gently sloping hill, stood the open-air pavilion where he had once seen *A Midsummer Night's Dream* performed. Light poured out of the western side of the pavilion.

Coming on the scene from the south, Chet saw people walking into the light and vanishing. When he angled to the west, he could see them filing through a doorway into a duplicate world where the light was honey gold and so clear the new world seemed more real than the original.

Afraid of being drawn into the beckoning light, Chet rooted himself to a spot off to one side. He had a good view of the doorway, which seemed to have been hewn from a single block of granite eons ago. And he had a good view of Bob's face looming out of a large-screen television balanced on the lintel.

"In this climate-controlled environment away from the reconstruction zone," Bob said, "you will be safe. You won't have any worries. Everything you need will be provided."

Though Bob spoke in a moderate tone, his voice carried for it had no competition. Chet heard none of the usual small talk that prevailed whenever people gathered. No gossip of weather, sports, work, food, fashion, celebrities, copulation. The only topic left on earth to discuss was the reconstruction, and people didn't know how to talk about anything that deep. So they remained silent.

When the cat gave him a quizzical look, Chet continued his thought aloud.

"You can't blame them. What is there to say? Either the renewal is an illusion and we're all crazy, or it's actually happening and life as we know it will never be the same."

"Do you mind, Chet?" Bob said. "I'm talking here."

Chet put his fingers to his mouth.

"Oops. Sorry." Speaking behind his hand, he said to the cat, "Let's get out of here."

He took a few steps then turned back. Might as well stay; he had nothing else to do.

Sucking on a lemon drop, he blocked out Bob's voice promising safety, and watched those waiting to go through the doorway. Most looked dazed, but some, like that brown-haired woman in jeans and a maroon jacket, seemed clear-eyed and calculating.

Chet winced. The woman reminded him of his mother, not in looks but in attitude, as if she assumed the world revolved around her and her problems. Interesting how people like that were the first to submit to authority. You'd think their self-absorption would make them strong and independent, though perhaps it was the other way around. Maybe their weakness and submissiveness made them self-absorbed. Either way, he had no respect for anyone who would choose safety over freedom.

A few people stepped out of line and shuffled off. Chet nodded his approval, but the brown-haired woman lifted her chin and wrinkled her nose as if the sight offended her. Apparently, like Isabel, she disdained those who didn't do what she thought right.

She moved forward with the line. A shaft of light made her hair gleam copper, and Chet recognized her: the business-suited woman who ran past his store on Friday. He remembered the look on her face. What had she been feeling? Fear? Horror?

He buried a twinge of sympathy under a shudder of contempt. Whatever she'd experienced couldn't have been bad enough to send her running to Bob, the being who probably caused the distress.

Suddenly, she spun out of line and raced past Chet.

"So I was wrong," he said, shrugging.

His gaze followed her. She really did have lovely hair. Was the light in the doorway making it gleam, or…

He glanced at the eastern horizon where the sun was rising in all its glory. Tension seeped from his body, and he realized how tightly he'd been holding to the thought that this day the sun might abdicate. He'd learned the lesson in childhood: by imagining something dreadful, he could keep it from happening.

He'd never imagined his father having a heart attack, and Michael had died. Afterward, terrified that his mother too would die, leaving him orphaned, he carefully stepped over sidewalk cracks to make sure he didn't break her back, and he haunted medical websites searching for all the ways a person could perish. And his mother had lived until her deletion, an end he had never imagined and could not imagine yet.

What had she felt in the seconds before she'd been deleted? Had she been afraid? Or had she simply blinked out with no warning? He hoped she hadn't suffered. Despite their difficulties, he never wished her ill; he'd simply wanted her out of his apartment. Well, he'd gotten his wish. But at what cost?

The sound of his name startled him.

He looked around. Only a few other people remained in the park—a man in an orange jumpsuit; an old woman with drawn-on eyebrows and rouged cheeks; a short Hispanic man with a thin mustache; a stocky, a dark-skinned woman with masses of shoulder-length black curls and a dress that did not become her; a ruddy blond wearing camouflage fatigues and a military haircut that made him look bald.

"Well, Chet?" Bob asked, a touch of impatience in his voice. "Are you coming?"

Chet folded his arms across his chest. "No."

"What about you, Ricky?"

The man in the orange jump shook his head.

"No way, man."

"It's a refuge, not a prison," Bob said. "You cannot even imagine what the world is going to be like when the heavy reconstruction begins."

Fear cramped Chet's stomach. Not even imagine? That meant anything could happen.

The Hispanic man smoothed his mustache with an index finger.

"Sounds like a prison to me, and I don't want to be no prisoner."

"You were always a prisoner, Esmeraldo."

"That's a stinking lie! Who you been talking to? I never went to jail."

"You humans were imprisoned many times over: imprisoned in your bodies, on earth, by your genetics."

Esmeraldo shrugged.

"Whatever. But we had free will."

Bob furrowed his brow.

"Who told you that? You never had free will. Remember when you were young, how you loved basketball?"

"Yeah, so?"

"You were good at it, and you wanted to be a professional basketball player when you grew up. Then all your classmates became taller than you. You did stretching exercises every day hoping they would make you tall. You wanted to be tall. You chose to be tall. You prayed to be tall. But are you?"

Esmeraldo glared at the television.

"Whose stinking fault is that?"

"I had nothing to do with it," Bob said. "That was the Left Hand of God's department."

"Oh, brother," the old woman muttered.

Bob fixed his gaze on her.

"Do you have something to say, Ellen?"

She put her hands over her head as if protecting herself.

"No."

The dark-skinned woman stepped forward.

"This is ridiculous. Right Hand of God. Left Hand of God. God. God. God. I don't even believe in God, so what's up with that?"

Bob gave her a benign look.

"God believes in you, Tisha. The door will close in a few minutes. Are you coming?"

"I don't think so."

"Well, I'm not going in there," the man in camouflage said. "Freedom is everything and I will remain free."

"Ah, Lance. What separates you humans from the other animals are your illusions. Or your delusions, which comes to the same thing—being deceived or mislead by erroneous perceptions of the truth. You humans were always so easy to lead because you believed the lies. In your elections, you voted for the lie, and every time the politicians gave you something other than what you voted for, yet you never learned. You kept electing lying politicians, and they kept sending poor boys off to fight for the purposes of the rich."

"No, sir," Lance said. "I fought for freedom."

"You ran off to fight for a cause that did not exist. It's the job of leaders to convince the people they are free when they are not, and to convince them to fight for that illusion of freedom. And the teachers propagated the lies. Yours wasn't the first civilization on earth, nor was it the greatest, yet your teachers kept the truth from you. That they themselves believed the lies did not mitigate the damage. It's all an illusion. Ellen, how much did you spend on cosmetics in your lifetime?"

Ellen ducked her head.

"A lot."

"Two hundred thirty thousand dollars and fifty-two cents," Bob said. "You wanted to be an actress, but you weren't pretty enough to be the star, and you weren't quirky enough to be the best friend. So you bought into the cosmetic industry's lies that their products would make you beautiful. You blamed yourself when they didn't do the job, but the cosmetics were sold by girls who were already beautiful. And they were twenty years old. They didn't need what they were selling."

The old woman shook her head, but the expression on her face told Chet that Bob's words hit home.

"And Tisha," Bob continued, "you went into debt buying clothes, but the latest fashions were shown off by skinny girls who seldom ate. The clothes looked wonderful on them, but when you put them on, they looked like the same garments your mother used to wear. And your mother had no fashion sense.

"But clothes, cosmetics, armies no longer have a place in your world. You humans could afford to be what you were and to indulge your rude concerns because your society was set up in such a way as to protect you. But that society is gone. In the old world, you all had pets. You will not be friends with the animals in the reconstructed world. You will be prey."

"Prey?" Ellen said, her voice rising to a squeak of horror. "You mean food?"

"I mean food."

"I'm out of here," Tisha said.

Esmeraldo and Ellen spoke at the same time.

"Me too."

One by one, they stepped through the doorway.

"Idiots," Lance muttered.

He turned on his heel and marched away from the door.

The woman with the coppery highlights in her brown hair lumbered toward them, a duffel bag, a canvas tote, and a black satchel hanging from her shoulders.

"Wait for me!"

Without slowing, she entered the new world. Chet felt no twinge of triumph at being right about her, only sadness. How could freedom mean so little to her, to all of them? Lance, at least, knew its value.

Ricky grinned at Chet.

"Bob sure is long-winded, isn't he?"

"Have your jape," Bob said. "I speak the truth."

Chet studied Ricky, trying to figure out why he seemed familiar. Maybe because they bore a faint resemblance to each other, like distant cousins. Both were about five-ten, had light brown hair, hazel eyes, and a slim build. Ricky, however, looked fit, and Chet had developed a paunch. He smiled ruefully to himself.

"What you laughing at?" Ricky pointed to his face. "You making fun of my moles?"

Chet held out a palm.

"Just wondering if we'd ever met."

"Maybe you were one of the kids in my class who stuck a pencil in my face and tried to connect the dots." He giggled. "I had fun with them."

Ricky was too far away for Chet to see moles on his face, but he had no intention of moving closer to check them out. The man's laugh gave him the creeps.

"Did I mention plumbing?" Bob said. "The sewage system is being dismantled as we speak."

Ricky grimaced. "Does a bear shit in the woods? Hell yes, but I'm no bear. So long, Chet. Nice meeting you."

As Ricky disappeared into the light, Chet saw the word "prisoner" on the back of the jumpsuit, and a connection clicked in his brain. No wonder the man seemed so familiar. He'd been on the news all the time back when televisions broadcast something other than The Bob Show. He'd been convicted of murdering and mutilating three women. He'd also killed men, men he'd gone to grade school with, but the state had not been able to make those cases.

Chet felt a tightening in his throat and chest.

"You...you..."

"Yes, Chet," Bob said.

"You deleted my mother and John and Rosemary, but you saved a serial killer? How could you?"

"God's ways are not the ways of man."

"I get that, but it doesn't answer my question."

"God is the ultimate landlord; the only thing that matters is the protection of the property."

"So?"

"Ricky always planted a tree over his victims' bodies after he buried them. What can I say? God was impressed."

"Well, I'm not. You can keep your area supervisor God."

Chet whirled and stalked away. The cat streaked off in another direction on business of its own.

Fuming and fretting, thinking of all the things he should have said to Bob, Chet made it halfway home without being cognizant of his surroundings. A foul odor, like a backed-up sewer, brought him out of his trance. In the middle of the grassy road, a scant ten feet ahead of him, steamed a knee-high mound of dung.

He broke out in a cold sweat. While he ambled along, paying no attention, some behemoth had crossed his path. He forced himself forward, one step at a time. With a hand over his mouth and nose, he studied the dung. No trace of vegetable matter. So the beast was a carnivore.

And humans were meat.

Chet took off running and did not stop until he reached his apartment. He locked the door, leaned against it to catch his breath, and then it hit him. He'd run up three flights of stairs. The building was now only four stories high.

# Chapter 8

BREATHING HEAVILY FROM his run, Chet propelled himself away from the door into the bathroom. After urinating, he flushed the toilet. A clank within the pipes caught his attention, and he remembered Bob's announcement. The toilet had flushed fine, though, so maybe the plumbing system was still intact. He watched the water seep into the bowl. One inch, two inches, three inches. A final gurgle, and the seepage stopped.

What was he going to do without plumbing? Go outside, like the cat? Panic seized him. And what about drinking water?

He ran to the kitchen, pulled every jar and bottle, mug and drinking glass out of the cabinets, and began filling them with water. When he was about half finished, the water slowed to a trickle, but he kept filling containers.

"Come on, come on," he said, bouncing on the balls of his feet. "Just a little more."

Slowly, painfully, the water levels rose.

He put the second to last bottle under the faucet. The pipes shuddered. One final drop of water formed but did not fall. He caught it on his finger and licked it, afraid of wasting even that single drop. Surveying his water supply, he figured he had enough drinking water for three or four days if he was careful, and then...

*Don't think about it. Take each day as it comes.*

Wanting not to be alone, he went in search of the marmalade

cat. He found it sitting on a sill in the guestroom, staring out the window, its body tensed.

"What do you see?"

He winced at the sound of his voice—harsh and overly loud as if he'd lost the ability to modulate his tone.

He tramped to the window and tracked the cat's gaze to a greenish-gray bird perched on a tree branch that just yesterday was ten feet below the apartment but now was eye-level. The bird, about the size of a sparrow, seemed to be all jutting angles with no curves to soften its lines.

Chet squinted, trying to get a better look at the alien creature. His eyes widened when he realized what he was seeing. Not an otherwordly animal but an othertimely one.

A miniature pterodactyl.

Where had it come from? Was Bob or God or the construction workers from the planet Xerxes recreating the world with a mosaic of time—an inland ocean from one age, a flock of pigeons from another, a pterodactyl from a third?

Or, being gods of a sort, were they recreating the world from nothing? Not that they'd need to. There was plenty of something that no longer existed to be used for reconstruction material.

He shied away from the thought of Rosemary and everyone else being disassembled atom by atom and reassembled into God only knew what, and attempted to picture Rosemary as she was the last time he'd seen her, but already her image was fading from his mind. He remembered her long black hair and how it felt when he slipped his fingers through it, and he remembered her breasts but not her nose. Had it been pert or straight? Had it been freckled?

They hadn't known each other well, but she might have become precious to him, at least for a while, if Bob hadn't meddled. He pawed through his memory searching for bits of Rosemary. Rosemary, whose favorite color was yellow, who loved most flowers but not marigolds, who liked salty foods better than sweet, who made love with abandon, and who moaned softly in her sleep.

*Were these few recollections all that remained of her? Or could the deleted ones have been shifted to another place in the galaxy as part of the galactic renewal program?*

All at once a breeze quickened, the pterodactyl flew away, and the cat jumped off the sill and gave Chet a stern "I'm hungry" look. By the time Chet opened a can of chicken and scraped it into a bowl for the cat, the breeze had whipped into a frenzy. Windows rattled, shingles flapped, tree branches flailed the building.

The wind picked up speed, roaring like unending cannonade, and the nostril-burning odor of brimstone filled the air. Black clouds roiled across the sky, turning morning to dusk.

Sucking on a lemon drop, Chet paced the apartment.

The windstorm became so violent he was sure it would blow the world apart. He clenched his hands, attempting to hold himself together, and he paced. He wanted to plan, but how could he prepare for the adjustments he was going to have to make when he didn't know what he'd have to adjust to? Not that it mattered. He was never going outside again. If only he could go back to the beginning of the change. Instead of sleeping his days away, he'd spend the time stockpiling food, water, toiletries, blankets.

Oh, hell. If he was going to wish, why not wish for what he really wanted: for everything to be back to normal.

He paced. The cat paced, too. He tried to assure it that they would be okay, but the wind killed the sound of his voice. The cat wouldn't have believed the lies, anyway.

Toward evening, he collapsed on his bed and fell into a fitful sleep with the cat curled up next to him.

He dreamed of creatures as big as houses that dumped knee-high mounds of dung. He woke, fell asleep again, and dreamed of Bob and shadowy Gods and an ever-changing carousel that whirled at dizzying speeds.

Quiet woke him. Groggy, aching all over, he sat up.

Was the storm over? What changes had it brought?

He tiptoed to the window and peeked out. It seemed to be early morning. Leaves and a few dead tree branches littered the ground, but otherwise the neighborhood looked the same as it had before the winds came. A surprising number of houses remained, giving the illusion of almost normalcy.

A young man in a black and purple wetsuit carried a surfboard past the apartment building. The sight seemed so incongruous that Chet felt his lips twitching, though he could not manage a full smile.

Maybe that's what he should do—take what was good in the new world and forget the rest. But what was good? Pissing in a jar? Needing to defecate and having no place to do it?

*Geez, why did I think that? Now I really have to shit.*

He rushed to the bathroom, lifted the lid of the toilet, but did not sit down. With no water to flush the feces away, it would pile up. He'd better grit his teeth and go outside.

He lowered the lid and trudged to the door.

A shriek, high and infinitely terrible, rose in the silence.

Chet froze. That scream sounded human. The surfer? He rushed to the window, but did not see the young man or anything that could have caused such agony. The scene looked peaceful. Nothing moved.

Well, one thing for sure: no way was he going outside.

He hurried into the kitchen, grabbed a pot, set it on a chair, and stared at it.

*This is ridiculous. If you just go out and do it, it will be over in a few minutes.*

He looked from the pot to the door.

"Do it," he said aloud.

Taking deep breaths, he went to the door, opened it, and stepped into the hall, which was much shorter than it used to be. Trying not to think of the agonized shriek, he tramped down the stairs and into the sunshine.

Behind a lilac bush, he dropped his trousers and squatted. Too late, he realized he hadn't brought any toilet paper.

*Fool! You'd better start paying attention to everything, or you're going to end up as animal shit.*

When he finished his duty, he reached for a handful of leaves. Something crawled out of the leaves and up his arm. He gaped at the bug. It was like nothing he'd ever seen before: rectangular, two inches long and a half inch wide, black with red spots, and three-inch feelers.

*Yuck!*

He shook his arm, but the bug continued its upward crawl. He scraped his arm on a lilac branch, and finally got rid of it. Though he'd always liked animals, he'd never felt any fondness for insects. He shuddered. Especially big ones.

The lower leaves of the bush began to tremble. Chet hurriedly wiped himself, then reached for a fallen tree limb. Gripping the stout, six-foot-long staff, he watched a brown creature begin to ooze out from under the bush. It paid no attention to him, but he couldn't take his eyes off the thing. What was it? Not a snake. It was too wide and had horseshoe-shaped feet—hundreds of them. And how long was it? Already eighteen inches had emerged from beneath the bush, and still it came.

Afraid to draw attention to himself, he crouched immobile, but he held the staff at the ready. If that thing were to turn on him...

He could see the entire body now, all seven feet of it. It seemed familiar, as if he'd seen something like it before. A picture on a website, perhaps. Of course—on a website for extinct creatures. A giant millipede.

How could he ever cope with the reconstruction if it was filled with bugs? He thought of all the horror movies he'd seen that featured giant insects such as ants, cockroaches, grasshoppers. They hadn't scared him because in the back of his mind he knew they were a trick of photography. But what if he were to meet a man-size cockroach in real life? He tightened his grip on the tree limb. It might not be much protection, but it was all he had.

He waited until the millipede had inched its way under another bush, then he stood and pulled up his pants. Carrying the staff, he headed for the door of the three-story building. He stopped. Three stories? It had been four stories a few minutes ago. Was the cat okay?

He studied the two remaining living room windows on the top floor. Was one of them his? Seeing the cat in the right one, he let out a pent-up breath. Oh, God. He didn't think he could handle any more of these shocks.

A single burst of unamused laughter escaped his lips. Oh, God? *Oh, Bob* was more like it.

A ringing came from his pocket. The cell phone. But he remembered placing it on the bedside table last night, and he hadn't touched it since.

He returned to his apartment, grabbed a towel, moistened a corner, and wiped his hands. Then he answered the still ringing phone.

Bob's face glowered at him.

"What now?"

"Nothing."

"You called me for nothing?"

"I didn't..." He sighed. Perhaps he had. Maybe invoking the name of a deity or the right hand of a deity constituted a call. "What do you have planned for me?"

"What makes you think I have anything planned for you?"

"I'm still here. You must have a reason."

"Must I?"

"You know what I mean. The world is changing all around me. My apartment building is shrinking. Are you testing me?"

"Why do you think I'm testing you?"

"Never mind," Chet said, thinking that Bob sounded like a psychotherapist or a not-bright child, responding to questions with questions. "Will you answer this at least? How are you making the changes?"

"I'm not making the changes. I told you, a development company on the planet Xerxes is making the changes."

"But how?"

"Do I look like a construction worker to you?"

The screen went dark. Chet snapped the phone shut and tossed it on the kitchen table.

While he fixed breakfast—granola and orange juice that smelled fermented—he thought about the reconstruction. If he had taken more science classes in college, maybe he'd understand it, but he didn't think so. The basic principles of science weren't applicable when the rules change. Mythology and theology classes probably wouldn't have helped his understanding either, and he was pretty sure they would not have explained Bob.

After breakfast, he resumed pacing, but all he could think of were animals in the zoo pacing in their cages. He had nothing else to do, though. He couldn't go for a walk outside, watch television, listen to the radio or CDs, use the computer, take a shower, play games. Wait a minute—he had a deck of cards somewhere. He could play solitaire.

He found the cards in a desk drawer. After playing two games, which he lost, he dealt a third hand. Putting the jack of spades on the queen of hearts, it hit him—this is really solitaire. As in solitary. Was he going to be alone for the rest of his life? Even though he saw himself as a lone coyote, he'd never seen himself as an only coyote, but now he had no friends, no family, no one to depend on but himself.

He gathered the cards, squared the edges, and looked around the living room for something to take his mind off his aloneness. His gaze settled on the bookcase, which was full of CDs, DVDs, video tapes and games, and a few books. He plucked *Nicholas Nickleby* off a shelf and settled on the couch with it.

The book had been required reading for a college literature course, but the pet store had been shorthanded back then, and he'd read cheat notes on the internet instead of the book. He promised himself that someday when he had time, he'd fulfill his obligation, and now he had nothing but time.

The cat jumped on the couch and sniffed the book.

"You want me to read to you?" Chet asked. "Okay. Here goes."

He opened the book, paged through a biography of Charles Dickens, the introduction, the acknowledgements, a note on the text, suggested further reading, a preface, the table of contents, and finally arrived at the first chapter.

"'There once lived in a sequestered part of the county of Devonshire, one Mr. Godfrey Nickleby, a worthy gentleman, who taking it into his head rather late in life that he must get married and not being young or rich enough to aspire to the hand of a lady of fortune, had wedded an old flame out of mere attachment, who in her turn had taken him for the same reason: thus two people who cannot afford to play cards for money, sometimes set down to a quiet game of love.'"

Chet slammed the book shut.

"That does it. Nothing out there can be worse than imprisoning myself in here." He snatched up his staff. "I'm going hunting for a supermarket. You coming?"

The cat beat him to the door.

Outside, Chet could hear the surf. Had it been the surfer who screamed? Maybe he should go look for him. Remembering the terror and pain he'd heard in that scream, he didn't think there was anything he could do to help. Besides, he had no idea where the person might be. The scream could have come from anywhere.

He looked to the mountains. The familiar jagged skyline made him long for everything that was ordinary, everything he'd taken for granted.

He turned east toward the remnant of the city. If there was a grocery store left in Denver, he was going to find it.

# Chapter 9

ANY ILLUSION OF normalcy disappeared before Chet walked two blocks. The houses became fewer and the fields between them larger. Though he saw no one, he had the uncomfortable feeling he was being watched, and a curtain twitching in one window of a wood-frame house confirmed his suspicion.

Is this what the remaining human population had come to—a blind distrust of its fellows? Modern society had always been blamed for isolating people from one another, but perhaps the reverse was true, that in some strange way civilization had given people the freedom to trust one another.

Odd to think that thousands of years of civilization, whether good or bad, had been annihilated practically overnight, and for what? Tourists.

An eerie, rhythmic sound interrupted his thoughts. He glanced over his shoulder. Trailing him were eight or ten adults dressed in belted and hooded brown robes that fell to their sandaled feet.

Heads down, palms together, they chanted, "Oh, Bob, Right Hand of God, holy is thy name."

Three of them might have been women, but shrouded as they were, Chet couldn't tell for sure.

He stifled an urge to laugh. Where had they gotten those costumes? Monks R Us? And how long had they been behind him?

A sigh of defeat blew away his amusement. He hadn't been

paying attention...again. He should have noticed when they started to follow him. They seemed harmless, but what if they weren't? How was he going to survive in this new world if he kept getting lost in his thoughts?

"I never considered myself to be introspective," he said to the cat padding by his side. "I better think about that."

The cat bounded into a field.

"That was a joke," he called after it, then clamped his lips shut.

*Probably not a good idea to draw attention to himself by talking so loudly.*

Catching site of Cherry Creek Mall a couple of blocks away, he quickened his step. With all those stores, including a supermarket, he should be able to get whatever he needed.

A half of a block from the mall, he stopped. Blinked. A sick, empty feeling he finally identified as fear filled his belly.

*What was he going to do now?*

He tried to will the mall back into existence, but all he could see was the reality: a plain of boulders that from a distance had looked like buildings.

He took in a shaky breath, let it out slowly.

If he followed Cherry Creek to Colorado Boulevard, he'd come to another grocery store. Or the ghost of one. Either way, he had to try. And since the cat hadn't returned from its side excursion, he'd have to go alone.

He marched across the plain to the creek, detouring around boulders as big as his apartment building. A forest, unlovely, dark, and deep, had sprung up on the other side of the swollen creek. Its trees were like nothing Chet had ever seen before. Perhaps two hundred feet tall, they had thick branches with broad leaves. Grafted onto those branches were sprigs of fern-like foliage. He wrinkled his nose. The forest smelled like a locker room full of ripe sweat socks.

Sandwiched between the plain of boulders and the forest, Chet felt as if he'd shrunk to a quarter of his size, and he couldn't prove to himself that he hadn't. Nothing in sight offered him normal perspective.

He walked beside the creek, feeling smaller and less real with every step. Before he shrank into nothingness, he came to a wide concrete overpass that spanned the creek and disappeared into the depths of the forest. Must be Colorado Boulevard, or what was left of it. One good thing—since the grocery store he sought no longer existed, he wouldn't have to enter that fetid forest.

On a long ago camping trip, his father had said, "Nothing in the woods will hurt you unless you hurt or frighten it first," but that was in another world where woods smelled of life and promise, not putrefaction.

The forest exhaled a sultry breath. Revolted by the touch of heat on his cheek, he stepped back, but a sweep of iridescent blue drew him forward again. What was it? If it were smaller, he'd think it was a feather, but no feather could possibly be four or five feet long.

Couldn't be that large? What was he thinking? Anything was possible now. What kind of bird could have lost such a feather? A great owl? A thunderbird? A teratorn? Whatever it was, he hoped it didn't fancy humans. He'd never be able to outrun a creature like that.

Squeals and the sounds of scuffling came from behind the tree. He froze. Two beasts tumbled into view. The size and color of brown bears, they looked like hamsters, and from the way they scuffled, tugging a mottled green object, he guessed they were babies. How big was the mother? *Where* was the mother? He glanced around but did not see her.

The cubs saw him, though. They dropped their plaything—a military boot with camouflage markings like the one worn by Lance, the soldier in Cheesman Park—and shambled toward Chet.

He fled.

Running blindly, he lost track of how many cross streets he passed. He slowed, trotted two more blocks then, hoping he was close to Fourteenth Avenue, he turned to the right. With the mountains at his back, he headed for Krameria Street and two rival supermarkets that had been built across the street from each other in the pre-deletion world.

Out here, east of Colorado Boulevard, little remained of Denver but a dozen houses clustered around a storefront. An odd-shaped cross, like the letter T painted red, hung over the door of the business, and a flickering light shone through the window. Above the rasp of his breath, Chet could hear singing. "Amazing Grace," it sounded like.

He trotted to the building and peered into the window. A dozen lit candles flanked a television centered on the counter. Three men, six women, and four children stood enraptured before the dark screen. The window vibrated with their song.

"'Twas Bob that brought us safe thus far, and Bob will lead us home."

The hymn ended, and a woman in a white gown and blond braids encircling her head like a halo, lifted her arms and cried, "Bob, Voice of God, we are waiting for your words. Speak to us, Oh Prophet."

Chet's upper lip curled in a sneer, but he couldn't help pitying the small congregation for putting their trust in Bob, that uncaring prophesier of doom. He sidled past the window and almost tripped on a broken board that looked like it had once been part of a sign. In faded red lettering, it proclaimed, "Tim's Plumbing."

He sped away from the makeshift church, running until a stitch in his side brought him up short. Surrounded by fields of purple-flowered weeds that smelled like sour milk, he trudged east in search of grocery stores he no longer had any hope of finding.

His breath had almost returned to normal when the earth rose and fell. He teetered. Planting his staff on the ground to keep his balance, he wondered if something was wrong with the earth or if he had lost his equilibrium. Ever since Bob had messed with his senses, he hadn't felt quite right.

The ground rose and fell again. He heard a loud crack, and the earth split open on the very spot where he stood. He hurled himself backward and smashed into a tree that hadn't been there a second ago. He wrapped his arms around the trunk and watched in disbelief as the rift widened and kept on widening. He wanted to clap his hands over his ears to block out the sounds of the earth wailing, the rocks popping and cracking like gunfire, but he had to cling to the tree to keep from sliding into the chasm.

A grumbling from the distance grew thunderous, and whitewater cascaded through the gorge. Gradually the earth stopped moving, the onrush of water slowed, and the gorge filled.

Chet stepped away from the tree and tried to shake some life back into his arms, but they were stiff and felt like clubs of ice. Trembling from an overdose of adrenaline, he stared at the newborn river. Had Bob tried to kill him? If the initial split had been a few inches wider, if his reflexes had been a second slower—

*What was that?*

He thought he heard a soft whine, but when he cupped an ear, all he heard was the river. Then he saw it.

A small brown and white creature was entangled in a branch that swept along with the river. The creature struggled to get free, but water kept engulfing it, and it was losing strength. Chet dove into the river and grabbed hold of the limb. The current was still strong, and he could feel himself being drawn downstream.

He scissored his legs, kicking as hard as he could, and managed to angle toward shore so overhanging tree roots could snag the branch.

Refusing to think about how tired he felt, he heaved himself out of the river and dragged the branch onto land. He reached for the creature but seeing its broad gargoyle face, he paused. Most pit bulls were friendly, but he had no way of knowing if this one had been bred for viciousness. Hoping it was too spent to attack, he freed it and backed away.

The dog shook the water off its coat. After staring at Chet for a moment, it sprang. The sixty-pound onslaught knocked Chet to the ground. The pit bull stood over him, licking his face.

A ringing intruded. Chet sat up and pulled the surprisingly dry phone out of his sodden pocket.

"What?"

"You sound testy," Bob said. "Is something wrong?"

"What could possibly be wrong?"

"Everything is on schedule at this end."

"Why don't you go talk to those people at Tim's Plumbing. *They* want to talk to you."

"All their prayers and all their hymns won't make a whit of difference. I can't undo what has been done."

"You can, but you won't." Chet snapped the phone shut and flung it into the river.

"Well, that's the end of that," he said to the dog.

He looked around for his staff. When he didn't see it, he figured he'd dropped it to hug the tree.

"We'll just have to go back. I'm sure I can find another stick, but I've grown attached to that one. We can rest there. Think you're up to it?"

The dog led the way. Despite its exhaustion, its gait was jaunty as if it expected to see something new and exciting any minute.

Ancient cottonwoods lined the river. Some had scars on their trunks from long ago traumas, and others had dead branches that creaked ominously in the breeze.

"You'd think they'd decorate a new river with new trees," Chet said, teeth chattering. His wet garments stuck to his skin, and the April sun brought no warmth. "I don't understand the purpose of creating trees that look like they're about ready for the great forest in the sky. Though maybe that is the point. Like builders on Earth who use artificially aged materials. I guess the Xerxes development company wants the tourists to think they're seeing the real thing, not some phony new reconstruction.

"Who are these tourists, anyway? Did Bob ever mention them to you?"

The pit bull grinned at him.

"I didn't think so. He's long on commentary, short on information, like some of those other guys on television."

The dog gave a joyful bark and bounded through the trees.

"Great conversationalist, Chet. Can't even keep a dog

entertained. Hey, here's the tree that saved me."

He patted the trunk of the tree. "Don't know how you appeared right where I needed you, but I do appreciate it." He looked around but didn't see his staff.

The pit bull returned, followed by an old man bent beneath a cumbersome backpack. The dog, looking pleased with itself, led him to Chet.

The man held out a calloused hand with thick, stubby fingers.

"Frank Rhoades. Retired rancher."

Chet grasped the outstretched hand. It felt rough as tree bark. He swayed, and Frank tightened his grip to steady him.

"Better sit down before you fall, young fellow. Better yet, take off those wet clothes. I have a blanket you can borrow."

Chet opened his mouth to protest, but Frank held up a hand.

"I owe you for saving Digby."

He shrugged off the pack, unstrapped a bedroll, and handed it to Chet.

Too tired and cold to worry about modesty, Chet stripped. He wrapped the blanket around himself, spread out his clothes to dry, then huddled in the sun.

Digby yawned and lay next to him. He scratched the dog behind the ears, and it made sounds of contentment.

Frank smiled at them, and Chet realized the man was younger than he thought. Perhaps a little over fifty. The deep lines around his eyes must have been etched by laughter and the sun, not just years.

The man's knees creaked as he settled on the ground. He leaned against the pack.

"I've seen a lot of strange things the past couple of days. An armadillo the size of a Volkswagen bug, A bird as big as a B-52. A town that turned to dust. But that river was the strangest. Cracked open and swept Digby away before I could grab him." He narrowed his eyes. "I don't believe you introduced yourself."

"Chet Thomlin. I used to own a pet store."

That was it, his whole life summed up in less than a dozen words.

"Pleased to meet you, though you could have been the devil himself, and I'd be pleased to meet you. Hardly see anyone. Where are you headed?"

Chet scowled at the river. Even if one of the grocery stores on Krameria remained, he couldn't get to it now.

"I've been trying to find a grocery store, but I'm not having any luck."

"I passed a small market about half a day's journey due north."

Chet brightened. Perhaps there was some hope of getting supplies after all.

"Of course," Frank said, "with the way things are changing, it might not be there much longer. Me? I'm working my way up to Canada. My boy married a Canadian girl. They live in Vancouver. At least they did. I want to find them if I can. A personal quest. One last look at this beautiful country before it's changed beyond recognition."

He rummaged in his pack and pulled out something that looked like old shoe leather.

"Want some beef jerky?"

Chet's stomach growled, but he shook his head.

Frank yanked off a piece with his big teeth and tucked it in his cheek like chewing tobacco. "You know about the doors to the refuge?"

"I saw one at Cheesman Park on Easter."

"But you didn't go through. There's no shame in being afraid of the unknown."

"I wasn't afraid." He spoke too loudly. Lowering his voice, he said, "You didn't go through, either."

"True. I was lined up like everyone else in Weld County, but when my turn came, I stood there like a tired old plow horse and didn't move. Couldn't see any reason to go into the refuge. Couldn't see any reason not to. If I was younger, I'd have gone for sure, but I have nothing left to live for."

"I know what you mean."

Frank's voice hardened.

"No you don't. Even before all this happened, my life was over. I used to have a contract with a government-funded meatpacking company that supplied beef for school lunch programs. My animals were clean, well cared for, and I thought I was doing a good thing feeding children. Then one year the beef got contaminated at the packing plant, and it all had to be recalled. Perhaps you remember the incident? It was the largest recall in history. Millions of pounds of beef."

His face looked stern and uncompromising.

"My entire herd destroyed. A total waste of all those lives for no reason. I had no heart for ranching after that. Reneged on the contract. Some snip of a girl from the government kept hounding me, trying to force me back into business. And while all that was going on, my wife died slowly and painfully from pancreatic cancer."

"I'm sorry."

Chet knew the words were feeble, but he couldn't think of anything else to say.

"Not your fault. But that's why this change means nothing to me. But you—you're a young man with your whole life ahead of you. You should have gone into the refuge."

"We only have Bob's word that the place is a refuge."

Chet thought of the ranch he'd dreamed about in the far away world of normalcy.

*Would the ranch have been a refuge or simply a bigger pen that gave the animals the illusion of freedom?*

Is that what Bob had been offering? An illusion? But he'd said everything was illusion. Did that mean illusion was reality? His head began to ache.

Frank gave him a shrewd look.

"Do you think Bob was lying about it being a refuge?"

"Not really. It's just that he twists words and plays games, and I never know what he means."

"But the doorway could lead to a refuge as Bob said."

"I suppose. Yes."

Frank stabbed a finger at him.

"If you have another opportunity to go through the doorway to the refuge, you take it. Hear? Save yourself. Someday things will get back to normal, and you can continue on with your life."

"Normal?" Chet snorted. "Do you really think things will ever get back to normal?"

Frank swept out an arm.

"Not there." He tapped his right temple. "Up here." He tilted his head. "Something's ringing. It seems to be coming from your clothes."

Chet winced.

"My cell."

"I thought phones no longer work."

"They don't."

Chet pushed himself upright, tramped to his pants, pulled the phone out of a pocket, and pitched it into the river.

He returned to his place in the sun. He tried to ignore Frank's questioning look, but he was wearing the man's blanket, after all.

"I don't have the strength to deal with him," he said.

"Him?"

"Bob."

Frank drew back.

"The Right Hand of God? That Bob?"

Chet nodded.

Frank stared at him.

"You just threw God into the river?"

"He's not God. He's an assistant. And his God isn't God, either. He's an area supervisor God—sort of a galactic landlord. All he cares about is his property. And anyway, I'm not sure Bob exists."

"Of course he does. I saw him."

"In real life?"

"On television."

"I've seen him on television, too. Also on my computer and the cell phone. It's always the same. Only a head. Nothing else. I think he's a recording or a virtual being or some sort of static created by electronic transmission."

77

"But he calls you and talks to you."

"So? If this whole change is being perpetrated by a being with phenomenal powers, then why couldn't he or she know what my response would be to anything Bob said, and program it accordingly?"

"If Bob isn't talking to you, who is programming the call? God?"

"Can't be." Chet sighed. "Maybe Bob does exist. But why would the right hand of God be talking to me?"

"Apparently you've been chosen."

"Chosen? No way. I'm nobody. I'm not religious. And, according to Bob, I'm not very bright."

Frank grinned.

"Bob said that?"

"He doesn't seem to like me very much."

"Sounds as though you feel guilty for being singled out when so many others didn't survive."

"I don't feel guilty and I don't feel singled out. I feel..." He paused, searching for the word. "Disconnected. Like none of this has anything to do with me. But I keep wondering why I wasn't deleted. What does Bob want with me?"

"Maybe you're being rewarded for something."

"Or punished."

Frank nodded.

"There is that."

Chet closed his eyes. What had he ever done, good or bad, to draw Bob's attention? Looking back, his life seemed blank, a wasteland of insignificant episodes.

His chin dropped to his chest. He heard Frank's voice, but couldn't focus enough to make sense of the words. He wanted to curl up, go to sleep, and wake in the normal world.

Feeling himself doze off, he jerked his head up.

Frank was staring at him, eyes bright, and he was chewing the wad of dried beef that had been tucked in his cheek.

Chet pulled the blanket tighter.

"Just wondering what it's like to be on a first name basis with The Right Hand of God."

"Damned uncomfortable. Like my skin doesn't fit anymore. Like…did you ever fry ants with a magnifying glass when you were a kid?"

"Nope. Can't say I ever wanted to."

"I did. Once. That's what I feel like. As if I'm under a magnifying glass." He frowned. "You don't think I'm being punished because I murdered an ant, do you?"

"Who knows? God must like ants. He made a lot of them."

"I was sorry I did it, and I never killed another creature." He took a deep breath. The smell of masticated meat, Frank's acrid sweat, and the pit bull's fishy breath turned his stomach. "My senses don't work right anymore. And I sleep all the time. That's why I need to find a grocery store. I was sleeping when I should have been stockpiling food." He gave a vague look around. "I better go before the market disappears."

The dog shot to his feet and dashed to where Chet's clothes were laid out to dry. He returned with the briefs, dropped the warm but still damp garment in Chet's lap, and sat back, tongue lolling.

Frank held up his bare left wrist with its band of untanned skin and glanced at it.

"It's time we were heading out."

Chet tugged on his briefs, shed the blanket, and scrambled for his clothes. Frank stowed the blanket. Digby ran circles around them, yipping with excitement. It stopped to lick Chet's face, then trotted south along the riverbank.

Frank shouldered his pack.

"Let me give you a bit of advice."

"I'm listening."

"If you're ever walking in the forest and you see a large animal wearing a bib and carrying a knife and fork. Run."

It took Chet a couple of seconds to realize the older man was joking. Or was he?

"That's it? After all you've gone through, that's the only bit of wisdom you have to impart?"

"Yep. That's it."

Frank strode away. Though his back was bowed under the weight of the pack, his step was as jaunty as his dog's.

# Chapter 10

NEITHER FRANK RHOADES nor Digby looked back. Chet watched them, surprised by the twinge of envy he felt. Frank seemed to be the young man with his whole life ahead of him, and Chet a graybeard at the end of his.

He stroked his chin. The bristles couldn't be called a beard, and they weren't gray. Yet. If life continued flinging trauma his way, soon he would look as old as he felt.

He reached into a pocket, half expecting to encounter the phone he'd twice thrown into the river, but all he found were his keys, a wet tissue, and the plastic bag of lemon drops. The zipper seal had been waterproof, and the candy remained dry. Bolstered by the tiny triumph as well as the sugar, he turned north.

A half day's journey. How far was that? Ten miles? Twelve? He squinted at the sun. It had moved past its zenith. Could he make it to the market before nightfall? He shuddered, imagining himself blundering into seven-foot-long bugs in the dark, and picked up his pace.

The trail let in a straight line through sour-milk prairie. He counted the blocks he'd traveled from Colorado Boulevard and decided he was on Eudora Street. Odd that even though roads were becoming indistinguishable from the fields where houses once stood, he still thought in terms of the city grid. What would he do when all traces of the grid disappeared? How would he ever find himself?

No time to think of that now. He opened his eyes and ears to any hint of danger, and speeded up to a double-time trot. Without dwelling on any one thing, he recognized that his clothes had dried, the river veered off to the northeast, he was getting thirsty, the sun dipped toward the horizon, and rocks littered the path.

What was that? He paused to listen, but his labored breathing drowned out the sound. He held his breath and heard it—a swish in the grass by a lichen-covered rock. Carefully, he let out his breath and took in another. Held it. Heard the swish again. Dread formed in the pit of his stomach. What sort of creature would he encounter?

*Oh, please. Not another bug.*

Then he heard an ominous rattle along with the swish. His breath burst out of him. Not a bug. A rattlesnake. What a relief! He could give the snake a wide berth, and they'd both continue their journeys in peace. He stepped to the side and accidentally kicked a rock out of his way. Heard a hiss. Felt a burn on his ankle. Another snake? He jumped back and stared at the path where the rock had been.

Steam shot out of a hole less than an inch in diameter. The hole widened. The air heated.

Chet wiped the sweat from his brow with a forearm. He tried to swallow, but his mouth was too dry to form saliva. How far away was the river now? A mile? Two? But if he detoured to the river for a drink, he'd never make it to the market. Maybe if he dug around the hole he'd find water. The steam had to come from somewhere, didn't it?

He focused his attention on the spot, and now he could see that the plume of steam shot from the top of a small mound. As he watched, the mound grew. He stepped back and kept stepping back as the mound continued to grow. If not for the sulphurous steam, he'd think monstrous ants were building a new home. How immense would ants have to be to build a six-foot mound in a few seconds? He pushed the thought away. Bob did a good enough job of tormenting him. He didn't need to do it to himself.

A faint boom came to him from deep within the growing

mound. The ground shuddered, and a dark mass billowed from the cone. A cry burst out of Chet when he realized the wondrous truth. A volcano was being born.

The black cloud spread, darkening the sky, and gray ash powdered the earth.

The cone of the new volcano glowed like fire.

Lava!

Chet turned and raced for home.

Chet clutched at his chest and slowed to a walk. His heart thudded against his ribs so painfully he thought he was having a heart attack. His left arm ached, but so did the rest of his body. So perhaps he wasn't having a heart attack. Could be he was out of shape. Until today, he hadn't run much, preferring to walk or climb stairs for exercise.

His heart rate slowed, and his breath settled into a more normal rhythm. How far had he sprinted? A mile? No, half that. He could still feel the heat of the volcano, but he'd outrun the lava. He looked back at the growing mountain and the glowing river.

Grand Mesa on the western slope had once been a lava river such as this. After millions of years, the land surrounding it had eroded, leaving the basalt formation behind. How long before this lava river became a towering mesa? A million years? A month?

Chet fumbled in his pocket for the bag of lemon drops, but put them back without eating one. He didn't have enough saliva to dissolve it.

He lifted his nose in the air. A sniff told him the river was close. He quickened his pace.

Then there it was. Cool. Serene. Timeless. He lay on his belly, cupped his hands, and drank the sweet liquid until his stomach distended. It seemed impossible that the liquid in this river and the fluid that used to come out of the tap at home were both called water; they were as different as cocoa and vinegar.

Perhaps he should pitch camp here for the night? From the far recesses of his mind came an echo of his father's bedtime admonition.

"Don't let the bedbugs bite." He shivered, thinking of sleeping in the open where monstrous bugs could munch on him.

He splashed water on his face and arms, guzzled one more handful of water, and heaved himself upright.

The water in his belly sloshed as he walked. Did camels' humps slosh? Did camels still exist?

Realizing he was getting lightheaded from lack of food, he stuffed a lemon drop in his mouth and focused his mind on the tang.

Prairie gradually gave way to the city, though what remained of Denver could not be called a city, not even a settlement. With the way buildings were disappearing, it seemed more of an unsettlement.

*What was he going to do when all traces of civilization disappeared?*

Panic, like bile, rose in Chet's throat. He turned his attention to the lingering citrus taste in his mouth, and pictured himself sitting with his father at the kitchen table, the lemon jar between them.

A familiar chant yanked him into the present.

"Oh, Bob, Right Hand of God, holy is thy name."

Long shadows swallowed the feet of the brown-robed monks, making it appear as if they were gliding effortlessly on the rough path.

Chet's legs felt stiff and lifeless, and every footfall jarred him to the top of his head. He'd like to call Bob a lot of names, but holy wasn't one of them.

A cat's shadow crept from an alley between two rows of frame houses. The sun slinking behind the mountains magnified the shadow and distorted it to look like that of a prehistoric beast.

Chet felt a lightening of his step. The orange cat was coming to meet him.

The monks reached the alley at the same time Chet did. He stepped out of the way to let them pass.

Too quick for Chet to comprehend, the shadow leapt. A blur of golden orange. A gush of blood. High-pitched shrieks.

Chet froze. All but one of the monks continued their forward glide, seemingly oblivious to the screams of their fallen member.

The screams stopped abruptly.

This wasn't real. It couldn't be.

But the smell—blood, guts, raw meat, feces, urine, and a powerful musky odor emanating from the beast—told Chet the truth.

The cat, sword-like fangs stained with monk blood, looked up from its meal. For one timeless moment, Chet stared into the amber eyes, eyes no human had seen for more than ten thousand years. Though his heart pounded wildly, he felt no fear. The saber-tooth tiger, with its strong forelegs built for springing, could take him down in an instant, but since it had food, it had no reason to go after more food.

When the beast bowed to its meal again, Chet sidled away.

Chet dropped onto the couch and, using both hands, hoisted first one of his legs and then the other onto the coffee table. The orange cat—which had been asleep at the other end of the couch—opened one eye, yawned loudly, then fell asleep again.

"Easy for you to say," Chet grumbled.

He watched the cat for a moment, marveling that any creature could be so relaxed while the world went through such staggering changes.

At least he was home now. Chet looked around the room. The silent television the bookshelves, the off-white wall, the tan carpet seemed different. It took him a minute to realize that they were the same—he was different. A failure. After all his travels that day, after all the traumas and dramas, what had he accomplished?

Not a dang thing.

Chet woke like a log: heavy, wooden, and with a tongue that felt like bark. He lumbered to his feet, looked around the living room, and wondered how he came to be sleeping on the couch. All in a rush, he remembered. Bob. Bugs. River. Digby. Rhoades. Volcano. Tiger. Exhaustion.

He dragged himself down the single remaining flight of stairs, relieved himself behind a bush, then crouched down to evacuate his bowels. Disgusted that once again he had forgotten to bring toilet paper, he picked up a handful of leaves and inspected them before cleaning himself.

Perhaps he could forgive Bob the river, the volcano, maybe even the bugs, but he'd never forgive the loss of plumbing. Shitting in the open was demeaning, unsanitary, and dangerous. With pants down around his ankles and hindquarters exposed, he was vulnerable to attack from any man-eating beast that may wander by.

Back in his second-floor apartment, Chet washed his hands and gulped a mouthful of water. He almost spit it out but caught himself in time. No matter how acrid, water was as precious as gold had once been.

He opened a can of tuna for the cat and fixed himself a bowl of dry granola. The cereal tasted delicious, but still, he'd give almost anything for a splash of orange juice.

Chet gazed out the living room window. Overnight, the prairie had swallowed all but a few distant houses. Did anyone live in them, or were they merely decoration?

*Was he the last person left alive?*

He cocked his head listening to the apartment below. Not a sound. He'd known the occupant only by the CDs he or she had played—loud metallic screeching that used to keep him awake far into the night. Even if he wanted to, there seemed no point in trying to make contact. Tomorrow, a single apartment would remain of the building that had once contained a hundred. And the day after that...

Chet took a deep breath to crowd out the thought, and inhaled a lungful of sea air. Energized, he gulped in more breaths, then he charged for the door, waited for the cat, and raced it outside.

The raw, mid-morning light made him squint. The end of the world should be murky, like old photographs, not this impossible brightness that hurt his eyes.

He slanted a look at the volcano. It stood stark against the incandescent sky, a perfect cone with the tip scooped out. Wisps of steam or ash drifted upward, and fire-colored lava rolled down the side. Without the enveloping clouds of ash, black skies, earth tremors, and storms that should have accompanied the erupting volcano, it looked like a child's science project.

For now, anyway, he wouldn't have to worry about ending up in some future Pompeiish archeological dig.

He and the cat trotted the four short blocks to the seashore. Four blocks? The ocean had been a mile away on Saturday when the blue flowers had called it forth. At the rate the water was closing in on his building, waves would be lapping at the front door in two days.

The hell with it. The rest of the new earth might be a horror show, but this place felt safe. Secure. The waves washing in from the mountains whispered a welcome, and gulls glided overhead.

The cat scampered along the beach—or what was becoming a beach. Chet reached down, picked up a handful of smooth pebbles, and let them trickle between his fingers. Not yet sand. But soon.

The cat crept to the edge of the ocean and stared down into the water.

"What did you find?" Chet called out.

A sea breeze blew his words away.

He knelt next to his feline companion. Colorful fish darted from one side of a tide pool to the other, as if trying to escape.

"They must have washed in on high tide and got caught," Chet said. "I wonder if they'd mind if I joined them for a swim."

The cat looked out over the ocean. Suddenly its fur stood on end, and it froze. Chet turned to follow its gaze.

"What? I don't see anything."

And then he did. Something was rising out of the depths, something monstrous and reptilian. It bore no resemblance to the Loch Ness monster, and no one would ever give it an affectionate name such as Nessie. The creature focused its slime-brown eyes on Chet, opened its razor-toothed mouth, and let out a sound like a chorus of damned souls.

Chet's stomach churned. He wanted to run, needed to run, but he could not move.

The leviathan bellowed once more, then slipped back into the water.

Chet swallowed.

"So much for swimming."

The cat washed behind an ear.

"Don't act all innocent," Chet said. "You were as scared as me. What was that thing?"

He struggled to his feet. Shook life into first·one leg than the other.

When he thought he could walk without staggering, he said, "Let's get out of here."

The cat washed behind its other ear.

"I need to go foraging for food, but I don't know how. Will you help?"

The cat reached a paw into the pool.

"No fish," Chet said.

The cat streaked off.

"No mice, either!"

It stopped, swiveled its head around, and gave Chet a bewildered look. Then it slinked back to his side.

"I have nothing against mice," Chet said, "but I'm a vegetarian. I guess that means I have to go grubbing for roots."

But where? The putrid forest? He'd rather die than eat anything that came from there. With a shock, he realized that if he didn't find a food source before his supplies gave out, he would die.

How spoiled he'd been in the pre-reconstruction era when all he had to do was stroll into a grocery store and fill a cart with whatever he wished. And yet shopping had seemed such a chore.

An unexpected sense of loss slammed into him, doubling him over. He wrapped his arms around his midsection.

The cat studied him, head at an angle.

"It's a human thing," Chet said. "Don't worry about it. But we better go before I change my mind."

They were a tenth of a mile from the forest when Chet felt a disturbance behind him, like the quickening of a breeze.

He glanced over his right shoulder. An abnormal cloud swirled lazily in the southeastern sky.

"But how can you tell if something is abnormal when abnormal has become the norm?" he said.

His companion did not respond.

Wind plastered Chet's shirt to his back. He stole another look behind. The cloud swirled like a cyclone. He blinked, and then there were three clouds swirling faster and faster, sucking up prairie grasses and weeds, whipping them into dark masses.

The masses grew smaller and tighter the faster they whirled. They descended, hurtling straight for him.

Chet dashed out of the whirlwind's path.

"Run," he yelled. The cat sat on its haunches. "Come on!"

He ran a few more yards then looked back. Two of the whirlwinds had swerved in his direction; the third swept toward the sitting feline.

Chet raced for the cat. Moments before he reached his friend, the air tore, like a great swathe of wallpaper. He stopped short.

Head and tail held high, the cat marched through the opening.

"No!" Chet cried. He started to follow, but backpedaled when he caught a glimpse of what the new world held. The whirlwinds swooped, rocking his body. He threw himself face down on the ground and covered his head with his arms.

The whirlwinds shred his shirt and yanked off a shoe as they sped soundlessly by. He imagined them scooping him into their embrace and pureeing him into a bloody cocktail. Maybe he should have followed the traitorous cat into the new world, but how could he after what he'd seen?

Sure, he'd be safe. Safe as the animals would have been in the refuge he'd planned. But his refuge would have provided privacy for its inmates. Bob's refuge seemed more like a zoo. Inside a vast fenced area, people milled or huddled together. Above the enclosure revolved a saucer-shaped vehicle girdled with windows. He had seen faces pressed to the windows, faces that did not belong to humans. And he had heard a few words: "To the left you will see..." It made no sense. Why would the guide be speaking English to the alien tourists? But if the guide wasn't speaking English, how could he have understood what it said? Unless Bob was messing with him again.

He peeked out from beneath his arm. He could not see even a hint of where the rend in the air had been.

Realizing the worst of the winds had passed, he dragged himself upright.

*This is growing old. How many times in the past few days have I ended up on the ground?*

But there were worse things. He watched the whirlwinds rip through the forest, uprooting trees, sending leaves flying. Overhead, two yellow leaves pirouetted around each other, descending so slowly he could almost see the double helix they drew in the air. Six feet from the ground, the leaves flitted off in different directions. Chet shook his head to clear it.

"You'd think by now I'd be used to such things as leaves metamorphosing into butterflies," he said.

*See what you've done to me?* he added silently to the cat.

*You've got me talking to myself. At least you're where you chose to be. Take care of yourself.*

Holding himself stiffly, he hobbled for home to get another shirt and pair of shoes. He breathed through his mouth so he wouldn't smell the nauseating odor emanating from the forest. After a few inhalations, he had to close his mouth; the foulness furred his tongue. He summoned what saliva he could and tried to spit out the stench, but it lingered on his palate, in his nostrils, on his tattered clothes.

He breathed shallowly. When he detected a different smell underlying the putrescence, he choked in a deeper breath. An orange scent mingled with the forest odor, like perfume on a corpse.

He lifted his nose, concentrated on the orange, and followed it to an unpruned privet hedge hidden in the shadows at the edge of the forest. He skirted the hedge until he came to a splintery wooden gate. He gave the gate a push, steeling himself for the squeak, but it swung open without a sound.

A two-story stone house stood surrounded by a riotous garden of roses and tulips, lilacs and petunias, crocuses and dahlias, all blooming at once.

*Where was the orange tree?*

Thinking of how good the cool citrus juice would feel in his dry mouth, Chet slipped into the yard and hunted the scent. He found it in an untamed brush of flat yellow roses. Orange-smelling roses? No fair!

"Jimmy?"

The quavery voice startled him. He spun to face the old woman clad in jeans and a man's shirt who scuttled toward him, arms outstretched.

"Jimmy, oh Jimmy," she cried. "They told me you were dead, but I knew you'd come back to me."

# Chapter 11

THE OLD WOMAN threw her arms around Chet. Her cheek rested on his shoulder, and her tears dampened his shirt. Too surprised to react, he stood, hands dangling at his side.

Surprise gave way to pity. After a moment's hesitation, he patted her on the back. He couldn't remember the last time he'd been enfolded in a maternal embrace—Isabel hadn't like to touch or be touched.

Eyes stinging, he relaxed into the borrowed hug that smelled of apples and cinnamon and uncomplicated times.

Finally, she stepped away and smiled at him. The smile smoothed the wrinkles around her mouth and crinkled her laugh lines, and Chet could see in that age-ravaged face the young woman she had been.

"It's so good to have you home again, Jimmy. I waited for you— I wanted to see you one last time."

"I'm not…"

Chet let the sentence die.

*Would it be so terrible to let the woman think he was her Jimmy?*

She gazed expectantly at him. "Not what, dear?"

Lucky Jimmy to have a mother who actually paid attention when he spoke. Chet scrabbled about in his mind for a response.

"Not staying long," he finished lamely.

"It will be long enough, you'll see." She studied him, giving a wry shake of her head. "You always were hard on your clothes. Some of your old things should still fit. Come. I was just about to take a bath, but it looks like you need it more than I do."

Without quite knowing how it happened, Chet found himself sitting in a large copper tub filled with hot water, set in the middle of the black and white checkerboard kitchen floor.

*Like a stewing chicken.*

Feeling silly, but unable to stop himself, he peered over the rim of the tub. Satisfied that it wasn't resting on hot coals, he settled back, but had a hard time relaxing. Gradually, the hot water erased the tension in his muscles.

*Not a good idea to stay here,* he scolded himself. *You need to be strong for what's ahead, and pampering will make you weak.*

But it felt so good to let go.

He woke to the sound of the old woman's voice. "—towels on the table," she called to him from the other side of the kitchen door.

Shivering, Chet grabbed a towel and stepped out of the cold water. He dried himself, then looked for his clothes. They weren't where he dumped them, on the padded turquoise seat of a chrome chair. He wrapped a towel around his midsection, draped another over his shoulders, and went in search of the old woman.

He found her in the dining room, sitting at a blond wood table covered with a vinyl lace tablecloth. She was paging through a thick photograph album, a half-smile curving her lips.

"Where are my clothes?" Chet asked.

"Upstairs, in your room. Everything is the way you left it."

"I mean my clothes. The clothes I was wearing."

She wrinkled her nose. "I threw the shirt and shoes in the trash, and I've got the rest of your things soaking in the laundry room."

His stomach lurched at the thought of being trapped here until his clothes dried. Putting on someone else's garments seemed almost as frightful, but no way was he going to hang around wearing nothing but a couple of towels.

He took three strides toward the dining room door, then stopped and looked back.

"You go on and get dressed," she said. "I'll be up in a minute."

Chet crossed the threshold into the living room. Decorated in orange and yellow and avocado, the spotless room seemed more like a movie set than a place where people lived. Not a single dust mote danced in the shaft of sunlight slanting through the window opposite the wide staircase.

Chet padded up the stairs. The avocado runner muffled his steps, and only the ticking of the mantle clock broke the silence.

On the landing, five doors faced him. He opened one door and exposed a linen closet, sheets and towels neatly arranged. He opened another door, and his lips parted in surprise. Unlike the rest of the well-kept house, this room looked a mess. Magazines, books, roadmaps, and jumbles of clothes littered the floor and the unmade bed. Undergarments spilled from open drawers, and dirty dishes covered the dresser top. The old woman's scent hung in the air.

Feeling like a voyeur, Chet hastily closed the door and opened another.

A boy's room. A twin bed neatly made with a white chenille bedspread jutted from a faded sea-green wall, and a model airplane hung from the white ceiling. Framed baseball cards—Mickey Mantle and Roger Maris—sat on the dresser next to a portable record player and a collection of 45s. Chet flipped through the discs. Johnny Horton. Gene Vincent. Eddie Cochran.

How long had the old woman kept this room sacrosanct? Forty years? What would it have been like to be raised by such a devoted mother? Four days after he left for college, Isabel had cleaned out his room and turned it into a gym.

Chet opened a drawer, grabbed a pair of blue-and white-striped boxer shorts two sizes too big. They looked new and old at the same time, and smelled of laundry soap. He dangled them from a finger, then reminding himself that wearing secondhand undershorts did not mean the end of the world—already there—he pulled them on and went rummaging through the closet.

A few minutes later, the old woman rapped on the door and called out, "You decent?"

He expected her to burst into the room without an invitation the way Isabel always did, but she waited for him to open the door.

She beamed.

"My, don't you look handsome."

Dressed in an oversize tee-shirt, jeans with the legs folded up like cuffs, socks that had lost their elasticity decades ago, and shoes too long and narrow for his feet, he knew he looked ridiculous.

She touched his cheek with the back of a hand.

"You still have the same sweet face. You were such an adorable child. People used to stop and stare." She let her hand fall, and her voice grew brisk. "I'll bet you're hungry. And I know just what you want."

She shooed him down the stairs and into a high-backed dining room chair.

"Back in a jiffy."

The seconds ticked away.

Chet glanced around the room, but found little of interest—the ivory-colored walls were free of adornment. His gaze fell on the photograph album lying open at the end of the table. Ears tuned to the sounds of the woman bustling in the kitchen, he drew the album close.

Black and white snapshots with scalloped edges showed a skinny boy in shorts and a horizontally striped tee-shirt squinting in the sunlight. If this was Jimmy, his mother either suffered from delusions or she loved him very much. With ears sticking out, eyes set too close together, and a gap between his front teeth, the poor kid had anything but a sweet face. Nor did he resemble the one picture Chet had of himself as a child.

Chet turned the pages, watching the boy grow and fill out. The final photo, three-fourths of the way through the book, showed the boy as a young man in a soldier's uniform. Riffling through the empty back pages, Chet found a yellowed letter from the United States government.

"We regret to inform you…"

Before he could read more, he heard the woman's footsteps

heading his way. He thrust the letter back into the album.

"You saw that silly letter," she said. "They should be ashamed of themselves trying to scare me like that. But it didn't work. I could tell you were still alive. I'm a mother—I know these things." She set a glass of water, a plate of sandwiches, and a smaller plate of chocolate chip cookies in front of him. "Your favorites." A look of uncertainty crossed her face. "I don't have any milk. Something's wrong with the car, and I haven't been able to get to the store."

Chet stuffed the corner of a sandwich in his mouth to keep from blurting the truth. After a couple of chews, all thought of the reconstruction fled. The symphony of crunchy peanut butter, strawberry preserves, and homemade whole wheat bread made his taste buds sing.

While he ate, they chatted of small matters—the food, the garden, the lovely day—and he could feel the woman's world wrapping around him like a much-loved comforter.

*What would it be like to stay here, to be Jimmy?*

He and the old woman could look after each other, create a reality separate from Bob's.

Be a family.

When Chet finished his meal, he pushed aside his plate and slumped in post-prandial bliss.

The old woman scraped back her chair.

"You have to go."

Chet stared at her stupidly, unable to make the mental shift.

"Go?"

"It's time."

"Time?"

"Come."

She scurried into the kitchen, swept the jars of peanut butter and preserves into a paper bag along with what remained of the bread and cookies, and thrust it into his arms.

She stood on tiptoe, kissed him on the cheek. He could hear a few words sighing against his skin before she pulled away.

"You're a good son. I wish..."

Dry-eyed, she nudged him outside.

"Don't look back."

She stepped further into the house and shut the door.

He stared at the closed door. What just happened? Was she nuts? Or did she know something he didn't?

He hesitated for several seconds, then he turned and trudged through the garden. The scent of orange was so strong it seemed a palpable presence, a companion. It followed him as he slipped through the gate, and it followed him as he limped past the hedge, heels already blistering from the ill-fitting shoes.

Abruptly, between two heartbeats, the scent of orange vanished.

His step faltered, but he did not look back.

# Chapter 12

CHET LAY IN bed, listening to the surf. No matter what he did, it wouldn't make a bit of difference, so why bother getting up? He closed his eyes and tried to will himself back to sleep, but his body felt effervescent, as if carbonated blood fizzed through his veins.

First too little energy, now too much. Would he ever again feel at home in his body?

He knew he should be thankful that he still had a body and a home, but he hated feeling grateful to Bob for anything. What the gods give, the gods take away. And take away. And take away more.

Yet by languishing in bed, wasn't he yielding to Bob?

He bit his bottom lip to keep from letting out a sigh. Forget the metaphysical crap. The physical was hard enough to deal with.

He threw back the sheet and thin blanket that covered him, pulled on his clothes, grabbed a roll of toilet paper, and opened his apartment door. Instead of leading to a hallway, it led directly outside. He stepped onto a white sand beach. The aqua ocean lay a scant block to the west. The putrefied forest lay a half block to the south and east, and the lava river moved in on him from the north.

He had a sudden vision of the ocean, forest, lava converging, burying him alive, and he felt his bowels loosen.

The bushes he'd been using for a privy had disappeared, and he'd never make it to the forest in time. Feeling like a cat in a vast litterbox, he scooped a hollow in the sand, crouched over the hole, did his business, then covered the mess with sand.

Invisible fingers seemed to pat him on the head, but it was only a salty breeze tousling his hair.

He went back inside his abode—now a single-story unit with all the charm of a cinderblock bunker. He washed his hands, made a peanut butter and jelly sandwich, and ambled to the ocean. He stood on the beach, waves breaking at his feet, and munched his breakfast. A disturbance in the water where he and the cat had been yesterday morning reminded him of the sea beast. He shivered.

*How could he have forgotten?*

So many changes. He'd never be able to keep track of them all. He looked to the mountains, the one constant in his life, but even they seemed diminished.

He turned his back on the mountains and headed for the forest, so deep in thought he didn't register his surroundings. If he couldn't count on the mountains always being the same, what could he count on to anchor him? The sky perhaps. So far, he hadn't noticed any changes in the sky.

He tilted his head back. And looked up at the ground. For a second, he could not fathom what he was seeing. No way could he be looking up at the ground unless…he glanced at his feet, which seemed to be striding along a cloud.

Stomach sinking, head spinning, arms windmilling to keep from falling up, he screamed, "Bob!"

A flat television screen, with Bob upside down and wearing a blue fright wig, materialized before him.

"Something's wrong," Bob said.

Chet gritted his teeth.

"Get me down."

"Oh, I know what the problem is."

Chet felt himself revolving head over heels. He could see nothing but a fine white mist, and he realized his head was in the clouds. The mist cleared. The ground lay far below, and Bob's face now appeared right side up, the blue hair shooting out in all directions."

"Nice wig, Bob. Now get me down."

"Wig? This is no wig. It's my own hair. And I'm not Bob. I'm Bill, the Right Hand of the Right Hand of God."

"I don't care who you are. Get. Me. Down."

"Bob's busy right now. He says he has more important things to do than respond to your every whine."

"My every whine?" Chet heard his voice rising to a shriek and forced himself to speak evenly. "This is more than a whine."

"What seems to be the problem now?"

Chet crooked a finger downward. The screen tilted, then righted itself.

"I see. You want your feet to be on the ground."

Chet started to nod, but stopped himself when he had a sudden vision of Bill stretching his legs until his feet touched the earth.

"I want to be on the ground."

"I don't know why. It's nice up here."

"Down. Now."

"Just a minute." Bill turned his head and spoke to someone or something off screen. Chet had never heard the language before—it sounded like water over rocks—but still he understood Bill asking, "What's going on?"

He didn't hear the response.

Bill faced Chet again. "They're tweaking the gravity. Some of the tourists find your gravity a bit hard to take, so the engineers are upgrading to a high-tech system. You might experience a few glitches until all the bugs are worked out."

"Bugs? Glitches?"

"Don't worry. I have something that will get you down."

A remote control device materialized in the space between Chet and the screen. Chet heard a click. The screen disappeared.

"Oops," came Bill's dematerialized voice.

The remote swiveled around to point at Chet. Another click.

Chet did not feel himself descend, but all at once he sprawled on the ground in a forest clearing. A self-assured young woman in a leopard skin skirt and a gold turtleneck sat on a nearby boulder, a strappy high-heeled shoe dangling from a long-nailed finger. Her eyes were a changeable green, her hair the color of orange marmalade, and her voice a purr.

"It's been a long time since I've had anyone fall at my feet."

Chet gaped at her.

"Cat got your tongue?" She smiled, showing small white teeth and too much gum line. "I like that in a man."

Chet managed to close his mouth, but he found no words. Of all the incongruous things he'd seen during the past week, this brassy, ultra-urban sophisticate sitting on the rock in the primeval forest seemed the most out of place and out of time. He scrambled to his feet. "I have to go—" He waved a hand, picking a direction at random, "—that way."

"Not a good idea. There's something big in there and it was making a lot of noise." She tilted her head, a forefinger at her chin. "That is so cute. You're afraid of little old me. Honey, you got nothing to worry about. I don't eat little boys for breakfast. Big boys, either." She gave a sultry laugh. "Unless they want me to."

Chet shifted his weight from one foot to the other, remembering why he seldom went to bars or parties. He never knew how to deal with sexual innuendo.

She scooted over, making room on the loveseat-sized boulder.

"Stay and talk to me a minute."

The brassiness was gone from her voice, and Chet heard a hint of loneliness. He perched on the rock.

"Don't you just love what they've done with the place?" she said. "I'd offer you a drink, but bartenders seem in short supply."

"I'm fine," Chet said.

"You sure are, honey."

Her breasts brushed against his arm, and his penis twitched in response. He edged away from her, thinking there was no point in letting himself rise to the occasion if he didn't plan to follow through.

She gave another deep-throated laugh. His face grew warm. Just what he needed, a manipulative witch who could read his mind.

"Who are you?" he asked, his tone more formal than he

intended. "Where did you come from?"

"Madison."

"You came from Wisconsin?"

"My name's Madison. I'm from Chicago. Been living in Denver for…oh, I don't know. With all the changes, does it matter?"

"I guess not." The heat of her thigh reached out for him. He wanted to move further away, but knew she'd only laugh at him again. "Where were you when the world changed?"

"At a party. Okay. Several parties. At least I think there were several—my memory is a bit fuzzy. I passed out, and when I woke, nothing was left but outdoors. I don't even know where I am. Could be Kansas. Could be Jupiter."

"We're still in Denver. I recognize the mountains."

"Yeah, like that means anything. The mountains could have been moved."

For one sickening moment, Chet felt as if he were upside down again. Had Bob moved the mountains? If so, then Madison was right; they could be in Kansas or Jupiter or anywhere.

"Things are looking better now." She slanted a speculative glance at him. "You really are adorable. I could have done a lot worse."

Chet jumped up, his heart pounding out a primitive beat.

"I'm sorry, but you're not my type."

"Honey, I just became your type." She cupped his crotch. "What other choice do you have?"

Against his will, he felt himself growing hard. Maybe she wasn't his type, but as she said, what choice did he have? He could spend his days alone, or he could spend them with this maddeningly provocative and seductive creature. Would that be so wrong?

A satisfied smile spread across Madison's face. Belatedly, Chet stumbled beyond her reach. Her smile broadened.

"Do you realize we might be the last people left on Earth? You know what that means, don't you? The survival of the species depends on us."

Chet blinked. Is this what Bob had in mind for him? Is this why he'd been saved from deletion? It couldn't be. Madison seemed as unlikely an Eve as he an Adam. And anyway, didn't he have the right to choose his own mate?

He took a hesitant step toward the trees. A loud thump, like the footfall of a massive beast, reverberated through the forest.

*Caught between a monster in the brush and a sexually charged woman sitting on a rock. Even I can make this decision.*

Chet plopped down on the rock next to Madison. Maybe this is the way it was meant to be.

"What do you think is going on?" Madison asked, sounding subdued.

Chet leaned sideways, touching his shoulder to hers.

"I don't know. It makes less sense to me every day, and I certainly am not getting any information from Bob. He only seems interested in taunting me."

"Bob? Bob who?"

"You know. Bob. The Right Hand of God."

"Don't be silly."

He gaped at her.

"You haven't heard of Bob? He appeared on television every night before the change."

"I was partying. So who is he? And what is going on?"

"All I know is what he said—that he's The Right Hand of God and that God accepted an offer from a development company on the planet Xerxes to turn Earth into a theme park for aliens."

Madison inspected a blue-enameled fingernail then let out a sigh.

"Sure. Why not? Seems as good an explanation as any. But where did everyone go?"

"Most people were deleted, and the ones who were left went to some sort of refuge."

"Whatever. At least we have each other. That's not so bad, is it?"

Somewhere deep inside, Chet felt a lessening of tension, like a laugh set free.

"Not bad at all."

"What do you miss most?"

Chet didn't hesitate.

"Grocery stores. It's funny—I hated them. Hated everything about them—the crowds, the displays in the aisles that made it hard to get around, the surly clerks who couldn't be bothered to say thank you—yet I'd give anything for one more trip to a grocery store."

"I didn't go to grocery stores. I mostly ate out or ordered in. You know what I miss most?"

"Chocolate? Shopping for shoes? Indoor plumbing?"

She laughed.

"You know me well. Of course I miss those, but what I miss most is my parents tucking me into bed at night when I was a child. They made me feel safe and warm and loved. I'll never have that feeling again."

Chet covered her left hand with his right. She didn't move, didn't say anything for several seconds, then she kissed his cheek.

"I'll be right back. I have to go to the little girl's room."

Chet knew he should look away, but he couldn't take his eyes off her. Amazing how she could swivel her hips so seductively while hobbling, one shoe on and one shoe off.

She paused at a bush, looked over a shoulder, and winked at him.

Heat pooled in his groin.

He averted his gaze, but when he heard a loud thump in the forest beyond her, he glanced her way. She seemed unperturbed by the noise. She stood, skirt raised, hands in front of her crotch like a man at a urinal.

Glimpsing the fleshy protuberance she held, Chet let out a strangled cry and took off running.

*Oh, God.*

He'd been flirting with a man. If Madison hadn't needed to pee, they'd probably be kissing right now.

He swished saliva around his mouth and spit it out. How much worse could his life get? And why was Bob doing this to him?

Side aching, lungs burning, Chet slowed to a walk. He shouldn't have run away, even if Bob had played a terrible trick on him. It wasn't fair to Madison.

Chet stopped. Did it really matter if Madison's gender was ambiguous? Isn't being with someone more important than being alone? He thought of her wanting to be tucked in again, wanting to feel warm and safe and loved, and his heart went out to her. She shouldn't be alone, especially with a monster so near.

Chet trotted back to the clearing. He clenched his fists when he saw the unoccupied boulder.

*Had something happened to Madison?*

He skirted the boulder, heading for the trees, and stumbled over a leg. Madison sprawled between the boulder and a grayish-green rock the size of a bowling ball. Blood and intestines spilled from a jagged hole in her midsection. Retching, Chet fell to his knees, touched his fingers to the side of her neck, and felt for a pulse. His fingers felt hot against her cooling skin. She must have died within seconds of his running away.

*If he had stayed, could he have saved her? Or would they both be dead?*

He folded his arms over his belly, holding his own entrails in place, and let out a whimper. Madison and he could not have had a lasting relationship—he doubted she would have been willing to settle for the simple companionship he had to offer—but he felt as if something in addition to a fellow human had died here. Hope, perhaps.

He rose and squinted at the forest. The beast that had killed Madison must still be close; it had eaten very little of its food.

Without warning, a heavy object rammed into his chest, and he went flying. He came down on his right hip. Pain shot through his body, and the air whooshed from his lungs. Dazed, he struggled to his feet. What happened? He'd been paying attention; how could he not have seen what hit him?

His head drooped, and he happened to notice the bowling-ball-sized rock launch itself at his chest.

He scuttled out of the way. The rock bounded past him, and he saw that it wasn't a rock but a fanged creature with the dry, warty body of a toad and the powerful hind legs of a frog.

The creature turned as it landed, and immediately launched itself at Chet again.

Chet dived behind the boulder. He lighted on his sore right side. An involuntary cry escaped his lips. He clamped his mouth shut, spared a swift regret for his lost staff, and scrabbled about for a weapon. All he found were stones.

The creature sailed over the boulder. Chet pelted its underbody with the stones, but they bounced off the thick skin without doing any damage.

Panic closed Chet's throat. He imagined himself killed and eaten by the beast. The creature landed ten feet away, then hunkered down and stared at Chet. Chet forced a breath through his constricted throat, and a fierce determination gripped him. He hadn't survived Bob's machinations so he could die by toad, no matter how monstrous and malevolent.

He thought how frightening it was when death came from below, and all at once he knew what to do.

He squatted, back braced against the boulder, and waited. The toad sprang. Chet waited one more beat, then hit the ground rolling. The toad rammed headfirst into the boulder.

Chet scrambled to his feet and dashed from the clearing. After sprinting a tenth of a mile, he took a chance and looked back. He didn't see the toad, but over his gasping breaths, he heard an airplane, or at least something that sounded like one, and it was gaining on him.

A bird flew out of the trees and hovered, its foot-long, sword-like beak inches from his face. The wings beat so rapidly that Chet could barely see them, and the sound they generated deafened him. The size of the hummingbird made it seem like another terrorist, and he'd had enough. He ran. It chased him all the way home.

Chet leaned against the door of his apartment. He could hear the engine sound of the hummingbird outside. Inside, the only noise came from his labored breathing. His legs trembled with exhaustion.

He reached into his pocket for a lemon drop, but found only the empty bag. He pushed himself away from the door, limped to the table where the lemon jar held pride of place, and groped for another bag of candy. His fingers encountered the smooth bottom and sides of the jar. Nothing else. He picked up the container and peered into it.

Empty.

He howled and threw the jar across the room. It shattered against the wall. Still howling, he grabbed a chair and threw that, too.

"Enough," he screamed. "Enough!"

He upended the table and kicked it. He wanted to keep on kicking it, but could not summon the strength.

His shoulders sagged.

"No more."

The words were barely a whisper.

A breeze ruffled his hair. He lifted his head.

The door to his apartment gaped wide. Beside it, a second door stood open, and Chet could see the zoo in the near distance, but he didn't see Bob, and he didn't hear the ringing of a phone that signaled Bob's desire to talk to him.

Still, he got the message: choose. But how could he? One door led to freedom and the threat of death. The other led to safety and the promise of incarceration.

He folded his arms across his chest and planted his feet. Then he noticed that the doors seemed to be drawing nearer. He closed his eyes and joggled his head to dispel the illusion. He opened his eyes and watched the room close in on him.

He had to choose. Now.

With a hand in his pocket grasping the empty candy bag, he took two paces forward and stepped across the threshold.

# Chapter 13

A CREATURE WITH a man-like body and the head and pelt of a sheep waited for Chet on the other side of the door.

The sheep spoke in an alien tongue, voice high and nasal, but Chet understood the single word. Even if he hadn't, the sheep's curt gesture would have told him the same thing.

"Come."

Moving with a rapid, high stepping mince, the sheep creature herded Chet toward the compound.

Chet clenched his jaw, wondering how he was going to get through this ordeal. He didn't like anyone or anything ordering him around, but he owed it to himself to do whatever he could to survive until things got back to normal and he could continue on with his life. Assuming Frank Rhoades was right about that.

At least this world felt the same as the one he'd come from, so there shouldn't be many adjustments on that front. The place even looked like Colorado, with distant mountains, deep blue skies, and wide-open spaces. Maybe he hadn't crossed a threshold into a new world; maybe he'd crossed into a different part of Colorado—the southeastern part of the state, perhaps.

In the quiet, he could hear his tied laces flapping against his shoes. Then, out of the still air, a dust storm shrieked into existence. It was everywhere at once, blotting out the sky, the earth. He tried to protect his face, but the storm sandblasted his skin. Grit built up in his ears, his nostrils, his slitted eyes. Particles even found a way into his closed mouth, and he could taste the loam.

Unable to see more than a few inches in front of him, he stopped. He felt a hard push on his back and realized the sheep was prodding him with a hand-like hoof. Or a hoof-like hand.

His brain seemed to skip a cog, and for a moment he had the light-headed feeling that none of this was real—not Bob, not the re-creation, not the storm, and certainly not the sheepish humanoid.

Another prod from the sheep. The cog slipped back into place, and he bowed under the weight of reality.

He moved forward, and stepped out of the storm. He blinked the grit from his eyes. The sheep had disappeared, leaving him standing by himself in the enclosure. The storm still raged outside the chain link fence and gusted through the entrance, but the compound appeared tranquil. If it weren't for the people kneeling before a television set perched on a large, flat rock, he'd think he entered a park. Groups of humans ambled about the lush grounds, sat under trees, played ball. Children chased each other, whooping with laughter.

A burly man with long hair and a bushy beard glared at Chet. The man wore a tank top, but he had so many tattoos on his arms, he appeared to be wearing a long-sleeved shirt.

He shouted, but Chet could not make out the words over the shriek of the storm.

The man stalked past Chet.

"I said, close the gate, asshole."

He gave the gate a shove. It clanged shut.

Though Chet could see dust swirling on the other side of the fence, he could no longer hear the storm. Hope surged through him. Maybe this place offered refuge after all.

A saucer-shaped tour bus passed overhead, and the truth froze him. No matter how pleasant, the place was a zoo.

Beings of light shone through the windows of the vehicle. One spoke in a voice like a canyon echo.

"On your right is a typical male whose ancestors came from

Northern Europe. Notice his belly, which mimics that of a pregnant woman, and his civilized-soft buttocks."

"He looks rather dim to me," one of the beings said.

"Not bright at all," another agreed.

Chet felt an involuntary smile tug at his lips.

The tattooed man narrowed his eyes at Chet.

"What are you laughing at?"

Chet raised a hand to point at the ship but turned the gesture into a shrug. If others couldn't understand the aliens, he didn't want to be singled out as different.

The tour bus moved on, but Chet still had the twitchy feeling of being stared at. He glanced around. Most of the people in the nearby groups were gazing at him.

He hunched his shoulders and stifled a childish urge to yell, "Don't look at me." He felt assaulted by their stares, and he worried about the danger of having so many people focused on him at the same time—they might bring him to the attention of someone or something unfriendly.

At first one, then dozens of the onlookers rushed at him.

In a parody of a press conference, they all shouted questions. Only the cameras and microphones were missing.

"What's happening to the world?"

"Is anything left of Colorado?"

"Did you see my baby?"

"How many people are still alive?"

"Is my dog okay?"

"Where did you come from?"

"Did you bring whisky? Gin? Anything?"

The crowd, smelling like warm beeswax, pressed in on Chet. He could feel the fence at this back, feel it swaying. With an odd sense of detachment, he wondered if the barricade would hold. If the fence went down, they'd all go with it, and he'd be suffocated under the crush of bodies. How ironic to survive a killer river, newborn volcano, saber-tooth tiger, devil toad, whirlwinds, and giant bugs to be felled by his own kind.

A harsh noise penetrated the confusion. It seemed familiar to Chet—yet not—and he had a hard time placing it. Then the answer came to him: the sound of an electric can-opener amplified.

Several people licked their lips, and one man drooled. All looked at the sky.

Chet squinted, trying to see what caught their attention. A shimmer materialized into something resembling a long trough. The crush around him thinned as people hurried toward the descending object.

"What's going on?" he asked.

An old woman, gray roots showing through pink hair, paused to say "Lunch," then she followed the crowd.

Finally only Chet and a skinny man with a huge head remained.

"They act like they're starving, but there's always plenty to go around." The man held out a massive hand. "Malcolm Barnstable. Barney for short."

"Chet Thomlin."

He gave Barney's outstretched hand one brief shake, then slipped his fingers out of the other man's clutch. An archaic ritual in the old world, shaking hands seemed totally bizarre in the new one. But perhaps, for Barney, the simple rite represented a way of hanging on to his humanity. It would be all too easy to let go in here and become a zoo animal for real.

*Not going to happen*, Chet thought. *I won't let this place change me.*

Barney flung a hand in the direction of the trough.

"You coming? The food looks like crap, but it's great. The pibble tastes like graham crackers and the peatable tastes like meat and gravy. At least that's what it's like for me. It's different for everyone."

"Pibble? Peatable?"

"Short for people kibble and people eatable. That's what Ricky Warneke calls the stuff."

Chet compressed his lips. He'd forgotten about the serial killer when he made the decision to come here.

Barney chuckled.

"Funny guy, that Warneke. You'll like him."

"Yeah. Sure," Chet said, vowing to stay as far from the killer as possible.

He didn't think Warneke had changed in the three days since they'd met, and if the guy happened to kill another inmate, he doubted Bob would care. Would probably consider it entertainment for the tourists.

As they headed for the trough, Barney rattled on about the funny things Ricky Warneke had done, though Chet didn't see anything humorous about stealing clothes from a bathing woman or dipping pibble in feces and feeding it to a kid. This place could be worse than he imagined—more like grade school than a holding pen.

Barney elbowed his way through the crowd around the trough, but Chet held back and watched the jostling humans. All that pushing and shoving didn't seem worth it for something called pibble. Barney reached into the trough, scooped up enough tan nuggets to fill a bucket, and joined Chet.

An image flashed through Chet's mind of future generations of students being taught how their oversized hands evolved: "Those with big hands could grab more food than those with little hands, so big hands were naturally selected."

When he caught Barney flashing him a puzzled look, he realized he was smiling again. He didn't know what his problem was, but he'd have to be more careful about how he arranged his face.

Barney held out his hands.

"Have some."

With the tips of a thumb and a forefinger, Chet picked a bit of pibble and brought it to his nose to sniff. It smelled like cinnamon and orange granola. He popped it in his mouth, closed his eyes, and chewed. It tasted fantastic; a perfect blend of sweet and tart.

Barney gave a nod of satisfaction.

"What did I tell you?"

He crammed half a handful of the pibble into his maw.

"You seem to have adapted well to this place," Chet said.

Barney's bobbing Adam's apple looked as large as a Macintosh in that skinny neck. He finished swallowing.

"It's okay. There's no weather, and the temperature is always just right. No place to sit or sleep except the ground, but it's comfortable enough."

"Don't you get bored?"

"Sure. Then I remember what's out there. Boredom's a small price to pay for safety." He stuffed more pibble in his mouth, spraying crumbs as he talked. "There I was, driving down Sixth Avenue, taking the wife to her diet and exercise class—the doctor told her she had to lose a hundred pounds or she'd die young—when she disappeared. Mid-sentence. One second, she's whining that she's hungry and wants to stop for donuts and the next second...gone. Not even poof. Just gone. Then the car vanished, and I tumbled onto the street. The street started to disintegrate, and I got so freaked out I picked myself up and ran the best I could." He swung his right leg. "I thought my knee was trashed, but it's okay now."

"I might have seen you," Chet said. "Were you wearing a cream-colored sweater?"

"That's right."

"I remember wondering if we were the last people left on earth."

"Near as I can figure, there's about a thousand of us here. From all over the west. Some guy passed through here a couple of weeks ago—"

"Can't be. It's only been ten days since the re-creation started."

"You sure?"

"Positive. Bob showed up on April first, and today's the eleventh. The first door to this place opened on the eighth."

"Well, I'll be..." Barney scratched his head. "This is only the eleventh? I could have sworn we'd been here a month."

"About the guy?" Chet said.

"He told us he'd heard there's still a city down south somewhere." Barney made a vague gesture that might have indicated a southerly direction. "See, the developers want all sorts of different habitats to show the tourists how we lived. Like Frontiertown and

Tomorrowland."

"Did he say anything else about these habitats? Like where they are?"

"I don't know. I didn't actually talk to the guy. Trip talked to him. You know Trip. He's the guy with all the tattoos." Barney laughed. "Do you know what Trip's real name is? Moonstar. Makes no sense, does it? A moon isn't a star. Makes you wonder what his mother was like."

Chet winced. What an awful name to saddle a little boy with. No wonder the guy had such an appalling attitude.

"You were telling me about the habitats," he said.

Barney's eyes glinted, and for just a second, Chet thought he could see the far-off city reflected in the man's pupils.

"Habitats? Oh. Right. Trip said one of the cities was made of gold."

"Can you imagine how lovely that would be?" Barney's voice dropped to a barely audible whisper, as if speaking to himself. "I would have liked to see a city of gold before I died."

A wave of exhaustion hit Chet, and his legs wobbled. He decided he'd better sit before he fell.

Barney peered down at him.

"You okay? You don't look so good. I should take you to the doc."

"The doc?"

"Francie Myles. She's really a nurse. No doctors survived that we know of."

Chet let out a weak laugh.

"Bet there aren't any lawyers, either."

Barney ducked his head.

"Just me, but I wasn't a very good one."

"Where did you have your offices?"

"On West Colfax, but I spent most of my time hanging around the courthouse and emergency rooms." He gobbled the rest of the pibble. "Be right back."

Chet watched him shove his way into the throng. The crowd

didn't seem quite so faceless now. He even recognized a few people who had gone into the light at Cheesman Park on Easter Sunday. Esmeraldo, the short Hispanic man who didn't want to be a prisoner, still had a mustache, but it looked wild and unruly and in need of a trim. The dark-skinned woman—Trisha? No, Tisha—tugged at her wrinkled dress with one hand while plucking pibble from the trough with the other. Ellen, the old woman who'd been so clownishly made up with drawn-on eyebrows and rouged cheeks, looked younger and prettier with her unadorned face and mussed hair.

He ran his fingers through his own mop, wondering how he'd keep it untangled without a comb. Seeing the woman with the lovely burnished copper highlights in her brown hair, he remembered how contemptuous he'd been of her, yet here they both were. And she'd probably been smart enough to bring a comb.

A man grinned at him as if privy to Chet's thoughts. Chet smiled back, but when he got a glimpse of prison-orange, he let his face go slack. Just what he needed to make this day complete—a close encounter with a serial killer.

He shifted his gaze, and it fell on the woman again. She was feeding pibble to a small child balanced on her hip.

Odd how few children of any age survived. What could an entire generation of young people have done in the future to merit deletion now? He'd read that they were the most environmentally conscious generation, but perhaps they had only been conscious of the problem and hadn't done anything about it. Or maybe their efforts to protect the environment and stop global warming only made things worse. Well, if humans ever thought they had control of the environment—or anything else in their lives—this re-creation sure disabused them of that notion.

"Here you go." Barney handed Chet a receptacle a bit larger than a yogurt container. Barney pulled the top off his and used the flat cover to scoop brown chunks into his mouth. "Go on. Try it."

Chet held out the container to return it to Barney. "I don't eat meat."

"It's not meat."

115

"Are you sure?"

He studied the label. Under *Scientifically Formulated People Food*, in tiny letters, it read: *contains no animal or vegetable matter.*

"If it's not animal or vegetable, what is it?"

"Mineral? Chemical? All I care is that it tastes great and is filling."

Chet rotated the receptacle. Long strings of strange symbols filled the back label. Apparently when Bob addled his senses, he'd given him the ability to understand spoken alien languages but not written ones.

His stomach growled. Gingerly, he lifted the lid off the container, scooped up a morsel, and nibbled it. The taste of garbanzo burger with Bermuda onion delighted his tongue. Suddenly ravenous, he shoveled the food into his mouth, eating as greedily as Barney.

When Chet finished, he looked around for somewhere to dump the container and saw Esmeraldo toss his off to the side.

Ricky grabbed the carton before it hit the ground. "Don't you want your dessert?" He took a bite out of the small container.

*Such childish behavior.*

Chet's thought must have shown on his face because Barney laughed.

"The thing really is edible. Tastes like strawberry shortcake. And no trash to take out. The wife was always on me to take out the trash. I hated that."

He munched on the carton, a beatific look in his eyes.

Chet took a bite out of his container. Cherry pie. It even seemed to have the texture of cherry pie. What chemical could trick one's mind into thinking one thing was another? Were they being drugged? Perhaps. Everyone seemed way too content with this untenable situation.

He started to set the container on the ground.

"Don't." Barney shot out an arm to block Chet's downward motion. "If you're not going to eat it, give it to me."

"I was planning on saving it for later."

"If you put it on the ground, the earth will eat it. It biodegrades real fast and acts as some kind of fertilizer. See?"

He dropped the last bite of his dessert. Within three seconds, the carton fragment disappeared, and the grass where it had landed looked greener.

Losing all interest in his dessert, Chet gave the container to Barney. He leaned back on his hands. The grass felt soft and warm, vibrant and springy, and he could feel the earth's vitality seeping up his arms.

"You mentioned before that a thousand people live here, but I see only about three hundred," he said.

"That's because we're divided up into four groups."

"Why?"

"No reason. We all hang around the gate we came in." Barney laughed, a short burst that sounded like a bark. "I guess we're waiting for things to get back to normal. As if that's going to happen."

"Do people change groups?"

"Not much. The Westie Besties are militaristic—they have drills and talk about taking over the world when we get out of here. The Westies who don't like that sort of crap joined us, but everyone else pretty much sticks with their group. A lot of prejudice here. When you're new, you're allowed to roam around to see if you'd prefer a different group, but after that, it's frowned on."

"Who made up these rules? Bob?"

"No one made them up. They're tradition."

"Tradition? In three days?"

"I told you, it feels like we've been here for a month."

"So what are we?"

"Northies. The others don't like us because we have no agenda. The Southie Mouthies reminisce all the time. They say they're creating an oral tradition, but they just like to yap. The Eastie Beasties are into contact sports." He shuddered. "Stay away from them."

A voice rose out of the crowd around the trough.

"Where's the new guy?"

"Over here," Barney shouted. He gave Chet an apologetic look. "Might as well get it over with. At least now they're stuffed and will be sedate."

As in sedated? Chet made a mental note to continue his quest to find a food source. Besides, if he did in here what he had done in world outside the enclosure, maybe he wouldn't feel like a prisoner.

A young couple, hand in hand, slipped away from the trough. Two little boys ran off, chasing each other. Five or six adults drifted toward the television. Everyone else crowded around Chet.

"Let the little ones sit up front."

Imperiousness marred the pleasant timbre of the female voice. The brown-haired woman pushed through the bodies, making room for the children. She bustled around until all the dozen of them were sitting in a semi-circle before Chet.

Barney nudged him.

"That's Francie."

She always had to be in control, Chet thought. *Always?* He didn't even know her. Then he realized she was mixed up in his mind with his mother. They seemed two of a kind.

Not wanting to think about Isabel, Chet focused on the crowd. Some sat on the grass behind the children. Some remained standing on the periphery. All stared at him with glittering eyes that reminded him of the way the saber-tooth tiger had regarded him.

Tiger. Cat.

"Has anyone seen an orange cat?" he asked. "It came through a doorway to this place a couple of days ago."

He stopped, confused. The cat had been with him yesterday morning, so it couldn't have entered the doorway two days ago. He'd been here but an hour, and already he was losing track of time.

The hundreds of heads shaking no made him feel seasick, adding to his confusion.

"There aren't any animals in here." Barney grinned. "Except us."

"What's it like out there?" Tisha asked.

Chet folded his arms across his chest. Deciding that the pose made him look defensive, he laid his hands in his lap, but that made him feel vulnerable.

Finally, gripping his knees, he said, "There's nothing left of the city. An ocean covers the area from East Denver to the mountains." Giving in to a petty desire to shock his listeners out of their complacency, he added, "A monster with razor teeth lives in the depths. It's so big, it could have swallowed me in a single gulp."

The glittering eyes devoured him, and he realized this is what the people wanted: the horrific details so they could prove to themselves that they had done the right thing by entering the refuge.

A tour bus glided overhead. Chet blocked out the voice of the tour guide, who was droning on about the human need for stories and storytellers.

Saving the wonder of the new world for himself, Chet spoke of the terrors. People nodded self-righteously when he told them of the saber-tooth tiger gutting the monk. They smiled when he told them about the river that almost killed him, and they grimaced pleasurably when he told them about the bugs, the devil toad, the pile of dung.

Before he could mention the giant cubs playing with the combat boot, his voice gave out.

The word barely scraped through his desiccated throat.

"Water?"

"We have a brook and a few pools," Barney said. "I'll show you."

He rose, waited for Chet to clamber to his feet, and led him through the crowd.

The trough had disappeared, and the grass showed no signs of having been trampled. Chet could feel eyes focused on him as he shambled along beside Barney, but he didn't look around to see if those eyes belonged to his fellow inmates or to a group of tourists.

When Chet realized Barney was taking him to a forested area, he slowed his steps and steeled himself for the attack on his nostrils, but the woods smelled sweet and clean. He breathed as deeply as he could, and peace descended on his soul.

A pool glistened like gold in the mellow light of the forest glade. Chet dropped to his knees, cupped his hands, and drank the wonderfully cool nectar. It reminded him of something. He paused, holding his dripping hands above the water, and tried to capture the thought. Then it came to him. When he first heard of champagne, he'd formed an idea of how it would taste—invigorating, magical, with a lingering hint of peach—but the reality had never lived up to the fancy.

He wished he had a crystal goblet for this champagne-like water; it seemed sacrilegious to be drinking from his grubby hands. After slaking his thirst, he wiped his hands on his chinos, rose effortlessly, and slowly swung around in a circle, feasting his eyes on the beautiful scenery. The glade looked like a postcard from a dream vacation.

Dream? He stopped and whacked himself on the head with the heel of a palm. What an idiot! He was letting himself be seduced by the whole Eden scenario.

"You really should go see the doc."

Chet started. He'd been so wrapped up in his own seduction, he'd forgotten Barney.

"I'm fine," he said. And that was the problem, though he didn't know if he could explain his fear of giving in to the soporificness. Was soporificness even a word? He sighed. Since dictionaries no longer existed, he'd never know.

"You'll get used to it."

An odd pitch in Barney's voice made Chet give him a sharp look. Maybe Barney would understand his fear, but the moment for expressing it had passed.

"Now what?" he asked.

Barney shrugged. "Take a nap or gamble."

"Gambling? In here? With what?"

"You know that stupid kid's game—rock, scissors, paper? Well, three play and everyone else bets on the outcome. Sports, too. Some folks play baseball, and there's plenty of side action. I owe Esmeraldo four thousand bucks." He gave a sour laugh. "Not that I'll ever have to pay off. But I still hate owing that little creep anything, even if it is only air money."

Chet blinked. He'd considered Esmeraldo to be more pathetic than unpleasant. He'd have to be careful how he judged people in here. Since he didn't want to trust the wrong person, he'd be better off not trusting anyone.

He yawned so hugely his eyes watered.

"Looks like you could use a nap," Barney said.

He bounced on the balls of his feet as if suddenly he couldn't wait to be shucked of Chet.

"You're right." Chet lowered himself to the ground and leaned against a tree. When Barney remained hovering over him, he waved a hand. "You go. I'll be fine."

"You sure?" Barney called over his shoulder as he scampered back the way they came.

Chet dipped his chin in an effort to nod, but he couldn't raise his head to complete the motion.

Chet awoke. Without opening his eyes, he stretched his arms above his head. He didn't remember the last time he'd felt this good. Maybe the new mattress helped as Isabel said it would. But why was he sleeping sitting up?

He opened his eyes. Reality slammed into him with such force that he gasped.

A pink and white snake that smelled like peppermint stood on end, no more than two feet away, and stared at him. Apparently deciding Chet wasn't anything special, the reptile sank into a coil and slithered under a rock.

So it was true. The world really had come to an end, and he now lived in a zoo with impossibly colored snakes. But Barney had said there were no animals here. Did that mean the snake was a hallucination? Or an alien tourist who'd snuck off on its own?

Wondering how long it would take him to become as blasé about the aliens as the other humans seemed to be, he staggered out of the forest into the late afternoon sun. He heard singing—a soft voice murmuring about two cats in the yard—and he followed the sound to a tree with broad leaves that formed a canopy like a weeping willow.

A woman puttered beneath the canopy, arranging bottles and jars, bandages and small tubes of what looked like topical medicine on a table-like rock, folding clothes and placing them in a neat pile on another rock.

Captivated by the domestic scene, Chet did not move or make a sound, but he must have done something to attract her attention. She lifted her head and gazed at him with unwelcoming eyes, and he recognized her. Francie.

"Can I help you with something?" she asked.

"No. I'm fine."

A quick frown.

"You don't look fine."

"What? This?" He touched a hand to his face, which was still raw from the earlier sandblasting. "It's nothing."

"Then why are you standing there staring at me?"

"I wasn't—" He stopped. Perhaps he had been staring. "Sorry."

As he ambled toward the vast open space where everyone seemed to hang out, he heard her mutter, "Can't a person have any privacy?"

He nodded to himself. Yep. Just like Isabel. Always had to have the last word. Except with Bob. Bob was the only one who had ever managed to beat his mother to the final comment.

The name "Bob" drifted to him from the worshipers by the television. The crowd around the rock had swelled. Did Bob put in a nightly appearance? He turned his back on the rock, not wanting to hear anything Bob had to say.

The harsh noise announcing a feed grated on his ears, and the trough descended. He could feel the saliva gathering in his mouth.

*Fool! When will you ever learn? You're still sleeping when you should be working to find food sources.*

Vowing to spend the next day in search of food, Chet strolled toward the dinner crowd. A waving hand caught his attention.

"Over here," Barney called. "I saved you a place."

Chet squeezed in next to Barney and bellied up to the trough.

"What now?" Chet asked. The trough had ascended into the blue and the replete diners lounged on the ground.

"We do the where-were-you."

"The where-what?" Chet questioned sleepily.

He'd eaten too much vegetarian pizza pibble and wished only for another nap.

"The where-were-you when it happened." Barney laughed without amusement. "You'd think by now we'd be tired of hearing the same old stories, but it's become a nightly ritual, so we'll be doing the where-were-you long after we've forgotten what it all means."

Tisha sat up straight, looking regal in the fading light.

"I was sitting at my desk at work. My boss stood over me, bitching because I didn't install the new software like he told me to. He wouldn't let me order it, said I wasn't qualified, like it took a masters degree to fill out the requisition. 'I told you I wanted it installed today,' he yelled. 'So order it,' I said. Then he got all pissy, going on and on about how I wasn't a team player. Whatever that is. I sat there wishing I knew voodoo so I could put a mojo on him and make him disappear. And then he vanished. I thought he was playing some kind of trick on me, so I waited a minute. When he didn't reappear, I took my coffee break."

She smiled. "It was the best day of my life."

"It was the worst stinking day of mine," Esmeraldo said. "My girlfriend broke up with me. Said I was too short." His matter-of-fact voice changed to a whine. "What did she mean? I was the same height as when she met me."

"Maybe she grew," Ellen said.

"Yeah." Ricky laughed. "Grew tired of you, Ezzie."

From the pained look Esmeraldo shot at the two of them, Chet surmised that these comments were part of the where-were-you.

"Let Esmeraldo tell his story." Tisha sounded resigned, as if she'd spoken the words many times before.

"Yeah. I'm talking here." Esmeraldo puffed out his chest. "Heather from work told me I was a perfect height. She said she been waiting her whole life to meet a guy like me."

"A short guy," Ricky said sotto voce.

Esmeraldo kept talking as if Ricky hadn't interrupted.

"We went to a motel, got undressed and into bed. The next thing I know, she and the motel disappeared, and I was lying in a stinking field wearing only a condom."

"Tough shit," Ricky Warneke said. "Wait until you end up in prison, and then you'll know how bad things can really get. But that day was a good one. We were out in the prison yard, guys screaming and yelling, guards strutting like armed peacocks waiting to shoot someone. Typical organized mayhem. Then all went quiet. No noise. No guards. No prison. No fence. I hoofed it to the highway. Some girl picked me up." He laughed. "I couldn't believe it. There I was in this orange jumpsuit, standing next to a sign that said, 'Prison complex. Do not stop for hitchhikers.'"

He flexed his hands.

"People make it so easy."

# Chapter 14

CHET WOKE BEFORE the sun came up. He turned on one side then the other, but could not get comfortable. His skin itched, his limbs twitched, and he felt that his body no longer fit. There was something wrong with the air, he realized. It seemed to contain too much electricity as if it were gathering its reserves for…what?

Dread cramped his belly. He was sure something unimaginable would soon take place. Bob had promised a refuge, safe from the reconstruction zone, but he tended to play loose with the truth. Look at the way he'd enticed Ricky Warneke into the refuge by announcing the loss of plumbing, yet here they were, still having to shit in the woods.

Blowing out a heavy sigh, Chet went in search of a secluded area. The person who claimed that only death and taxes were inevitable must have been constipated. As he passed the glade where most people spent the night, he couldn't help wincing at the snores and grunts and whistled breaths. Amazing that anyone could sleep through the racket.

He squatted behind a bush that looked like a cross between a rose and a fern, and wondered how people had survived this particular indignity for hundreds of thousands of years. He washed his hands in the brook, shook them dry, and ran in place for a minute to get warm.

The sky brightened, and the sun rose, a dark maroon ball that cast a blushing glow over the earth.

*Red sky at night, sailor's delight. Red sky at morning, sailors take warning.*

Chet shivered. He'd take warning all right. A sun the color of dried blood could only bring an evil day.

He walked eastward, thinking it better not to turn his back on the abomination, but the strangeness of it made him feel off balance, as if any second he'd fall off a cliff into another world, and he had all he could do to handle this one. He veered to the left and headed for the fence.

Arms wide, fingers hooked through the warm steel links, he stared out onto the dark red earth. The land rose and fell, forming hills, valley, gulches. Winds gusted, lashing saplings like whips. In this place of safety, where he no longer had to fear for his life, wonder swamped him. He'd actually walked on land while God was creating it. Or re-creating it, which came to the same thing: a newly formed world. No one witnessed the first creation, but he got to witness the second.

*How cool is that!*

A dark spot appeared on the horizon. He studied the expanding spot, thinking clouds were about to blanket the sky. Instead, a bird bigger than any plane, bigger than an ocean liner grew from the darkness. The bird spanned the undulating terrain in seconds. What did a bird that big eat? Chet smiled humorlessly, thinking of the punch line of an old joke: anything it wants. He plastered himself against the fence, hoping the bird did not want to eat him.

The bird skimmed the last bit of land to the fence, then turned sharply and flew north.

Chet jerked away from the fence. Had the metal emitted some sort of force field that repelled the creature? He put a hand to his chest and felt his heartbeat. It seemed normal, if a bit fast.

All of a sudden, fingers closed around his throat. Writhing frantically, he tried to pry loose, but the chokehold grew tighter. Just when he thought he'd pass out, he heard a laugh and the fingers loosened.

Gasping for air, he reeled and beheld Ricky Warneke.

"I wish I could have seen your face," Ricky said. "I bet your eyes about popped out."

"You could have killed me."

Ricky flexed his fingers.

"So?"

Chet massaged his throat and tried to think of a retort, but the lack of oxygen must have addled his senses; he couldn't think of a single thing to say.

Ricky smirked. "I could have done it. Kill you, I mean."

"I know."

"But I didn't want to." For a second, bewilderment shadowed Ricky's eyes, then the glitter of amusement returned. "Maybe someday."

Chet shrank from him.

Ricky guffawed.

"Just funning you. God, you're easy. Like shooting fish in a barrel." With another of his quick-fire mood changes, he clenched his hands into white-knuckled fists. "That's what we are. Fish in a barrel waiting for those freakish tourists to pick us off."

"Do you think that's going to happen?"

"Got you again."

Ricky laughed, but his hands did not unclench.

"As amusing as this is," Chet said, "I have to go."

"People to do? Places to meet?"

Chet nodded and started to walk away, but Ricky grabbed his left arm.

"I want to talk to you."

"Let go of me."

Ricky raised his hands and showed his palms.

"I'll be good."

"What did you want to talk about?"

"That day in Cheesman Park. Do you believe the shit Bob told us about our being dupes?"

"Dupes?"

"Don't be stupid. You know what I mean. He told us our leaders deluded us, that we got conned into buying worthless crap, and that we never had free will."

Chet didn't want to answer, but Ricky's intense gaze seemed to drag the truth from him.

"I didn't believe much of it at the time, but now I can see that he's right about our not having free will. I feel like one of those wooden dummies sitting on a cosmic lap. I don't even know anymore if what I say and think comes from me or some celestial ventriloquist."

"But you chose to come here."

Chet thought of those last moments in his apartment and the side-by-side doors that had closed in on him.

"Did I? Or did circumstances choose for me?"

"So basically you're saying that we do the things we do because circumstances force us into it? Could be our genetics are circumstances, too. That Esmeraldo couldn't play basketball because his genetics told him he couldn't, and I killed because my genetics told me I could." Ricky nodded slowly. "That's why I'm here. I did what God wanted me to do."

A smile broke over his face, and he clapped Chet on the back.

"You're okay, kid, no matter what anyone says."

Chet watched him stride jauntily away. Had he really told a serial killer it was okay to have killed? Even if circumstances did force one into making a particular choice, didn't other things enter the equation? Like responsibility, for example.

Shoulders bowed, he trudged in the opposite direction from the one Ricky had taken. At least he wouldn't be responsible for more killings. Either the food or the ambience seemed to deflect the man's murderous inclination into a penchant for cruel jokes.

The sun rose higher. It brightened from a dark maroon to a blood-gushing red.

Chet's heart beat faster, and drops of perspiration formed on his brow. Inexplicably, anger surged through him, pure and uncomplicated. If he'd known he'd still have to deal with the ever-plastic earth, he would have stayed home.

He trod on a stone.

*What were rocks doing in this place anyway? What purpose did they serve?*

He snatched it, thinking to throw it over the fence, and it drew blood. Sucking on the cut finger, he studied the stone. One edge smooth and rounded, one flattened like a blade, it fit neatly into his palm. He pitched it aside, then realizing its potential, he scrambled after it. Only a fraction of the flat edge seemed sharp, but he could probably hone it on another rock to make a serviceable weapon to protect himself. Ricky Warneke might have given up murder for the moment, but things had a way of changing rapidly nowadays.

He found the rock shining darkly beneath the orange red sun and stowed it in his pocket.

Invigorated, he marched along beside the fence. A faint jangle from the north caught his attention. The morning trough! Thinking he was hungry enough to eat all the pibble and peatable himself, he hurried back to the clearing. When he arrived, most of the others had finished their breakfast, but plenty remained for him. By the light of the orange sun, he ate his fill.

Hushed voices drifted toward him.

"It's Chet's fault."

"How can you blame it on Chet?" Barney demanded. "Are you saying he has the power to make the sun change color?"

"All I'm saying is that nothing like this happened until he got here."

A murmur of agreement, then Barney again.

"Coincidence."

Chet heard a hint of doubt in the word, and didn't blame Barney for the change of heart. For all he knew, it could be his fault. Maybe Bob was punishing him for throwing the phone in the river. Twice.

Where was Bob anyway? Though most of the Northies huddled around the television, it remained blank.

*Good.*

# Chapter 15

THE TANGERINE LIGHT faded to yellow. Chet focused his eyes on the ground so he wouldn't keep turning to gaze at the lemon sun, immense and vivid against the bright blue of the sky. He walked along the fence line, feeling optimistic and confident that in the end everything would work out. The air was sweet, the ground soft, the food plentiful. His mouth watered at the thought of the pibble, and he wondered how much longer until time to eat again.

A shimmer, like gold coins, in a nearby tangle of bushes caught his attention. A money tree? Here where gold had no value? Seemed like something Bob would find amusing. Chet cut toward the thicket. As he drew closer, the gold shimmer turned chartreuse, and he could see that the bushes were laden with a yellowish-green, plum-like fruit. He gave a shrug of disinterest and walked away. What need had he of such edibles anymore?

He stopped abruptly. How long had he been in this place? Less than twenty-four hours and already he'd become addicted to the scientifically formulated people food.

"Idiot!" he railed aloud. "It's one thing to choose safety, and another thing to let yourself become enslaved."

He approached the bushes, gingerly reached out a hand, and plucked a fruit. It felt warm and smelled enticing. He took a bite and chewed slowly. Wonder swept through his body at the incredible taste, a cross between the sweetest plum and a perfect apricot with a slight tang of lime.

*This must be ambrosia—the food of the gods.*

He lifted the plum to his mouth again, then froze. What was that sound? A footfall? He tilted his head to listen and thought he detected breathing but heard no other noise, as if someone or something on the far side of the bushes had also stopped to listen.

A second later, a well-muscled man stepped out from behind the thicket. His camouflage fatigues looked rumpled, his short blond hair ragged, his feet bare. The unnatural viridescent light turned his skin a sickly green.

Chet stared.

"Lance?"

Lance glowered at him.

"Do I know you?"

"I saw you at Cheesman Park."

Lance's glare darkened.

"What of it?"

"Nothing. It's just that the next day I saw a couple of creatures playing with a combat boot. I thought they'd...eaten you."

"They almost did. I was walking through the woods—" Lance shuddered. "I never smelled anything that bad, not even in Kuwait. Then all of a sudden, something that looked like a bear dropped out of a tree. It sank its teeth into the heel of my boot and wouldn't let go. I untied the laces, slipped my foot free, then another animal fell out of the tree. It chased me, but it moved so slow I barely had to double-time to get away. Don't think they were bears."

"They might be giant sloths," Chet said. "Good thing you didn't meet up with the mama."

"You mean those animals were babies?"

"They acted like cubs. So that's why you decided to come here?"

"No."

Lance clipped the word and clamped his mouth shut.

A stocky man with a dirt-streaked babyish face trotted out from behind the bushes. He carried a three-foot-long branch that had been stripped of bark and crudely sharpened to a splintery point. He

131

rammed the point against Chet's chest.

"What do we do with this trespasser, sir?"

"Nothing, Corporal Grady."

"I think he's the new guy Trip warned us about."

Lance narrowed his eyes at Chet and jerked his head toward the east.

"Go. And don't come back."

Corporal Grady pushed harder on the stick. It poked a hole in Chet's shirt, and Chet wondered if it would pierce his skin. Then the pressure eased.

"Yeah, go," Grady said. 'We don't want your kind around here."

Chet didn't move, though he had no idea why he acted so foolhardy.

"My kind?"

Grady spat out the word.

"Northie."

"I'm not anything. I just got here." Chet didn't notice any difference in what he could see of himself, but maybe being with the Northies was already making an imprint on him. "And anyway, isn't Trip a Northie? I thought you weren't allowed to associate with people from other groups."

Grady jabbed Chet again.

"Go. Or we'll make an example of you."

Chet felt no fear, but he couldn't see a reason to continue the conversation. Besides, the point hurt.

He stepped away from the stick and sauntered east.

"Be seeing you," he called over his shoulder.

Both men stared at him.

His lips quirked into a smile and, with a sense of well being, he continued on his way beneath the turquoise sun.

Chet heard the cheering long before he saw the humans making the racket. As he strode up a grassy hill dotted with trees and bushes, he could almost imagine himself in a Denver park on his way to an impromptu ball game. The sky-blue sun glistening against the cloudless blue sky shattered the illusion, as did the saucer-shaped craft hovering overhead.

He scrambled through a thicket of plum bushes, grabbing fruit and stuffing his pockets, then he crested the hill and saw the noisemakers. Most were standing pressed together on the hillside, their backs to him, their heads turning first in one direction then the other in sync with the men and women running back and forth at the base of the hill.

At first Chet thought the runners were playing touch football, then two men—one apparently from a team wearing shirts, one from a bare-chested team—rushed at each other from opposite ends of the field. Without slackening speed, they slammed into each other, bounced off, staggered, but did not fall. Another bare-chested man, gut hanging over his belt, rammed into the staggering "shirt," and the shirted player fell flat. The cheering crowd jumped up and down, screaming at the top of their lungs. So, not touch football. Maybe a bowling game where the goal was to mow down the other team.

In a momentary lull, Chet could hear the tour guide droning on about primitive religions, ritual self-sacrifice, and simplistic belief systems for the masses.

Feeling a vibration against his thigh, Chet rummaged among the plums in his pocket and pulled out a phone. He stared at the device, unable for the moment to comprehend what he saw. The object that had been so common in the old world seemed unutterably alien in this one. All at once the phone started ringing, a harsh and insistent demand.

The people closest to Chet stopped cheering and turned toward him. Then, like a wave, so did the rest of the crowd. Sensing that these Eastie Beasties regarded him as an unwelcome interloper, he dropped the phone and ran. He heard no sounds of anyone chasing him—perhaps the onlookers had already lost the will to do anything but watch others in action—but he didn't slacken his pace until the sun turned a soothing cobalt blue.

Chet feasted on plums. In the light of the indigo sun, the fruit looked ordinarily purple, but it still tasted like something meant for the gods.

He had drawn near enough to the Northie camp that he could hear the chanting of the evening prayer. He ambled slowly, in no hurry to return to the fold, and reflected on all that he had seen. The synapses of his brain seemed to be firing on all cylinders, his thinking clear, and he could almost make sense of what Bob and the reconstruction crews were trying to accomplish. The setting sun turned a bruising purple, then faded to violet. As the orb slid below the horizon, he had a flash of inspiration, but before he could grasp the concept, the sun disappeared, leaving behind a black streak of night above the lavender dusk. Then night fell, like a curtain rolling down after a stage play, and all went dark.

Chet followed the sound of chanting back to his new home.

"Oh, Bob," the Northies droned. "Right Hand of God, deliver us from evil and forgive us our sins."

Chet winced.

*Did these people think the changes on Earth were due to their petty transgressions? Were humans really so egocentric?*

"Chet, is that you?" came a whispered voice in the darkness.

"Barney?"

"Yeah. Just wanted to warn you—a lot of people think what happened today is your fault. Be careful."

"They need a scapegoat," Chet said softly, wondering how he knew.

*Could the awareness be a result of his clear thinking during the time of the indigo sun, or did it originate in the same part of his brain that now understood alien languages?*

He felt a moment of compassion for those who needed to heap all their fears and inadequacies, their rage and impotence onto an unwitting individual, but when it sunk in that they'd elected him to be the scapegoat, he hardened his heart. If that was the way they wanted it, then so be it. He didn't need them. He didn't need anyone.

"Maybe they'll forget all about you by tomorrow," Barney said, walking away.

"Thank you for the warning," Chet called after him.

"No problem. Just be careful."

Stars appeared in the sky—red, blue, yellow, green—and they offered enough light for Chet to scout the area. He found a tree with low hanging branches that would give him some privacy, and he settled beneath it with his back against the trunk. The spongy bark molded itself to his form and seemed to absorb his tension. Relaxed, he fell into a deep and dreamless sleep.

Shouts woke him. Raising his hands to rub the sleep from his eyes, he noticed that his skin looked green. He slid a glance at the sun and was surprised to see that it had returned to its usual state. So the color didn't come from the reflection of an abnormal light. He spit on his hands and tried to rub off the green, but his efforts only made the color darker.

He held out a hand like a woman admiring a wedding ring, and chuckled. It was a lovely color. Maybe being green would be fun for a while. At least it seemed a relatively innocuous change. An insistent pressure in his bladder caught his attention. He stepped behind the tree and unzipped his pants. At the sight of his leaf green penis nestled in a tangle of spinach green curls, his giddiness evaporated and a frisson of fear passed through his body. Could Bob be turning him into something resembling vegetation? The hot dribble of urine looked normal, so perhaps the green was merely a surface condition rather than a physiological change.

Chet heard running footsteps and Barney yelling his name. He zipped up his pants and stepped out into the open.

"We need you," Barney said, gasping for breath.

His mint green skin glistened with sweat, and his avocado hair stood on end.

"Why?"

"Bob won't talk to us until everyone in our quadrant is present. He says he'll explain only once."

"He won't notice I'm gone."

"The thing is..." Barney looked up, down, sideways,

everywhere but at Chet. "We told him we were all present, but he said he didn't see you. Let's go. We're all waiting." He hurried off toward the Northie camp then, apparently realizing Chet wasn't following, he stopped and looked back. "Aren't you coming?"

"No."

"Don't you see? Once Bob explains what's going on, no one will blame you anymore."

"Oh, yeah. Right. Like being singled out by the so-called Right Hand of God is going to make me popular."

Barney's forest green eyes grew round, and he sucked in a breath.

"So-called? You better be careful. Some people might think you're being sacrilegious."

"Let them think what they want. Humans always do."

"Whatever. Just come, okay? Everything will be fine."

Chet studied the lawyer, wondering if Barney really could be that naïve. He shrugged. What difference did it make? If the humans didn't make his life miserable, then Bob was sure to take up the slack.

When Chet and Barney arrived at the clearing, only a few people glanced at them. Most kept their heads turned toward the television, which had grown as big as a movie screen. Bob's face filled the screen, and he did not look happy.

"Well, look who finally decided to put in an appearance," Bob said, his voice grating. "So glad you took time out of your busy schedule, Chet."

"What's going on?" Tisha demanded.

"It's not really any of your concern," Bob said, "but if you must know, God's been experimenting with the lighting, trying to find the best way to illuminate the theme park. He never really liked that pale gold sun—too dull."

"The hell with the sun." Ricky lifted his pea-green arms. "What about us? Why are we green? I hate green. Reminds me of my sixth-grade teacher." He lowered his arms and softened his voice. "The only green she's wearing now is grass."

He laughed, sounding as carefree as a child.

Chet shivered and reminded himself once again to stay away from the killer.

"Green?" Bob said. "Oh, that. God decided the light was just fine. It's you people he doesn't like. He always considered you rather a mistake—never quite got the color right. Too undercooked, if you know what I mean."

Tisha thrust out a celery-colored arm.

"So why am I green? I wasn't undercooked."

"Overcooked," Bob said.

Esmeraldo lifted his lime green head and straightened his shoulders.

Bob rolled his eyes skyward and blew out a breath.

"You people just don't get it. To God, you all look the same. It's not your individual color that counts, but your appearance en masse, and God finds it boring." He stroked his chin. "Hmm. Maybe you'd look better in fuchsia. Or polka dots."

The screen went black.

The television shrank and kept on shrinking until it disappeared.

As one, the crowd turned toward Chet.

Chet ran.

# Chapter 16

A SHRIEK LIKE that of a jungle beast in pain woke Chet. He rolled over onto his back, too tired to wonder who or what could be making such a racket. Dry leaves scratched his bare skin. What happened to his shirt? He patted the ground beside him thinking that perhaps the buttons had somehow come undone during the night, but he didn't feel any fabric.

More shrieks and shouts. This time the screeches sounded decidedly human.

He squinted at the sun. It seemed to be lower on the eastern horizon than when he'd run from the mob. Could the sun be moving backward? He closed his eyes and tried to remember what he'd done after he stopped running, but all he could recall was creeping back to his quadrant and collapsing under this very same tree. Slowly it dawned on him that he must have slept round the clock. But clocks didn't exist anymore. Letting out a soft groan, he wondered how long such outdated expressions would linger.

A breeze ruffled the hair on his thighs. He raised his head and stared at his legs. When he fell asleep yesterday—was it yesterday? It could just as easily have been a week ago—he'd been fully dressed.

He caught a glimpse of hot pink and lime green between his thighs. He jerked his torso upright and stared at the polka-dotted-fur loincloth tied around his hips.

*Polka dots, Bob? Really? And where are my clothes?*

He looked all around him, but couldn't see so much as a thread. With any luck, this particular phase of the re-creation would be as short-lived as the color-changing sun, and his clothes would miraculously reappear on the morrow.

Unless they had been deleted like so much else in on Earth.

He blinked away the tears that bleared his eyes. Not a single thing remained of his life. *His life?* Who was he trying to kid? He didn't own his life anymore. It belonged to Bob, to the tourists, to the capriciousness of the reconstruction workers.

As he started to lie back down, his hand came to rest on a sharp stone. A jolt of pure satisfaction coursed through his body. He did have something. Something of this new world; something that could not be deleted. The sharp-edged rock might not be much of a foundation to build a life on, but it was a start.

A voice popped his bubble of optimism.

Francie. Behind him. Coming closer.

"Tell me where he lives, Barney."

"I don't know. I think he hangs out around here," Barney all but whined.

Francie, wearing a one-shouldered cave girl dress that matched his loincloth, stepped out from behind the tree and glared at Chet.

"There you are. What's going on?"

Chet stared back at her for a second before letting his glance slide away.

"Why are you asking me? You know as much as I do. You heard Bob say he wanted to try polka-dots."

"That's not what I'm talking about."

Barney sidled into view. He twitched as if in discomfort, but Chet couldn't tell if the discomfort came from being dressed in nothing but the silly pink and lime green loincloth or from having led Francie to Chet's lair.

Chet held out a placating hand to let Barney know it was okay. Barney acknowledged the gesture with a sheepish shrug.

"Are you listening to me, Chet?" Francie shrieked. "You tell Bob I want my stuff back." Without pausing or even taking a breath to signal the change of pace, her voice softened. "What did you do?"

"I didn't do anything," Chet protested. "I have no control over the re-creation."

"No. Your hand. What did you do to your hand?"

Only then did Chet feel the sting of a small cut on his palm and notice the drop of blood oozing from his closed fist. He tried to hide his hand behind his back, but Francie grabbed his wrist.

She pried his fingers open.

"What's this?"

"Just a rock."

She stared at him as if trying to bore into his brain for a deeper truth, then flung his wrist away from her.

"There's nothing I can do about that cut, and it's your fault."

"I don't know what the big deal is. I've had worse cuts from paper."

He smiled to show he was making a small joke, but she pressed her lips into a thin line and folded her arms across her chest.

Chet looked from Francie to Barney, who was trying to edge away.

"What am I missing?"

"It's not what you're missing," Francie said. "It's what I'm missing. What happened to my stuff?"

"It's gone?" Chet asked.

Francie glared.

"As if you don't know."

Chet remembered the clothes, first aid supplies, and various other items that Francie had arranged so neatly in her makeshift room.

"It's all gone? Everything from the old world? Not just our clothes?"

"Everything."

"I tried to tell people it's not your fault," Barney said. "But they don't care. They say you knew what was going to happen and didn't tell us."

Chet sighed.

"I don't know why that surprises me. You'd think by now I'd be used to the idiocies of the masses."

"So you don't know what happened to my stuff?" Francie asked.

Chet stabbed a finger in her direction.

"What do you think?"

One silent second went by. Then another. And another.

Finally, Francie whispered, "I think we're screwed."

"So that's what the screaming was about?" Chet asked. "Nothing more serious?"

Francie opened her mouth, but the sound of the descending food trough seemed to make her forget whatever outraged remark she'd planned to lambaste Chet with. By the time she refocused her attention on him, he'd lost any interest in speaking with her. Or anyone.

He lay down on his side, and huddled into himself.

"Aren't you coming to eat?" Francie asked. "No matter what happens, you have to keep up your strength."

He didn't respond, couldn't respond even if he wanted to because a lump of tears formed in his throat and threatened to spill over.

*Go away.*

He heard the soft pad of bare feet moving away from him, and he let the tears spill over.

A few minutes or a few hours later, he heard someone say, "Eat this."

Chet opened his eyes a crack and peered at the tear-blurred woman crouching beside him.

Francie tried to force a piece of pibble between his clenched teeth.

"Eat this," she repeated. "It will make you feel better."

"I don't want to feel better."

"Stop being so childish. How do you think it makes everyone feel to see you carrying on this way?"

"Feel? They don't feel anything—except happy." He batted her hand away. "I do not want to feel happy, at least not because of some drug."

"We don't know this is a drug. It could be—"

He waited for her to continue, then gave a brief nod.

"That's what I thought. You don't know. None of us knows. It could be a virus that's mutating us into playthings for the tourists. It could be a parasite that eats our brains and turns us into zombies."

Francie glowered at him.

"You're being silly. Why would Bob want to turn us into zombies?"

"Why does Bob do anything?"

The question seemed to stop her for a moment.

Finally, she said, "If Bob wanted us to turn into zombies, we'd *be* zombies." She snapped her fingers. "Just like that. He wouldn't need to use parasites."

"Unless he's keeping us as food for the parasites. Maybe the parasites are the point."

Francie munched a bit of pibble.

"Now you're making me depressed, too."

"I'm not depressed. I'm grieving." Chet waved a hand toward the fence. "All the months I lived out there after the deletion—"

"Not months," Francie said. "Days."

Chet sat up and cradled his head in his hands.

"Sheesh. I haven't eaten very much of the pibble or the peatable and already I'm turning into a zombie."

"You're not a zombie. It's this place. It has a feel of eternity, as if time doesn't exist, never did exist. Everything seems to last forever, even things that happened before we got here."

"I can barely remember what it was like before," Chet said. "That's why I can't eat Bob's food. I need to remember. All those billions of people—gone. All of civilization—gone. Though I'm not sure how much of a loss that is. In retrospect, it doesn't make sense. What did wars and economic growth, shopping centers and fancy restaurants have to do with reality? With truth? With freedom? With anything important?"

He slanted a glance at Francie, waiting for her comeback, but she lowered her head and did not respond.

"Even if our civilization didn't mean anything," he continued after a moment, "it's all gone. I never mourned the loss of my world. I never mourned the loss of my store, my animals, my friends, my mother. I either slept or went searching for a grocery store. It's like...I didn't care."

Francie lifted her head and gave him an unwavering look.

"You were in shock. It's the normal reaction to a major loss. Your mind shuts down so you don't feel the pain."

Chet plucked a piece of pibble from Francie's hand, crumbled it, and dropped the fragments on the grass. The blades stood straighter, brightened, became greener.

"I need to feel the pain. If I don't, there will always be a wall between me and my feelings." He tapped his forehead. "And I'll never be able to get back to normal in here."

"Maybe that's a good thing."

The corners of her mouth turned upward, and Chet realized she'd made a joke, but there might be some truth in her words. He hadn't always been a good son, hadn't always been nice, hadn't always done the right thing. Still, he needed to be himself, be true to himself, and the only way to do that was to knock down the wall around his emotions and let his grief take him where he needed to be.

"We've been kept alive for some reason only Bob knows," Chet said. "But I have to find my own reason, and I can only do that if I know who I am—good or bad."

"I'm sure there's some good in you," Francie said without a hint of humor. "And I appreciate your angst. We all have a lot to grieve, but this is not the place for it. You have no idea what can happen to us if we don't act like the sheep they want us to be."

"Do *you* know what will happen?"

"Not exactly, but I'm sure they'd start by putting us back in the cages."

Chet reared back.

"Cages?"

"When we first got here, this place was set up like a chicken farm with cages stacked on top of cages, and we were forced inside them. You wouldn't believe the screeching. Sounded like the bird house at the zoo. We all felt betrayed. We thought we were coming to an Eden but ended up in our worst nightmare, and we let them know how we felt. They did feed us well, though. The sheeple—"

"Sheeple?" Chet asked.

"The guards. The sheeplike creatures that brought you here. There were hundreds of them and they'd come around two or three times a day with fruits, vegetables, nuts, seeds."

Chet looked around at the park-like setting, trying to imagine the torment of the experience, but the image melted into the morass of horrific memories engendered by Bob's brave new world order and didn't make an impact.

"What happened?"

"Scientifically formulated people food happened. We all calmed down. The cages disappeared. The sheeple left. And now you're here, stirring things up again. It makes me very uncomfortable."

Francie popped a piece of pibble in her mouth, and held out the rest to Chet. He shook his head more violently than the offer warranted, but the thought of being forever in Bob's thrall turned his stomach.

"What are you going to eat?" Francie asked.

"I found some green fruit that's edible," Chet responded. "I'm sure I'll find other things."

Francie gave him a sad smile.

"And who provides the fruit?"

It took Chet a second to realize what she meant.

"I know Bob provides the fruit trees, but the fruit doesn't seem to be infected with the zombie gene otherwise you wouldn't be trying to force the pibble on me to make me feel better."

"It could be infected with a virus, bacteria, molds, parasites, whatever. You don't know what the long-term effect will be."

Chet shrugged.

"Right now, I have no other choice."

Francie narrowed her gaze on him.

"Just be careful, okay?"

For moment Chet felt warmed by her concern, then she opened her mouth again.

"I don't want you dying of food poisoning and stinking up the place with your rotting carcass."

He studied her, trying to figure out if she really was that callous. Considering the way she took care of everyone, the remark didn't seem in character. Could she have made such a sick joke? That didn't seem in character, either, but then, he had to admit he didn't know her well enough to understand what was in character. And since they were barefoot, he couldn't walk a mile in her shoes to find out.

A glower contorted Francie's face.

"What are you grinning at?"

He put a finger to the corner of his lips, surprised to think he'd been smiling.

"Nothing. Shoes."

Her glower deepened.

"Shoes are no laughing matter."

A sudden thought struck him.

"*Could* someone die in here?"

She cocked her head and slanted a glance at him.

"What makes you ask? You're not thinking of killing yourself, are you?"

The word burst out, shocking him with its force.

"No. If I had wanted to die, I would have stayed out there." He waved a hand in the general direction of the fence. "I just wondered what would happen if someone died in here. Would the carcass rot like you said or would it be subsumed into the soil like the pibble?"

They both glanced at the bright green blades of grass where the pibble had fallen, stared at each other, then looked away.

Some things did not bear thinking about.

# Chapter 17

THE POLKA-DOTTED LOINCLOTHS and cave girl outfits did not disappear, but Bob did. Or rather, he did not reappear. The vanishing of all the accoutrements of civilization seemed to signal an end to something, or perhaps a beginning, but in Chet's personal corner of reality, nothing changed.

Well, except for one thing.

Over the span of a single night, the bottoms of his feet hardened to something resembling shoe leather, and from what he overheard from his fellow Northies, it sounded as if it had happened to everyone at the same time. He wondered what other changes the re-creators were making to human physiology, but for the sake of his sanity, he filed the thought away with the rest of the things that did not bear thinking about.

Other than that, everything seemed to remain the same. People still alternately avoided him as if he were the cause of all their woes or sought him out as if he could repair the damage to their world. Even more than their clothes, they wanted the television back. To him, the television had symbolized the deletion of all that mattered to him, and he was glad not to have to see it, but apparently, to the others, the television had been a sign of something greater than themselves, and they refused to believe him when he said he had no way to get in touch with Bob.

Thinking that it would be good to be around people who

remembered the old life—people who did not know him—he wandered down to the Southie encampment to check it out, but the cacophony of all those voices talking at once, recalling every tiny detail of that defunct existence disturbed him. Despite what he'd said to Francie, maybe it wasn't important to remember. Maybe it was more important to live in the present, whatever that present might be.

With nothing else to do, Chet spent more and more time foraging for food. He feasted on green plums; fat mushrooms that smelled like roasting meat but had no discernible flavor; and orange bean-like seeds that grew in a long pod and tasted like peanuts.

He spent hours sharpening his stone until it had a knife edge. He whittled a skinny stick into a large needle, and using thin vines for thread and leather-like leaves for fabric, he made a sheath for the knife and attached it under the flap of his loincloth.

Although he spent his days alone, he spent the nights beneath his tree near the Northie encampment. Having a familiar place to return to helped dispel the sensation of being suspended in time and brought him a modicum of comfort.

One night he returned to find someone in his space. He started to creep away again, but Barney's voice stopped him.

"We need you, Chet," Barney said.

Chet clenched his hands into fists.

"Why? Has Bob returned?"

"No. That's the problem. People are worried they did something wrong."

"They don't get it." Chet let the tension seep from his hands and body. "It's not about them."

"Please, Chet," Barney begged. "Please try once more to contact Bob. I promised the others I'd ask you. They need him. He brought us here, and now they feel abandoned."

"What about you?" Chet asked.

Barney hung his head.

"Me too. Why did Bob do this to us? I thought we were special. Chosen."

"Chosen as a means to his unhumanly end," Chet said harshly. "Why can't anyone understand that he doesn't care?"

Barney sucked in a breath.

"Are you saying God doesn't care about us?"

"I don't know anything about God. The real God. All I know is what Bob told us. That he works for an area supervisor God. And neither Bob nor his God care about us."

A crafty look narrowed Barney's eyes.

"If you do this, I'm sure everyone will see what a good guy you are, and they will treat you better."

Chet laughed. He couldn't help it. Barney was very good at wheedling, and very bad at understanding what motivated humans.

Or perhaps he was good at both, because Chet found himself saying, "Okay, fine. I'll do it."

He followed Barney to the large rock where the television had perched. People crowded him so he could barely breathe. He stifled his panic. He wouldn't die in here. Couldn't die. At least he didn't think he could.

"Move back." Trip elbowed his way through the crowd. "Give me room."

When he reached Chet, he bent down and formed a cradle with his hands.

"What the heck," Chet said.

"I'm going to boost you up."

"Great," Chet muttered.

He placed one foot gingerly onto Trip's hands, and in a moment he was lying awkwardly on the rock. He scrambled to his feet and stared out at his audience. He felt so sorry for them and their desperate need for some sort of salvation that he wished he'd kept the phone so he could call Bob, but all he had was his voice.

"Bob!" he shouted. "Bob!"

And everyone raised their voices.

"Bob!"

Chet shot his arms toward the sky.

"Please hear us, Bob!"

The crowd echoed him.

"Hear us."

Remembering the makeshift chapel he'd seen in the Tim's Plumbing building and the way those folks had talked, Chet called out, "Bob, Voice of God, we are waiting for your words. Speak to us, Oh Prophet."

And the crowd screamed, "Speak to us, Oh Prophet."

Bob did not respond, and the fanatical look in the Northies' eyes changed to hunger. They reached out for Chet. Chet inched to the center of the rock. Luckily, most of the Northies were still sedated on their morning pibble and peatable so they didn't do anything beyond making that one feeble attempt to grab him. But they did not leave, either.

They just stared at him.

"What do you want from me?" he rasped. "I'm no different from any of you. Just one of Bob's dupes."

"That's right," Ricky Warneke yelled. "He's a dupe. Can't do anything for us."

Chet held out his palms.

"I'm sorry."

"Sorry doesn't do us any good," Tisha said, looking imperial in the cave girl outfit.

Ellen slumped her shoulders.

"What do we do now?"

"It's your life, not Bob's," Chet said. "Stay. Leave. Whatever. You need to find something of your own, something that will keep you going."

"Sheesh," Esmeraldo said. "What a stinking idiot."

"Maybe I'll start killing again," Ricky said, sounding pensive. "That gave my life meaning. And it gave meaning to the folks I killed. There, at the end, they knew what was important."

Barney laughed.

"You're so funny, Ricky."

An unsmiling Francie regarded Ricky for a moment, then ushered the young ones from the crowd.

"Come, children. Let's go play a game."

"Yay!" screamed the children.

Realizing that no one was paying attention to him, Chet slid down the back of the rock, and slipped away. He did not return to his tree, but found a cave-like bush to crawl under. He thought himself well hidden, but in the early morning hours, a foot prodded him awake.

"Come." Francie grabbed Chet's hand and hauled him upright. "I need you."

She ran, pulling him along in her wake.

"What's wrong?"

"A girl is having a baby."

He slipped his hand out of her grasp and sped up to match his step to hers.

"How?"

"The usual way. How do you think it happened?"

"I don't remember seeing a pregnant woman."

"She's a Southie."

"And they want you to deliver the baby?"

"You don't have to sound so disbelieving." She puffed out the words. "I know you don't like me and I don't like you—"

"I didn't mean to offend you. I was referring to the prejudice in here."

"Are complications," she gasped, running faster.

The poor girl must really be in trouble if the Southies had broken tradition and made contact with the Northies. The sound of distant screams made him wince in sympathy. The screams grew louder. As they approached the southern sector, a man came running to meet them.

"The messenger found you. Good. I'm Christopher. Mara's my fiancée. Don't let her die."

"No...one's...going...to...die," Francie huffed. "Are you the father?"

"Not the birth father. Met her here."

Mara, who looked to be no more than sixteen, writhed on the

ground, trying to escape the three women holding her down.

"Let her go," Francie demanded.

Two of the women stepped back, but the third, a haggard-looking woman of uncertain years, kept the girl's hands captive. She acknowledged Francie's presence with a brisk nod.

"She's trying to rip out her baby."

"We're here now," Francie said.

Chet felt pride bloom in his chest. Francie exuded a quiet confidence that seemed to reach out and touch everyone in the vicinity. She knelt and placed her hand on the girl's abdomen.

Mara lay still, her screams fading to moans. The haggard woman kept hold of the girl's hands, but she loosened her white-knuckled grip.

Mara's gaze locked onto Francie's.

"Will I lose my baby?"

"You'll be fine. Let me look." She waved the others back, and spread the girl's upraised knees. "You're dilated enough, but the baby is coming out the wrong way."

The girl let out a scream.

"Don't push, honey. It's just wearing you out."

She motioned for Christopher to go to his fiancée. The haggard woman stepped away and let Christopher take her place. He held Mara's hand and whispered soothingly into her ear.

Chet stood watching, feeling like a voyeur. Francie didn't need his help. She seemed capable of delivering even this breech baby without breaking a sweat.

Francie craned her neck to look at him.

"I need to turn the baby. Would you keep her still? This will hurt, and if she jerks, she could harm the baby."

It seemed to Chet as if the three women had been doing fine keeping Mara from moving, but he knelt beside her, placed a hand on either side of her belly, and held her gently but firmly in place. He closed his ears to her screams and concentrated instead on Francie, increasing his grip when he sensed her efforts, relaxing when she did.

Francie leaned backwards and stretched.

"That should do it. You can push now."

Mara sobbed.

"I can't. Too tired."

Remembering how he'd once helped deliver a litter of baby seals, Chet scooped up the girl, staggered to the nearby pool, and climbed down the bank.

Francie jumped in beside him. Together, they supported the girl as she crouched in the water.

"Feels good," Mara mumbled. Then, a minute later, "It's coming."

Francie squatted beside her, and the baby slid into her hands. Chet motioned for Christopher to take his place at Mara's side, then he fumbled in his pouch for his makeshift knife, and handed it to Francie.

She cut the cord and returned the knife to him with a small smile, and he realized that's what she'd wanted from him all along. His knife. He slid the sharp stone back into the pouch, and accepted the newborn Francie held out to him.

While Francie and Christopher helped Mara out of the water and settled her in a reclining position against a rock, Chet studied the baby in his arms.

She looked perfect, this first child born into the recreated world. What would happen to her? Would she have a good life? She'd be safe here in this enclosure, but would she ever know the joy of overcoming a challenge? Would she ever know the heartache of unrequited love? How could she stretch beyond the bounds of this place? Residing here, she'd never know anything of life.

Nor would he.

In a flash of understanding, he knew that coming here had been a death. He needed to live, to be born again, to become a child of the re-creation. Until that very moment, he hadn't seen the promise of the creation, but now it lay before him in all its glory.

*If God can recreate the world, then I can recreate myself.*

Mara held out her arms for the baby. Chet handed the child to her and stepped back. The expression on Mara's face mirrored the one he'd seen in dozens of paintings in the pre-deleted world, the beatific expression of Madonna and child.

He felt an urgent need to put his arms around both of them, to hold them tight against life's cruelty, but he kept his hands to himself.

They had their journey, and he had his.

# Chapter 18

THE WORLD BEYOND the chain link fence flickered as if it couldn't decide what it wanted to be—desert or rain forest, plains or mountain terrain—but none of the scenes seemed particularly volatile. At least the vicious sand storms had passed. Chet didn't know how long his resolve to leave would last if he had to contend with being sandblasted half to death.

He touched the fence with one finger. The force it emitted to keep the birds and other creatures away still didn't seem to have any effect on him. He looked up at the top of the fence. No barbed wire. Just a basic fence that should be easy enough to climb if he could find no other way out of the enclosure.

A small breeze rattled the gate, and Chet realized that nothing but a simple latch held the gate closed. He chuckled to himself. He'd spent days trying to come up with a plan to escape and never considered the possibility of simply walking out the way he came in.

*Could it be that easy?*

He drew in a deep breath and put out a hand, but he could not force himself to touch the latch. He released the breath, and sagged against the fence. If he went outside, would the sheeple be waiting for him to herd him back into the enclosure? If he were caught, would they put him in a cage? And even if he managed to escape, how could he survive? He could only carry enough food for a couple of days, and then he'd be on his own. And what if the flickering scenes took him somewhere he didn't want to go? What if terrible things waited for him? Maybe he should stay inside.

But if he stayed, then what?

No, better to brave whatever torments that waited beyond the refuge than continue living this half life.

Holding his breath, he opened the latch. The gate swung open. The flickering worlds made him dizzy, so he closed his eyes as he stepped outside. His step felt solid. Looking from beneath half-closed lids, he noticed no flickering. He opened his eyes and took another step away from the enclosure. The world stretching beyond him looked like a rain forest and smelled fecund. No sheeple. No punishment. Nothing holding him back but his own fear.

The gate slammed shut. Chet whirled. Ricky Warneke stood on the inside the fence, giggling to himself.

Chet felt like vomiting. He wasn't ready to face the new world yet. All he'd wanted was to see if it were possible to leave. And his provisions were cached beside a brook in the enclosure. He slammed his body against the gate but it didn't open.

Panic blinded him. He forced himself to take deep a deep breath, hold it, and let it out. After he'd repeated this rhythm two or three times, the answer came to him.

The latch.

Wondering how he'd ever be able to survive outside the refuge if he gave way to panic so easily, he unlatched the gate.

Still giggling, Ricky stepped back so Chet could enter.

"I got you good, didn't I? You should have seen your face!"

He turned and trotted toward the south, his purposeful bearing indicating he had something more on his mind than exercise.

Chet clung to the fence until his pounding heart slowed to normal, then he followed the killer at a distance.

A group of people waited for Rickey in the center of the compound near a stand of trees. They were gesturing wildly, as if arguing.

Chet jogged to the trees. Using the trunks to hide behind, he slipped closer to the group. It didn't take long for him to realize they, too, were thinking of leaving, but not for the same reason. They seemed to think the city of gold was real, and that they could find it if only they could agree on how to escape the compound.

"We can make a ladder from tree branches held together with vines," Esmeraldo said.

Grady rolled his eyes.

"We don't need a ladder. It's a chain-link fence, for Bob's sake. We can climb it. Even girls can climb this fence."

Tisha glared at him but, apparently deciding to fight one battle at a time, she didn't say anything.

Barney held his right hand to his chest and pointed his right forefinger to the sky, as if hiding the gesture.

"What about the force field?"

Esmeraldo, Grady, Trip, Ricky, Helen, and Lance all spoke at once, and Chet could not make out a single word of what they were saying, but from their gestures, he understood they were bickering about the best way to get over the fence.

Francie's voice rose above the din.

"This isn't helping. We need to keep focused on finding a way to get out of here."

"If we can't get along in here," Barney said, "how will we get along out there when our lives depend on it?"

"And how will we trust each other to share the gold evenly when we find it?" Ellen asked

Tisha clapped her hands. All heads turned toward here, even Chet's. Despite her silly purple polka-dot one-shouldered dress, she looked commanding enough to rule the world, not just one small group of squabblers.

"Esmeraldo. Grady. Barney. You three get together after the meeting and figure out how to get out of here."

Chet stepped from the protection of the trees.

"What's he doing here?" Lance said.

"Yeah." Grady glared at Chet. "We don't need his kind."

Tisha tapped a foot.

"We're in a closed-door meeting, Chet."

"Closed door?" Christopher muttered. "There's no doors here. Just that darned gate."

For the space of three heartbeats, Chet thought about letting these people spend the rest of their lives trying to devise an unnecessarily complicated way out of this place, but if he was going to leave, he'd be better off in a group. Even if that group had no fondness for him.

Tisha looked pointedly at her wrist as if she were wearing a watch.

"Well?"

"You don't need to figure out a way to escape," Chet said.

Lance jumped to his feet. He planted himself in a fighter's stance, legs wide, fists in front of his face.

"You don't know what you're talking about. Did Bob send you to spy on us?"

"Can't we all just get along?" Barney said plaintively.

Tisha silenced them with a royal wave, then focused her attention on Chet.

"I hope you have something important to say."

"Just that you don't need to plan an escape. The gate isn't locked. Nothing is keeping us in here but our own fears."

They all looked at him as if he'd suggested jumping into a black hole, and Chet realized that for them, simply walking out the gate would feel like stepping into nothingness. They needed their elaborate plans to give them the courage to act and at the same time gave them a reason not to act. Regretting his impulse to get involved, he turned to walk away.

Trip grabbed his arm.

"What fears?"

Chet jerked his arm free.

"All I meant was that when I came here, it was you, Trip, who closed the gate. Not the guard."

Trip's face looked pinched.

"You were letting in all that wind."

"We can't leave by the gate," Barney said. "It's off limits."

Chet shrugged.

"No one told me that."

"No one told me that, either," Francie said. "I just presumed..." She looked at Chet without any of the hostility the others were displaying. "We can walk out of here without any trouble?"

"I did."

Stunned silence greeted Chet's words, followed immediately by a wall of sound as everyone in the group talked at once.

Trip's voice rose above the rest.

"He's lying!"

"No, he isn't," Ricky said. "I just saw him. I closed the gate behind him and tried to lock him out. I thought it would be funny. But there's no lock on the gate. Nothing but a latch."

Lance glowered at Chet.

"If you left, why did you come back?"

"For the same reason I came here in the first place," Chet said. "For the same reason all of you came."

"Well, don't expect to leave with us," Trip said. "We don't need you."

"What about Bob?" Barney asked. "Maybe we will need to contact him, and Chet was the only one Bob talked to."

*Bob.* Chet mentally slapped himself on the forehead. How could he have forgotten Bob? He glanced at each person in the group, and realized he knew every one of them. How was that possible? Could Bob somehow be working behind the scene to manipulate him? But why? To get him to leave?

But it had been Bob who had engineered his presence in the compound in the first place.

"We don't need Bob."

Ricky looked pleased by the collective indrawn breath his words elicited and even more pleased by the titters that followed. He grinned at Chet as if sharing a private joke.

The others might not remember that Ricky had been convicted of murdering and mutilating three women, but Chet could not forget. Nor could he forget Ricky's expressed desire to kill again someday. He had no doubts the murderer would surrender to that desire once he left the soporific influence of this place. If Chet left with the group, could he save them from Ricky's murderous impulses? Could he save himself?

"And anyway," Tisha said, "Bob's gone. It's just us now."

"So, see?" Trip said to Barney. "We don't need Chet after all."

Ellen shrugged.

"It's okay with me if Chet travels with us."

"It's okay with me, too," Francie said.

Ricky smirked. "I can hardly wait to have some fun."

Chet thought Ricky was talking about him, but when he saw the look the killer slanted at Francie, a spasm of pain cramped Chet's stomach. Not Francie! The world needed Francie, needed her skills and her caring. Even if Bob was somehow manipulating him into an escape, he'd have to leave when these people did. They might shut him out, but they could not stop him from following behind.

He looked from Lance to Grady and realized the naïveté of his thought. Of course, they could stop him if they wanted to, but they were just superstitious enough to believe he had Bob on his side. If they knew the truth, they'd probably already have ground him to dust.

Grady growled.

"What are you laughing at?"

Chet wiped the ironic smile from his face.

"Nothing. Look. I just want to travel with you for a while. I have no interest in the city of gold."

Nor did he believe it existed. It seemed too much like the legend of El Dorado, but he would never tell them that. The belief would keep them on the move. Maybe—somewhere—a city did exist. And maybe they could stumble on it.

He tried to make his tone conciliatory.

"I'm leaving here to find a place where I can recreate myself. I've lived out there longer than any of you. I survived the deletion of our entire civilization. I survived the six-foot bugs. I survived the birth of a river and a volcano. I've even survived my grief. And now it's time for me to deal with what is, and move on. Let me know what you decide."

He strode past the group. He had no illusions they'd welcome him into their crowd—their hostility seemed to be an impenetrable wall—but it felt good to have stood up to them. And it felt even better to have reinforced his decision to leave.

Would he find a place out there where he could be part of the re-creation? Or would the forces of creation—and Bob—destroy him? In the end, it wouldn't matter, but until the end, he would be free. Free to make his own way in the new world. Free to create a life for himself. Free to become whoever he wanted to be.

He thought of Francie, of Mara and her baby, of Ellen, and he realized that with freedom came responsibility.

*I promise I'll do whatever I can to protect them.*

Laughter seemed to echo from deep within the universe, but the sound of hilarity only tightened his resolve.

# Chapter 19

NO ONE ACTUALLY said Chet could join their escapade. Nor did they say he couldn't. They simply avoided him.

He returned to camp after a day spent foraging—the green fruit, mushrooms, orange peanuts, roots that looked like onions and tasted like toasted almonds.

"Pass it on, but don't tell Chet."

The whispered words wafted to him on an air current. He looked for the speaker and saw Esmeraldo and Ellen with their heads together. Ellen nodded and scurried toward Barney.

"We're leaving tonight," Ellen whispered. "Pass it on, but don't tell Chet."

Chet watched the message being transferred from one of the would-be escapees to another. Were they that stupid that they'd doom their mission by leaving at dark? They still didn't seem to understand that only their own fears kept them encaged. Bob did not care what any of them did.

Everyone in the camp seemed strangely quiet that evening. Even those who weren't in the plan were silent, perhaps feeling a change in the air. In this place of constant sameness, any hint of change would be unsettling.

They did the where-were-you, the stories told with an added aura of nostalgia, as if this would be the last time the tales were told, and for some of them, it would be.

Chet studied the faces barely visible in the fading light and wondered if the people remaining behind would remember the ones who were leaving. Would the adventurers become part of the lore of this place, or would the absence go unremarked? If the groups were ever to meet again, would they know each other, or would both groups have changed all out of recognition?

Ricky rose with cat-like grace and melted into the shadows. Seconds later, Barney followed. One by one, Ellen, Trip, Esmeraldo, and Tisha headed toward the gate. Francie seemed hesitant, as if she weren't sure she wanted to go. She hugged the child sitting on her lap and murmured "good-bye" into his hair. The little boy slid off her lap and ran to the other children. Francie gazed after him.

Was she remembering a different time when the shrieks of children playing rang on the evening air? Was she wishing for a home and a child of her own? She scrubbed her face with her hands, and Chet realized she was crying. He turned away, feeling like a voyeur, but he could feel his own eyes watering.

What did he care what this woman felt? She meant nothing to him, and yet, for a second, he wished he could wrap his arms around her. Would he ever again feel the warmth of a woman's body next to his? Would he ever...

*No, better not think of such things.*

Pleasure and intimacy belonged in the old world. They had no place in the harsh environment of the re-creation.

Chet trudged to the gate, wondering if he felt up to dealing with the conspirators. Did it matter if they left at night? They'd made it clear they weren't interested in his opinion, yet didn't he have a responsibility to them since he knew the dangers and they didn't?

He spotted Lance talking to Grady by the gate, and he realized he wasn't the only one who knew what the group could expect. Lance had remained outside longer than anyone but Chet. He felt a lightening of his spirits. If they didn't need him, maybe he didn't need them. If he couldn't persuade them to wait until morning, he could wait and leave by himself.

Francie hurried past him.

"Where are Mara and the baby?"

Barney pointed to the south.

"Someone's coming."

The single moving shadow separated into two as it neared. Mara and her baby, and Christopher.

"Looks like we're all here," Tisha said. "Let's go."

No one moved, not even Tisha.

"Wait until morning," Chet said, drawing closer to the group. "It will be safer."

"Safer? For who?" Grady jeered. "For a pantywaist like you?"

"Safer for everyone," Chet responded mildly. "The darkness holds horrors you can't even imagine."

Ricky chuckled.

"Good thing I don't have an imagination."

"Keep it that way," Tisha said.

The remark confused Chet for a second until he realized Tisha had addressed her words to Ricky, and he understood she also had reservations about Ricky's ability to keep his murderous impulses under control outside of the enclosure.

"We have to leave at night." Esmeraldo pointed a finger upward and lowered his voice. "We don't want him to see we're leaving."

Chet closed his eyes and shook his head. Even after all this time, they still didn't get it.

"Bob does not care what we do."

"How do you know?" Lance demanded.

"He told me," Chet said simply.

The Northies murmured among themselves, but the Southies and Westies stared at Chet as if he were crazy. Apparently his fame as a contactee hadn't spread beyond the Northies.

Grady leaned forward, thrusting his face close to Chet's.

"You expect us to believe Bob talks to you?"

"It's true," Barney said.

Grady pulled himself upright.

"And what exactly did Bob tell you?"

"He said it's all about what's best for the tourists. I'm sure it will suit his purpose just fine if you're out there blundering around in the dark like the primitive life form he thinks we are. I'm sure the tourists will be much amused if you get hurt."

The sound of tittering came from above, and a dark shadow drifted over them.

Chet glanced up. Human faces stared out from the portholes of a tourist saucer, then one of the creatures removed the face to reveal a bovine-like countenance.

*What the...? Oh, a mask.*

The saucer passed out of sight.

Tisha pushed open the gate.

"Let's go before anyone notices we're here."

Chet stared at her. Hadn't she seen the tourist saucer passing overhead? Maybe the humans had become so inured to the antics of the tourists they no longer even saw the creatures.

No one moved. Suddenly, as one, the group rushed through the gate. Chet wanted to offer a silent prayer for their safety, but he no longer knew who to pray to. Francie looked back, and for a moment, their gazes locked. Then she followed the others into the darkness.

The gate shut with a resounding crash.

"Gotta keep this sucker closed," Trip said. "I keep telling you, but you don't listen."

"Trip?" Chet peered at him. "I thought you wanted to leave."

"Me?" Trip's bared teeth gleamed in the moonlight. "Whatever gave you that idea? And anyway, you're here, too. Didn't have the guts to leave, did you?"

"I'll go in the morning when I'm better prepared. You're welcome to come with me if you want."

As soon as the words escaped his lips, Chet wished he could call them back. Delete them. The only thing worse than contending with the re-creation again would be to do it accompanied by the surly Trip. But he needn't have worried.

"I have better things to do." Trip shook the gate. Apparently satisfied the latch held, he strode away.

Chet wandered back to camp. The tourist saucer hung above the site. What could those creatures find amusing about watching humans sleep? He lay under his usual tree and tried not to think of the watching creatures. Tried not to think of his coming journey.

Tried not to think of Francie at the mercy of Ricky.

# Chapter 20

IN THE GRAY of the predawn world, Chet rose from his place beneath the tree and stretched. He'd slept well. The ground had seemed as soft as a mattress, and he gave a fleeting sigh of regret at giving up that luxury. He had no doubt the ground outside the enclosure would feel like granite beneath his soon-to-be-aching bones, but for now, he had no aches, no pains, just an overwhelming craving for pibble.

He patted his belly at the thought of the food and wished the trough would hurry up and get there. Realizing the direction his thoughts were taking, he drew himself upright, sucked in a deep breath, and let it out slowly. The air seemed intoxicating, like champagne bubbling through his body.

*Stop it, Bob.*

He didn't say it aloud lest Bob hear and put in an appearance. Today would be hard enough without having to deal with the annoying entity. He remembered how awed he'd been as a child by all things religious. The boy that had been he would be appalled at his offhand dismissal of the Right Hand of God, but that boy was long gone. And so were the vast majority of the all people who had ever lived.

He wondered, as he so often did, what had happened to the deleted.

*Did they still exist somewhere, or were their atoms and energy recycled into God knows what?*

A horrifying thought struck him. The deleted couldn't have been recycled into the pibble and peatable, could they? "Scientifically formulated people food" could mean both "scientifically formulated people" and "scientifically formulated food." The label had specified "no animal or vegetable matter." In the strict sense, humans were animals, but in another sense—having been made in the image and likeness of God, they were not.

Nausea rose to his throat, but he focused on the brightening sky and waited for the feeling to subside. Grateful he'd eaten only a bit of the food from the gods, he went from one of his caches to another, gathering his supplies and putting them in a pouch he'd made from broad spongy leaves and cordlike vines. He hung the pouch from one shoulder, hung the three gourd canteens he'd made and filled with water from the other shoulder, and strode to the gate. His courage faltered as he pushed the gate open and confronted the flickering world, but he didn't pause. He marched through the portal and kept on going.

Yesterday when the others left, the landscape outside the enclosure had seemed like an extension of the vegetation inside, but now all around him lay desert. Sandy ground strewn with rocks. Creosote bushes. Joshua trees. Barrel and pear cactuses. Looked like photos he'd seen of the Mojave Desert.

*Which means scorpions and Mojave green rattlesnakes.*

Fear washed over him, but so did something else.

Exhilaration and a feeling of being reborn.

He stopped and turned around. It didn't seem as if he'd come far, only a few yards, but the enclosure looked distant. He imagined he saw the man he used to be standing by the gate, still in the womb-like pen. He could feel the tug to be reunited with that man, but he turned his back on his old self and ambled away, leaving himself behind.

He took it slow and easy. Though he did not believe in the city of gold and had no desire to live there even if it did exist, he headed south. If the reconstruction affected only the surface of the earth, then the basic geography remained the same. Coldest at the poles, hottest at the equator, with temperate climates somewhere between. Since he had no expectation of ever wearing clothes again—though that mirage up ahead did look like a shopping center—he'd need to find a place where he could live without even this silly polka-dot loin cloth.

The mirage turned out to be just that—a mirage. No shops filled with the vast array of merchandise he'd once been used to. Not that it mattered. At the moment, he had no need of anything, though a backpack might be nice. Or a delicious handful of pibble.

*Stop that!*

He rummaged in his pouch, pulled out a dried green plum, and popped it in his mouth. Chewing slowly, relishing the dried apricot flavor, he continued on his way.

A tourist saucer floated overhead. The starfish-like creatures leaned away from Chet, and seemed to be peering at a spot in the distance.

"Can you see them?" one of the creatures squawked.

"Yes, ahead of us," responded another in a whiny voice so high-pitched it lay just inside Chet's audible range.

"What are they doing?" trilled a third voice. "Are they hurt?"

"Only one of them," said the high-pitched voice.

"One is better than none," squeaked the first.

Chet had become used to the chattering of the tourists and didn't pay much attention to them anymore, but now he strained to hear their words.

"Is there much blood?" trilled the third.

"I don't see any," said the high-pitched whiner.

"Oh," the third trilled softly. "I hoped for more carnage."

The saucer drifted out of hearing range. Chet trotted after it, questions swirling in his mind like confetti. What happened? Who was hurt? One of the people who had left the enclosure yesterday? If so, why had they traveled such a short distance? Perhaps the starfish had been talking about some other creatures? But what? Coyotes? Rabbits?

The saucer hovered above a spot near a rocky knoll about a quarter of a mile away, then it accelerated and disappeared into the distance. Good. That meant there hadn't been enough damage to satisfy the bloodthirsty creatures.

Faint screams became deafening as Chet approached. Christopher rolled around on the ground, ignoring Francie's pleas to hold still. The others huddled off to the side. The eyes they turned to Chet had a blankness in their stare.

Chet rushed to Francie's side.

"What's going on?"

"I don't know. He tripped and fell an hour ago, or maybe two minutes or two hours. Out here, there seems to be no time."

"Did he break a bone?"

"No. He looks fine, but he won't stop screaming."

Chet knelt on one knee by Christopher, then immediately jumped up, his kneecap burning as if impaled with a thousand splinters. Gritting his teeth, he limped to a hassock-sized rock, perched on the edge of it, pulled his knee to his chest to study it, but could see nothing out of the ordinary.

"...wrong?" Francie said, the rest of her words drowned out by Christopher's screams.

Chet glanced at her and found her looking at him, a crease of concern between her brows.

He exaggerated the words so she could read his lips, and touched his knee to show here where he hurt.

"I don't know what's wrong."

The touch made him gasp with pain. He turned his knee toward the sun to get a better look, and he saw them—hundreds of tiny blond filaments sprouting from his skin. They came out easily; the hard part was finding them all. What were they? Leftovers from a furred plant that had disintegrated in the heat? Not that it mattered where they came from. Just something else to watch out for.

When he could finally touch his knee without hurting, he hunkered by Christopher's side and began removing the filaments. Francie's eyes grew wide with comprehension, then she too set to work.

Christopher's screams subsided to sobs then whimpers.

"What did you do to him?" Lance demanded.

Chet jerked his head upward. Lance glared at him, shifting his weight from foot to foot as if preparing to charge.

"Removing splinters," Chet said in the soothing tone he'd used to quiet agitated animals in his pet store.

"No. Before that. What did you do to make him scream?"

Chet's mouth dropped open in disbelief.

"I had nothing to do with Christopher's agony. I wasn't even here."

"Ignore him," Francie whispered. "He's itching for a fight."

"I wish he'd pick on someone his own size," Chet muttered.

Francie smiled. "You are his size."

"No."

"I guess you haven't seen yourself recently. You look…"

She bent over her task again, but Chet could see her cheeks turning pink.

But she didn't even like him. Nor did he like her, though he had come to respect her. She always stepped up to do whatever needed to be done.

He glanced at her and caught her stealing a look at him.

"Something's going on here that I don't like," Lance said.

"Give it a break," Tisha said, sounding tired.

Lance pointed at Chet.

"Every time he turns up, something goes wrong. We should never have let him come with us."

"He didn't come with us," Barney said. "I wish he had. Then maybe Ellen wouldn't have gotten caught in the pool of quicksand."

For the first time, Chet realized Ellen was missing from the group.

"Where is she?"

"Loose lips sink ships," Grady growled.

Ricky rubbed his hands together, a look of glee on his face.

"We couldn't get her out."

"We tried using Grady's stick, but she went under too quickly," Barney said.

"It wasn't a stick. It was a spear. And she took it with her." Grady glared at Chet. "So now we have no weapon."

Francie spoke as if to herself.

"I'll never forget the look in her eyes."

Chet didn't say anything, but he couldn't keep from gritting his teeth. If they'd left this morning as he'd suggested, maybe they could have seen the quicksand before Ellen stepped into it.

Esmeraldo yawned.

"I'm tired. Are we going to stop? We've been traveling all stinking night."

"We'll stop when we get to a safe place," Tisha said.

"I'm going back." Mara kissed the top of her baby's head. "It's too dangerous out here."

Grady stepped in front of her and crossed his arms over his chest.

"No one is leaving."

"I'm going with her." Christopher struggled to his feet.

"I thought you wanted to raise your baby in freedom." Francie went to Mara and draped an arm around the young mother's shoulders. "Don't let one or two setbacks stop you from doing what you want."

"I want—" Mara's voice broke. "I want her to live."

She ducked away from Francie's hold.

"The kid will live," Tisha said. "We all will."

"The kid? *The kid?*" Mara clutched the baby closer. "She's not The Kid. Her name is Eve."

"We'll keep Eve safe," Francie said.

"We couldn't keep Helen safe." Barney spoke so softly Chet didn't think anyone but he could hear the words. "How can we keep a fragile thing like Eve safe?"

Mara stared at Francie for a moment, then shook her head.

"She'll never be safe out here, not like at home."

"Home?" Grady sneered. "That place back there isn't your

home."

Christopher stepped to Mara's side.

"Wherever my family is, that's home."

Tisha waved a regal hand.

"Go."

Chet's gaze caught Francie's.

"Be careful."

"Are you going back?"

The alarm in Francie's voice made him smile. Maybe she didn't hate him after all.

"Not to stay. I want to make sure they get there safely."

"Good riddance," Lance said. "Now can we continue?"

Chet stood with Christopher, Mara, and Eve, and watched Francie, Tisha, Esmeraldo, Barney, Lance, Grady, and Ricky straggle across the bleak terrain. Barney turned around to wave at them. Chet lifted a hand in return.

The sun lay directly overhead when they arrived at the enclosure. The trip had been without incident. The small family could probably have made it back by themselves, but at least Chet didn't have to worry about them anymore. He waited outside the gate until they entered the enclosure and disappeared into the welcoming crowd, then he turned around and headed back across the desert.

The sound of a ringing phone came from inside Chet's pouch, but he ignored it and kept on walking. The pouch vibrated, and when he still didn't reach inside for the phone, the intensity of the vibration increased, banging the pouch painfully against his hip.

He grabbed the phone.

"What do you want?"

"Is that any way to speak to your God?"

"You're not my God."

"I'm the right hand of your God, so anything you say to me, you say to him."

"As if he cares," Chet grumbled.

"You're right. He doesn't. I'm just making conversation here."

"Well, go make conversation somewhere else."

"Do you know what I like about you, Chet?"

"Nothing."

"You got that right, Chet! Maybe you're not as stupid as you look."

Chet quickened his pace.

"Did you call just to insult me? If so, I have better things to do."

"Like catching up to that group of losers?"

"No."

"Liar."

Chet blew out a breath.

"Okay. So I am going to catch up to them. You satisfied?"

"I guess you are stupid after all. What will traveling with them get you? You don't seem to be the type to be seduced with fictions about cities of gold."

Something in Bob's voice, a slight emphasis on the word gold, caught Chet's attention.

"Are there other cities? Not cities of gold, but real cities?"

"Would you look for them if I said yes?"

The phone blazed with light, and Chet held it away from him to look at the image on the screen. Bob's cherubic face beamed at him, but the gleam in the being's eyes seemed like the same murderous glint of glee that Chet often saw in Rickey's eyes. Is that why Bob had kept Ricky alive? He'd recognized a kindred soul?

"Why are you calling me now?" Chet asked. "Why not that night when I needed you?"

A sound like a rusty chuckle emanated from the phone.

"Your performance as an evangelist was truly pathetic. I thought you were playing games. I didn't realize you actually wanted to talk to me."

A chill passed through Chet. It had never occurred to him that Bob had heard him that night on the rock. What would have happened if Bob had responded? Chet would never have been able to leave. Those people would have torn him apart if the pibble and peatable had let them. Or they would have all but imprisoned him with their neediness.

As if a switch had flipped on in Chet's brain, he suddenly understood he was actually bandying words with, if not a God, then an omniscient being. Why hadn't Bob smited him? Or smote him? Could Bob and his God have a plan for Chet?

"Do you get it now?" Bob asked.

The switch flipped off.

"Get what?" Chet asked crossly.

Bob gave Chet a mournful look.

"You of all people should know." He turned his head as if talking to someone almost out of the phone screen's range. "He's not ready."

Chet caught a glimpse of familiar orange fur behind Bob. Could Bob be talking to the orange cat? Could the tangerine cat be an alien or even an angel, perhaps come to earth as a scout for Bob or the development company? Or—the thought staggered him—could the cat be Bob's God? If so, what could it possibly have wanted with Chet? A home base and someone to feed it?

"We'll have to increase his training," Bob said to his companion.

"Training?" Chet yelped. "What training?"

Bob beamed at Chet, and the smile seemed to remain even as the phone disappeared.

"What do you want from me?" Chet screamed.

He waited for a response, but all he heard was the howl of a far-off coyote.

Chet trudged across the desert, muttering "What training?" and "What should I know?" and "That traitorous cat."

Finally, realizing he'd become overheated, he huddled in the shade of a creosote bush and drank one of his gourds of water. He dozed until the sun went down, then nibbled on his rations as he continued tramping across the desert in the long twilight.

He didn't see anyone from the refuge. Had they really made such good time? Last night, they'd gone hardly any distance at all, so he didn't think he'd have any trouble catching up with the group, but he saw no sign of them. No tracks in the loose sandy soil. No human scat.

Remembering the flickering scenes outside the enclosure, he wondered if they could they have ended up in a different world. But he'd been in the same world with them just that morning, and there hadn't been any flickerings since. Could Bob have switched him to a different world? Or could he have deleted Francie and the rest of her group?

"Where are they, Bob?" he screamed. "I know you hear me."

He wanted to cry, but dehydration kept the tears from flowing.

When full night finally descended, he collapsed beneath a Joshua tree, wrapped the darkness around him, and fell asleep to the rustlings of tiny creatures in the nearby bushes.

In the distance, way off to the right at the base of the hills he'd been using for a landmark, Chet glimpsed a swathe of silver and green glistening beneath the desert sun.

"It's a mirage," he mumbled through chapped lips. "You're not going to catch me that way, Bob. I don't need your stupid training to know you're playing with me."

And yet he found himself veering toward the silver. After two or perhaps three days of seemingly aimless wandering, his gourds were empty, his foods supply diminished, and without prickly pears or some other recognizable source of hydration and nourishment, the gamble of the silver being more than a mirage seemed worth taking.

The smell of fresh water drifting on a cool breeze quickened his step. Maybe this wasn't so much a gamble after all.

Gradually he became aware that the footsteps of a solitary hiker stretched before him. When had they appeared? And where was the hiker? Castigating himself for not paying attention, he looked back to see where the other footprints had originated, but all he saw were the prints of his own bare feet. He turned facing the side and looked first back to the left then ahead to the right, and it seemed as if his prints led from where he'd been all the way to the oasis.

He rubbed his glare-blinded eyes, certain the footprints ahead of him were an optical illusion, but when he studied the prints again, he couldn't avoid the truth. He was walking where he'd already walked. Had he been this way before? It didn't seem possible. Ever since he'd left the refuge, he'd kept the same hills in sight, knowing that as long as he followed the range, he'd never get lost. Besides, if he'd already been to the oasis, wouldn't he have replenished his food and water? And yet, there were those impossible footprints. But, he had to admit, in this newly recreated world, there didn't seem to be much difference between the possible and the impossible.

He tried to swerve to avoid walking in his footsteps, but he stumbled and found himself back in line. Too leaden to move, too fearful of going forward, he stood in place until his legs threatened to collapse beneath him. Finding a few shreds of courage, he managed to lurch toward the hills, his footprints both trailing him and leading him on.

Gradually, the mirage grew into an oasis, complete with green vegetation and palm trees surrounding what looked like a small lake. Birds circled overhead.

Chet tried to puzzle out the meaning of the oasis and the footprints that led him there. Could it have something to do with whatever training Bob intended? Could it be a trap? Thirst pushed the thoughts out of his head. If Bob intended to poison him with lake water, there wasn't much he could do about it. He filled his gourds, drank all his belly could hold, then filled the gourds again. He reached for a bunch of yellow fruit dangling on a vine from the nearest palm, and stuffed one in his mouth. A hard seed almost cracked a tooth, and he spit it out. The seed looked like the pit of a date, but the fruit was as crisp and as tart as an apple, though a lot sweeter.

After he finished his snack, he jumped in the water fully clothed, if that silly loincloth could be considered clothes. He was treading water when he noticed something hidden in the shadow of a palm tree. A rock? He climbed out of the water and crept closer. Not a rock. A woman with her arms around her knees, sitting very still and staring across the water.

Francie.

For just a second, his throat felt closed in, as if his collar were too tight, and then he smiled to himself, not just at the thought that he wasn't wearing a collar, but at the very sight of her. She wasn't lost!

But she certainly didn't seem approachable, either, not with how rigidly she held herself. Was she sad? Angry? Planning something?

He moved closer. The tears on her face stilled him. She seemed so vulnerable he wanted to put his arms around her and tell her everything would be okay, but he knew she wouldn't appreciate the lie, no matter how well meant.

She turned to him, eyes hard, all hint of softness gone.

"What?"

"Are you okay?"

Of course she wasn't all right, but he didn't know what else to say.

She brushed away the lingering wetness on her cheeks with a quick, impatient gesture.

"I'm fine."

"I just thought…"

"Well, don't." She did a double-take as if she'd just realized who he was. "Chet. What are you doing here?"

He wanted to ask her if she'd seen him before he ever arrived, but felt too foolish to voice the question. Instead, he shrugged.

"Oh, you know. The re-creation. Escaping. Oasis." He'd attempted a light tone to disarm her, but she didn't smile or speak, so he tried again. "I got here as soon as possible." Still no response. "Well, I'm glad to see you, anyway."

She spoke so quietly, it took him a moment to decipher her words.

"You don't even like me."

"I didn't at first," he admitted. "You reminded me of my mother."

"And that's not good?"

He thought of Francie meticulously arranging her meager possessions in the refuge, and his mother as meticulously rearranging his cabinets. Francie doing what she could to take care of the children, and his mother working two jobs to take care of him. Francie needing to be needed just as his mother had needed to be needed. A deep-seated tension of which he hadn't even been aware eased its grip.

"It *is* a good thing," he said.

She slanted a quick look at him, then went back to staring off into the distance, but it seemed to him as if her body lost some of its rigidity, and when he settled beside her, she didn't shift away from him.

They sat in silence for several long minutes.

Finally he asked, "Where is everyone?"

"On the other side of the lake. Fighting." Tears welled up in her eyes again. "We're out here all alone, and each of them acts as if the rest of us are the enemy."

"Well, I'm here now."

"What?" And then she made the connection. "It's mean, but true. The rest of us do get along better when we have you for a scapegoat."

"You've never scapegoated me."

"But I never stuck up for you either." She turned to face him. "You take your situation well."

He shrugged.

"What else am I going to do? Argue with them that I'm a good guy? Maybe I'm not. I don't know anymore."

"I don't think any of us are. Bob's idea of what is good and what isn't certainly doesn't fit how we were raised to believe."

"Does he scare you, too?" Chet asked, being careful not to evoke Ricky's name.

She didn't pretend to misconstrue his meaning.

"He terrifies me," she whispered as if she didn't want to admit the truth to herself. "I don't like how he looks at me. We finished what little the food we brought with us, and now the effects of the pibble and peatable are wearing off. He still makes jokes, but…"

*I'll protect you.*

But could he? Despite his brave determination to re-create

himself, he had more than a suspicion that events were beyond his control. He felt sure that whatever was going to happen would happen whether he willed it or no. But that didn't mean he'd give up. He'd live until he died, as free as possible.

"Are you going to stay with us?" Francie seemed uncharacteristically hesitant as though she didn't want to influence his decision.

"I'm planning on it." He felt a clunk in his mind as if a die had been cast. Well, so be it. "What can I do to help?"

She gave him a sad smile.

"Just be yourself."

*Myself. The scapegoat.*

His shoulders slumped. Moments ago, he'd acted blasé about his role of scapegoat, but oh, the burden weighed heavily. No one, especially not one of the very last folks on Earth, wanted to be shunned, but if it would help keep Francie and the others alive, he'd do it. There was nobody else.

He stiffened his spine.

"So tell me. What are they arguing about?"

"Not arguing. Fighting."

"As in beating each other up?"

Francie plucked a piece of thick grass, shredded it, and tossed the remains in the lake.

"Yes, as in beating each other up."

"Who? Lance and Grady? Ricky and…everyone?"

She surprised him by laughing, though the laugh was closer to a sob than a sound of amusement.

"Esmeraldo and Barney this time. They're fighting about us eating one another."

Chet's mind skittered away from the image her words evoked.

"Eating one another," he repeated in a flat voice.

"Yeah. Grady died…"

"What?" Chet jerked even straighter than he'd already been sitting. "How?"

Francie absently destroyed another blade of grass.

"Ricky was the only one who saw. He said a cactus reached out its arms and strangled Grady."

"A cactus with arms? You mean like a saguaro? I didn't see any."

"We passed a whole section of them."

"Sheesh. Murdering cactus and we still have all this desert to cross? That's enough to make anyone crazy. Or crazier." A sudden thought sent a splinter of cold up Chet's spine. "Could Ricky have killed Grady?"

Francie turned her head toward him. Her eyes were rimmed with purple shadows.

"Maybe. I don't know. Grady's body looked like it tangled with a cactus, but there's no way to know what happened. He could have been beaten. I wanted to bury the body, but Tisha said no. We'd seen this oasis, you see, and she wanted us to get here before night came."

"So what does that have to do Barney and Esmeraldo fighting?" Chet asked.

Francie shivered.

"Esmeraldo says we should have butchered the body."

"Butchered?" Chet felt his mouth go dry. "As in...meat?"

"We have food here." She swept a hand above her head, drawing his attention to the palm trees. "But Esmeraldo says we need meat, so he suggested that as we die off, we need to eat each other to keep up our strength. Barney said that he'd kill Esmeraldo if Esmeraldo ate him. When they started pounding on each other, Ricky made a joke about them tenderizing their meat for him, so they turned on him. Tisha tried to stop the fight and got smacked in the process. That's when I left."

Chet wanted to laugh, but thinking Francie wouldn't appreciate such a response to her tale of woe, he managed to keep a straight face.

"Why was meat such a volatile issue? They haven't been eating any meat at all."

"Grady found a flint or something like that to start fires and a slingshot he made to kill rabbits, so we've been eating meat all those weeks we wandered in the desert."

"Not weeks," he said. "We left two or three days ago."

She fixed him with a piercing intensity.

"Weeks."

A wave of vertigo washed over him. He put his hands to the ground on either side of his body trying to anchor himself to something that made sense.

"How is that possible?"

She gave a disbelieving laugh.

"You're asking me? Aren't you the expert on the re-creation?"

He hardened himself against the chill he felt from her.

"Did anyone collect the flint and the slingshot from Grady before you left him?"

She jumped to her feet.

"What is wrong with you men? Ricky and Lance accused each other of taking the tools. If Tisha hadn't stopped them, they might have killed each other. People are dying and all you guys care about is your stupid toys."

For just a second, she looked lost, like a little girl waiting for someone to take her hand and show her the way safely home, but then her face bunched with grief or perhaps anger, and she stalked off.

It wasn't until that moment, seeing her stiff back moving away from him, that he realized how desperately he had craved a connection with someone.

But he couldn't afford a connection.

Couldn't afford to love.

# Chapter 21

CHET PATTED HIMSELF to make sure he still existed.

*Am I invisible?*

For as much attention as the other humans paid him, he might as well have been a barren palm tree. When he rejoined the group a week ago, Barney had given him a quick welcoming smile, but no one else had glanced his way, not even Francie. He'd been braced for disparaging remarks from Lance and Ricky, been prepared to defend his decision to return to the group, and he didn't know what to make of being so completely shut out.

Oddly, it wasn't just he the other humans ignored. They also ignored the alien visitors. Out here, far from the fenced refuge, there seemed to be no restrictions on what the tourists could do. Tour buses of all shapes often parked in the nearby desert. The braver beings, clad in suits similar to those the Earth astronauts had once worn, toddled toward the oasis. The bravest of the beings didn't even bother with a suit, but perhaps for them it wasn't bravery so much as being acclimated to Earth's atmosphere.

A creature like a stretched-out purple kangaroo patted himself in mimicry of Chet, and made a twittering sound that could have signified laughter or disgust or nothing at all. Three of the astronaut-suited beings stood staring at the humans as if they felt superior to them, and Chet wondered what they knew that he didn't.

He laughed at his conceit. They probably knew a hell of lot more than he did. At the very least, they knew what they were doing at the oasis and why they were there.

The kangaroo creature mimicked Chet's laughter, then quivered all over as if in ecstasy.

What meaning were any of these beings attributing to the human activity they so avidly watched? Tisha, Francie, Barney, Ricky, and Esmeraldo sprawled in the shade and argued while Lance prowled around them as if waiting to pounce on anyone who displeased him.

"So messy," one of the suited aliens whispered.

The other two murmured agreement.

*Messy?*

Chet studied the other humans. Their hair was wild from being combed with only fingers, and longer than he remembered. Once clean-shaven, the men now had untamed beards. Cuts, scrapes, bruises, and even black eyes, decorated their faces. But they smelled fresh from swimming in the lake, their hair shone with the aloe they used to keep their locks manageable, and their loincloths and cave girl dresses were as spotless as the day the clothes appeared on their bodies. He thought they looked good considering how rapidly they'd been thrust into a primitive lifestyle, but since he probably looked the same as they did, would he know if they looked unkempt?

"We can't stay here," Esmeraldo said. "All we have to eat are dates and those stinking roots. We need meat."

Barney scooted away from him.

"Stop staring at me."

Esmeraldo sniffed.

"There's not enough meat on your bones anyway."

"We should stay." Francie maintained her equanimity, though Chet wondered how she refrained from slapping the two silly men. "This oasis is a refuge."

"Not much of a refuge," Tisha said. "It's like the place we came from, only without the fence and no protection from the...the tourists. We have no idea what sort of diseases we could catch from them."

Ricky laughed.

"Or what sort of diseases they could catch from us. Ever wonder why none of them try to munch on us? I bet they think we're toxic."

"You're the toxic one," Esmeraldo muttered. "I wouldn't eat you if you were the last man alive."

"Hah!" Ricky shot a finger at him like a gun. "If I were the last man alive, you couldn't eat me because you'd already be dead."

"We're all dead meat." As if suddenly realizing what he'd said, a look of horror passed over Barney's face. "I don't mean that, I meant—"

Lance overrode him.

"You're forgetting the city of gold."

"Not me." Tisha skimmed her body with her hands. "Pretty dresses. Stores. Shopping. Salons. We need to leave. Soon."

"Very soon," Chet said. "Have you noticed the mountain to the right of this oasis? The one that looks like a beast at rest? I think it really is some kind of living creature. I can hear it breathing at night. It seems like it's...waiting."

Tisha, Barney, and Esmeraldo laughed, but otherwise his words had no more effect than the wind in the rushes. Perhaps they thought he was trying to goad them into action? Well, he was, but he also told the truth as he saw it.

"This whole thing seems like a set-up, as if we're mice, and the water and dates are the cheese meant to entice us."

*But to what end? To feed the beast?*

He shivered at the thought.

Lance snorted.

"Why does anyone ever listen to this jerk? Oh, right. We don't."

Ricky winked at Chet.

"I'm supposed to be the funny one, remember?"

"It could be dangerous away from here."

Francie sounded hesitant. Of all of the people in the group, she'd seemed the most valiant, but something—perhaps the way Ricky so often leered at her—had made her shrink into herself.

But then, everyone in the group acted different from the way they'd behaved in the refuge.

Chet spoke simply, keeping any hint of censure out of his voice.

"Staying here is dangerous, too."

Despite what they'd been through, these folks still didn't seem to understand the horrors of the re-created world, where mountains could be monsters, havens could be hazardous, and uncertainty was the only certainty.

"I read a lot in the slammer," Ricky said. "And know what? People in the stories about the apocalypse always had a hard time. Those worlds were mostly empty. No animals or anything like that. And hardly any food. We have it easy."

"That's because we aren't dealing with the apocalypse," Barney said. "It's gentrification."

"I bet this is a trap of some kind, like a mousetrap." Lance pounded one hand into the other. "And we're the mice."

Francie shot a quick look at Chet. He shrugged. She turned away, a troubled expression on her face.

"Are you saying someone wants to kill us?" Esmeraldo asked. "Who? Bob?"

Ricky grinned, showing too many teeth.

"I'm the only one who wants to kill anyone."

Barney laughed, though no amusement showed on his face. Perhaps he, too, was learning to fear Ricky.

Tisha stood.

"So we leave."

"What?" Lance stopped pacing. "Right now?"

"Why not?" Tisha asked. "You have plans that need to be cancelled? A dental appointment you have to go to?"

Lance glowered at her.

"We need rations. You know what the desert's like."

The purple kangaroo hopped close to Chet and held out something that looked and smelled like dung. Chet backed away. The creature took a bite, stepped forward, and again shoved the ghastly mess toward Chet.

Chet took another step backward. Did the kangaroo understand what rations meant? Or was his offering the food at that particular moment a coincidence?

The kangaroo made a gesture that looked remarkably like a human shrug and stuffed the food in its mouth.

A loud twittering came from one of the saucer-shaped tour buses. If the twittering were a language, it was one Chet didn't understand, but apparently the sounds meant something. The kangaroo patted itself, flung out an arm out and touched Chet, then hopped toward the bus.

Chet was so caught up in the bizarre occurrence that it took him a moment to realize Ricky had spoken his name. He jerked his head around to focus on the killer.

Ricky was smirking at Lance.

"Are you talking to me?" Lance snarled.

"Why would I be talking to you?" Ricky said with exaggerated nonchalance. "I only said we didn't have to worry about rations. Chet has food."

"What kind of food?" Tisha asked warily.

"The kind you eat." Ricky gave a nasty-sounding laugh. "Such a busy little man, that Chet. Digging roots. Drying dates. All for us."

A wave of fear washed through Chet. So he hadn't been invisible after all. How long had Ricky been spying on him? More to the point, why hadn't he noticed the other man? Could Ricky really be that careful?

Of course, Ricky could be that careful. He'd been sneaking up on his victims for years before he'd gotten caught.

It didn't seem fair that they had to deal with a human killer as well as all the other unsociable elements of the recreated world, but what did fairness ever have to do with anything?

Realizing that the others were getting ready to set out, Chet cried, "No."

"He's too stingy to share his food?" Lance asked Ricky.

"I don't care about the food." Chet's legs sagged from sudden fatigue. Had he always had such a difficult time dealing with other people? He couldn't remember anymore, but perhaps that's why he'd gravitated toward the fur and feather folk. They didn't exhaust him. "I prepared the stuff for all of us. But look at the sky. The sun's almost directly overhead. In these clothes, well die of heatstroke before we get more than a few miles."

"Are you sure we should wait?" Francie asked Chet. "Aren't you the one who said we needed to travel during the day?"

"That was when we first left the refuge. The world was flickering and there was no way of knowing what we would encounter. Now we know what we will encounter—sun so hot during the day it could kill us." Chet turned from Francie to Lance. "You know it's the truth."

Lance placed a hand behind an ear.

"Did anyone hear that? Sounded like a gnat buzzing."

"Let's get some sleep," Tisha said. "We leave at dusk."

Esmeraldo clambered to his feet.

"Good idea. We'll die of heatstroke if we leave now. Wake me when you're ready to go."

Ricky chomped his teeth at him.

"Sure. If you're still alive."

Esmeraldo scurried behind a bush and disappeared.

"You're such a cut-up, Ricky," Barney said with a wobbly laugh.

Ricky giggled.

"You got that right. I cut things up real good."

Chet felt like banging his head on the trunk of a palm tree. If this is what his life was going to be from now on, maybe it would have been better if Bob had deleted him a long time ago.

Tisha and the men moved in various directions to find spots to sleep, but Francie remained regarding Chet, a tiny furrow between her brows.

"What?" he asked softly.

She shook her head and slipped away.

Despite his fear for Francie's safety and his unease over the strange group dynamic, Chet found himself smiling as he went to his own preferred place of rest in a cool grotto close to the lake.

# Chapter 22

WALKING IN THE desert twilight was like trudging on the most boring treadmill ever. The scenery never seemed to change, with the same shadowy horizon ahead, a few dark hills to right, and sparse vegetation throughout.

"Didn't we just pass this place?" Barney stopped and pointed to a single flower glowing in the dim light. "I'm sure I saw that orange flower before."

"It's a stinking poppy." Esmeraldo stooped to pick the blossom. "There are lots of them in California."

"Can't be a poppy, then." Barney arched his back, then bent forward to touch his toes. "This isn't California."

"How do you know?" Ricky asked. "We could be anywhere."

Lance squinted at the stars emerging overhead.

"We're still in the northern hemisphere."

"Unless Bob rotated the sky." Tisha shuddered. "He better not have. We need to be able to count on something."

Francie, who'd continued walking when everyone else had stopped, turned around.

"Shouldn't we keep going? Soon it will be too dark to walk."

Tisha strode past Francie.

"Let's go."

Esmeraldo tossed the flower aside, and followed her.

Francie carefully picked up the bloom and tucked it into her hair behind her left ear.

Chet couldn't help smiling at how gently she'd handled the once-living thing. At least one person hadn't become so jaded that she'd lost all reverence for life. It gave him hope for the future.

Assuming there was a future.

Assuming the desert would ever end.

He'd lost track of how long they'd traveled. Each day was exactly the same—walk in the early morning, sleep in the heat of the day, walk again in the evening, eating what they could when they could during their waking hours, then curl up against the cold in the darkest part of the night. He'd also lost track of how many times, just when they were ready to collapse from dehydration or hunger, Lance found a water or food source such as a seep, aloe plants, prickly pears, acacia trees, even a scraggly bush with raisin-like fruits that he claimed grew only in the Australian desert.

"They'd die without me," Lance grumbled, digging in the sandy soil where the poppy had been. "Can't they understand that a flower doesn't grow without moisture?"

He kept scooping the soil with his hands, and in a few minutes the small hole filled with water.

One by one, the travelers trooped back to drink the gritty water. When they all trekked off again, Chet scooped more dirt out of the hole to get enough water to fill the gourd bottles.

As Chet tagged along behind the straggling group, he had to admit Lance was probably right. Without the ex-soldier and the survival skills he'd learned in the military, they wouldn't have lasted this long. Still, Chet had the uneasy suspicion, one he had yet to voice, that they would have been okay no matter what. It seemed as if the water seeps and edible plants were strewn like breadcrumbs to lure them in a specific direction. If Lance hadn't been able to identify each crumb along the way, Chet felt sure there would have been some sign to help them interpret the clues, such as a note saying, "Eat me."

But where were they being lured? And why? Could this be part of his training? Was he supposed to pay attention to what Lance was doing so he could learn how to survive the desert? But why the desert? Surely there were more hospitable places left on Earth for him to settle down. Or maybe he was supposed to be a wanderer, eternally seeking rest and finding none. That prospect sounded even more pathetic than the other humans dreaming of an El Dorado. At least they were searching for something specific—a city of gold. He was just...rambling.

Strangely, other than the mountain beast and the strategically placed food and water sources, there were no signs of the re-creation, no horrors such as he had encountered before going into the refuge. There weren't even any visitations from Bob or the tourists. Could their dark flight from the oasis have confused the aliens? Their leaving in the night wouldn't have confused Bob, so maybe Bob had finally abandoned them. If so, were the water and food Lance found not enticements but naturally occurring resources?

And maybe, wandering the endless desert was making him crazy.

Gradually, over the next few days, the desert landscape segued into something resembling an arid plain—still inhospitable, but with a greater abundance of vegetation. Most of the plants were sun-dried, the grasses brown, but the very fact of the grass heartened Chet.

The whole group had been silent for a couple of hours when Esmeraldo burst out with, "If this land was just created, why is everything dying?"

Lance turned back and stared at Chet who was lagging behind as usual.

"Next time Chet talks to Bob, he should ask why God would create dead plants."

"Bob is gone," Tisha said emphatically. "It's only us."

"Maybe God likes dead things." Barney spoke quietly, but a breeze carried the words to Chet. "He created death, didn't he?"

"He created people who love to kill." Ricky slanted a glance at Francie. "And he created people to kill."

*Nooo*, Chet screamed silently.

Ricky combed his beard with his fingers for a second, then

nodded as if to himself.

"But not yet. The savor has to be there."

*Savor?*

Chet tried not to think what Ricky meant by the word, but still an image of the killer gloating over Francie's bloody body drifted across his mind.

*Please, please, please bring us to safety.*

Chet didn't know to whom he was sending his plea. Tisha, maybe, since she seemed to have elected herself leader. Or Lance, since he was the one who kept them fed. Or Bob. As much as he didn't want to have to deal with that annoying and confusing being, he wanted to make sure the group reached safety.

He patted his food pouch, but the bag remained empty. No phone. No food, either. The group had eaten the last of his offerings days ago, and so they were all dependent on Lance. At least Lance, for all of his military background, seemed to focus on life, not death.

Francie pointed in the direction they were walking.

"What's that?"

Chet squinted, but all he could see was something resembling a faint haze on the horizon.

"Fog?" Esmeraldo said. "There's a lot of fog in California, but not in the stinking desert, I don't think."

Lance held open fists to his eyes as if they were binoculars.

"It looks like a forest."

Chet made his own fist binoculars, and it did seem as if the horizon came a bit closer. But still, for a long time, all he could see was the haze.

And then, even with his arms swinging at his sides as he walked, the forest popped into focus.

The closer they got, the more he could make out the shapes of the individual trees, but not enough to say what species they were. After a few more miles, the trees became indistinct again, as if the forest were retreating, and it grew increasingly indistinct. A trick of the light? Or...

"I think the forest is running from us," Chet said.

Lance tilted his head.

"Did anyone else hear that gibberish?"

Esmeraldo laughed.

"Chet said the forest is running from us."

"Forests can't run." Barney let out a high-pitched giggle, then abruptly cut it off. "They can't, can they, not even in this world?"

"If you were a tree that discovered you could run," Chet said, "and you saw a bunch of humans, what would you do?"

"Nothing," Esmeraldo said. "Why would I be afraid of humans?"

For once Chet didn't bother to modulate his tone.

"Think! Practically the entire United States was once a forest. Every time pioneers settled on a bit of land, the first thing they did was cut down the trees. And we're still cutting down trees. Only five percent of America's original forest cover remains. If I were a tree with the ability to move, I sure as hell would run as far and as fast as I could from any human."

Ricky's eyes grew round.

"No wonder God loves me. I kill the tree killers. Wow. So cool!"

No one laughed, not even Barney.

"Don't listen to Chet," Tisha said. "He's just trying to scare us. None of the things that he said would happen have happened. I think he made it all up. The devil toads. The river. The volcano. All of it."

"I'm not scared." Esmeraldo coughed and cleared his voice. "I never believed any of that stuff he said."

Ricky grinned.

"Chet's just a wussy."

*Wussy?* Chet mouthed the word. Although he'd never heard that particular term before, he knew what Ricky meant. Maybe he did seem weak, maybe he even was weak, but that didn't negate all that he had been through. Nor did it matter what his companions believed. He sincerely hoped that the group would not have to deal with any of the nastier denizens of this re-created world, and if their luck continued to hold, they might not have to.

Tisha rallied the group, and they trooped onward.

They followed the trees for the rest of the day, never getting any closer, though they did come upon what looked like a plowed field that stretched all the way to the trees. Even when the group expressed confusion over a plowed field in the middle of nowhere, Chet kept his mouth shut. He knew the churned ground came from the desperately running trees, and the look Francie shot him made him think she suspected the same thing, but she also kept quiet.

The next day, the breadcrumbs led them to a small riparian area with a waterfall, though it wasn't so much a fall as an ooze. From no discernible source, a thin sheet of water moved down an eight-foot-high slab of rock into a pool not much bigger than a basin. Berry bushes, cottonwoods, wild grape vines, cattails, all crowded into the small, cool area.

Everyone except Lance stuffed berries into their mouths, heedless of the juices dripping down their chins and beards. Lance foraged among the cattails and plucked young shoots and small leaves, and ate them with more determination than enjoyment.

"Be careful," Francie said. "If you get sick, there's not much I can do about it."

Lance held out a handful of thin shoots.

"Try them. Cattails are the perfect survival food. Almost all parts are edible. The roots are a better source of starch than potatoes or rice or taro or just about anything, but they need to be cooked."

An unreadable expression flashed over Francie's face, and Chet had the feeling she wanted to say something but changed her mind. Maybe she'd been about to make a comment about the disappearance of Grady's flint. Having such a tool sure would be handy, but wouldn't Lance know how to make a fire? Chet had tried once when he was a boy, and even after an hour, he hadn't managed a single spark, so maybe Lance didn't want to attempt something he couldn't guarantee would work.

Or maybe he simply did not like cooked cattail roots.

After quenching his thirst, Chet made a bed of cattail leaves on his left hand, filled it with berries, grapes, and shoots, and went off to sit by himself and enjoy his meal in silence.

"No!"

The shouted word startled Chet. He jumped up, spilling the last few uneaten berries, and dashed the short distance to the waterfall.

Lance had Esmeraldo by the arm and was yanking him away from the pool. Esmeraldo's feet were wet.

"Don't you people know anything?" Lance bellowed. "You never bathe in drinking water."

Tisha put her hands on her hips and fixed Lance with a stern look.

"Let him go."

Lance dropped Esmeraldo's arm.

Esmeraldo stumbled away from him.

"I just wanted..."

"I know," Tisha said soothingly. "We all want to get clean. But in this one thing, we have to do as Lance says. He has wilderness survival skills that the rest of us don't."

"So what are we supposed to do?" Barney asked. "How do we use the water if we can't use the water?"

Tisha slanted her head in the military man's direction.

"Lance?"

"Use the gourd canteens," Lance growled. "Take the water far enough away from the pool so that your filth doesn't contaminate the drinking water."

Esmeraldo sidled up to Chet and held out his hands.

"Give me the stinking gourds."

Chet winced.

*The gourds.*

As if they were community property and not something he'd spent hours gouging out using only sticks and willpower. He managed a small smile, though, as he passed the makeshift water bottles to Esmeraldo, reminding himself he wanted the group to survive as best as it could. It's not as if he'd kept the food and water he carried to himself. He'd always shared what he had. He just wanted...what? Thanks? A pat on the back? A kind word? Respect?

Whatever it was he wanted, he wasn't getting, and might never get. It had to be enough that the group survived. He surreptitiously touched the small lump at his hips that meant the knife sheath hidden beneath his loincloth was still there. Although he was willing to share everything else, the stone knife was one thing he wanted everyone to forget existed. As far as he knew, only Francie was aware he'd made the thing, but what if the others with a penchant for spying, like Ricky, had seen him with the sharpened stone? It was best for everyone if he kept the stone hidden. Either Ricky or Lance could easily take it from him, and if any of the other two ganged up on him, they could take it too. They might use the knife for the good of the group, but they could also use it for other things. Fighting, maybe. Or murder.

Ricky smirked at him as if he knew what Chet was thinking.

He nodded his head toward Francie, who was gathering grapes and laying them on a rock in the sun, and mouthed, "She's mine."

Chet shivered. There was no way Ricky could really have known what had been in his mind. Or could he? Could some form of mental telepathy account for the man's phenomenal power over the women he had captured and brutalized?

*Cripes. Bob, what have you gotten me into?*

Fortunately, Bob did not respond, and even more fortunately, when Esmeraldo returned with the gourds, Ricky grabbed the makeshift bottles, filled them with water, and disappeared from sight.

# Chapter 23

THE TRAVELERS STAYED by the waterfall only long enough to rest and to dry enough grapes and berries to get them through a couple of days on the trail. Lance, Ricky, and Esmeraldo objected to Chet carrying the provisions, but since he refused to give up the bag, and they had no other way of carrying so many tiny bits of food, they finally let him be. Of course, they had no objection to his carrying the water. The gourds themselves were heavy since they so easily became saturated with water, and the water added another couple of pounds of weight to each gourd.

No one seemed to realize that the filled gourds would make great weapons, though Chet found that hard to believe. More likely, they assumed he was too weak or too stupid to appreciate the gourds' potential, and Chet had no problem letting them think whatever they wished. As far as he knew, in this re-created world, thinking had no more effect than it did in the previous one.

Still, taking no chances, Chet tried to keep his darker thoughts and suspicions at bay. Mostly he kept quiet, which seemed to suit everyone, including him. The others talked about the city of gold and what they would do once they got there, but mostly they fell into endless conversations about the drudgery of the trek, with Tisha issuing commands, Esmeraldo whining, Lance grumbling at the others' stupidity, Ricky giggling to himself, Barney begging them to get along, and Francie encouraging them to remain upbeat and focused on the day.

Occasionally Chet heard his name or caught a backward glance, and he knew they were discussing once again his report of the horrors he'd supposedly experienced before he went into the enclosure. All of them had some knowledge of the remodeling of the earth—every night in the refuge they had held the where-were-you, each of them telling their story of where they were and what they were doing when the first great change and the massive deletions took place, so the possibility of deleterious events should not be easily dismissed.

Chet sighed. Animals seemed to have more of a realistic sense of danger than people did. Apparently, civilization had skewed the human survival instinct to such an extent that killers were more to be feted than the Cassandras, even if the doomsayers told the truth.

But, being honest with himself, he had to admit that if all he had to go by were the things the others had seen, he might not be concerned either.

Ellen slipping into the quicksand could be considered a normal accident. Grady's death could also be considered an ordinary mishap if one discounted Ricky's tale of a cactus strangling the man. Both the monster mountain and the fearful forest could be chalked up to an overheated imagination.

Understanding the group's state of mind didn't help make his self-imposed protection duty sit any easier on his shoulders, and he found himself lagging further and further behind.

The group topped a small mount and, as they disappeared from sight, Chet's Bob-enhanced hearing detected the soft pounding of their bare feet as they ran down the slope. Chet picked up his pace and soon reached the hilltop. Far below, in a bowl formed by a ring of hills, grew the most astonishing garden he had ever seen with every sort of flower blooming all at once, regardless of climate or season. Despite the beauty and the sense of awe that stole over him, he felt uneasy. And then it hit him. It wasn't his enhanced vision that was making each flower so visible—it was the size of the flowers. They must be huge, with some of the stems as tall and thick as an old oak tree.

A loud whirring sound, like that of a nearby a helicopter, rent the air. Chet cupped his hands around his mouth.

"Come back," he yelled. "Come back."

Francie stopped and turned to look at him, but the others ran heedlessly on.

Wanting nothing more than to stay where he was, Chet half-ran, half-slid down the hill to where Francie waited.

"This better be good, Chet," she said.

"Not good at all." He panted for breath. "What pollinates massive flowers?"

Her mouth opened, and her eyes widened.

"Bees," she whispered.

He nodded.

"*Enormous* bees. And wasps."

"Oh, no." She charged down the hill, screaming, "Come back. You have to come back. Bees. Wasps."

Tisha turned around and shouted, "What?"

"Bees," Chet and Francie yelled.

Tisha scuttled back up the hill.

"I'm allergic."

Chet let out an unamused snort.

"Allergies would be the least of your worries. Stingers on bees large enough to pollinate those flowers would be as big and as sharp as swords."

Staring at him, Tisha stumbled.

"Oh. My. Bob."

Both Barney and Esmeraldo slowed as they neared the colossal garden. They turned to each other as if conferring, looked up to where Chet and the women stood beckoning them, then trudged back up the hill.

"What were you yelling?" Barney asked.

"Bees." Tisha shivered.

"So?"

Esmeraldo looked at Barney, and the two of them shrugged.

"Giant flowers," Francie said. "Giant bees."

198

"Ouch." Barney pointed to the small figures of Ricky and Lance disappearing into the jungle of flowers. "Someone should go down there and warn them."

"Don't look at me," Esmeraldo said. "I'm not going."

Hoping he looked more composed than he felt, Chet trotted down the hill.

"Don't go, Chet," Francie called to him. "You don't have to be a hero."

"Not a hero," he called back. Too low for anyone but himself to hear, he repeated, "Not a hero." And then even lower, "A fool."

The helicopter-like sound as well as deeper rumblings and high-pitched screeches grew louder the closer Chet drew to the jungle. Even worse was the smell. In a small dose, such as normal flowers in a normal garden in a normal time, the smell would have been delightful, but such a powerfully sweet aroma with a strong undertone of decay and rich loamy soil made him feel as if his sinuses were about to explode.

Even before he reached the jungle of flowers, he could feel the damp heat generated by the respiring plants, and his steps faltered. Lance and Ricky would be okay if he didn't go searching for them, wouldn't they? They were smart enough not to engage in combat with giant insects, weren't they?

He heard a human scream. Before he could react, Ricky came dashing out of the jungle and sideswiped Chet, spinning him around. Lance came out a second later and ran full into Chet. Chet went down.

Lance stood over him, chest heaving.

"What the hell do you think you're doing? Are you stupid? Don't you know there are giant insects in there? Ants as big a cats. Grasshoppers the size of horses."

Ricky gave a start as if he had just that moment seen the other two men.

"What's this jerk doing here?" he asked Lance.

"Being an ass." Lance trotted up the hill, muttering, "Cripes, I get tired of looking after all these knuckle-draggers."

Chet struggled to his feet and brushed himself off.

Ricky grinned at him, though his eyes looked haunted as if they were still focused on the horrors among the flowers.

"This is something new for me, Chet old boy. Rescuing people instead of killing them." He poked a finger at Chet's chest. "But don't expect me to do it again."

Chet watched Lance and Ricky ascend the hill.

*Is that how they saw what just happened? That they rescued him?*

He felt a breath on the back of his neck as if the flowers were growing toward him, and he realized how foolish he was being. What did it matter what anyone thought? No one had gotten hurt or absorbed into the vile garden.

As he ran up the hill to join the others, he heard Ricky brag about the worm that almost ate him.

"Worm?" Lance spun to face Ricky. "You saw worms?"

Ricky nodded.

"Big ones. As big as the snake in that movie."

Lance started back down the hill.

"What are you doing?" Tisha demanded.

"Getting a worm." Lance sounded as matter-of-fact as if he'd just announced he were going to get a drink of water. "Worms are full of protein. They're good to eat once you squeeze out all the dirt."

A clatter of sound as Tisha, Barney, and Esmeraldo spoke at the same time.

"No one is going in that place again," Tisha said.

"Worms?" Barney said. "Eeew."

"I'm not eating no stinking worm," Esmeraldo said.

"And you, Chet?" Francie asked. "Would you eat the worm?"

Chet shook his head.

"I'm a vegetarian."

Lance stopped short.

"A vegetarian? I should have known. Real men eat meat."

Ricky giggled.

"Real men eat worms. And women."

A look that could only be terror passed over Francie's face. She edged away from the killer.

"What if you were starving, Chet? Or someone you loved was starving? Could you still hold to your principles?"

Chet answered reluctantly, not wanting to face one more unpalatable truth.

"Being a vegetarian is an ethical choice. But I don't know if we will have the luxury of being ethical anymore."

"No worms," Tisha pointed to Lance as if she were the Red Queen and he a subject about to lose his head. "We have no way to kill them or cut them up or cook them."

Lance grumbled, but Chet got the impression the man was glad to have an excuse not to enter the unholy garden again to hunt for a gargantuan worm.

The group had appeared carefree as they had run down the slope, but now, trudging along the ridge of the hills, they seemed leaden. Chet felt bad about dampening their spirits until he heard them laughing at him.

"Bees," Ricky chortled. "Did that brain-dead jerk really say there were bees down there?"

Esmeraldo snickered.

"Yep. Sure did. I didn't see no stinking bees though."

Chet hardened his heart. Couldn't they hear the helicopter-buzz of the bees below? Couldn't they see the creatures flitting from plant to plant? Admittedly, from up here, the bees looked their normal size, so perhaps the others couldn't see the insects, but still, logic should have prevailed.

He lagged further and further behind, trying to distance himself from the other humans. Why should he care if they didn't make it to the city of gold or wherever they wanted to go? Why should he care if they were stung by humongous bees? Why should he care if they didn't believe him? Why should he keep offering himself up as the sacrificial goat just so the group wouldn't tear itself apart?

He vowed to strike out on his own. He even meant it, but somehow, he found himself straggling after the group as they hiked to the far side of the flower bowl and down into a woodland. These trees did not run from them, but the place seemed dark and inhospitable and cold as if it had shut itself off from the humans.

The travelers rushed through the darkness, and then stopped abruptly when they reached the light at the end of the woods.

What now? Chet hurried to catch up to the group, and when he did, he too stopped and stared at the wondrous sight. Not an unnatural garden. Not a city of gold. But something as fabled.

A log cabin.

# Chapter 24

CHET FOLLOWED THE others into the cabin. Much of the chinking between logs was missing, and ribbons of light patterned the floor, but the building seemed sturdy enough to keep out the worst of the weather and most of the predators. He looked longingly at the faded patchwork quilts piled in an open trunk. How wonderful it would be to roll himself into a quilt and let the stress and worry seep from his body. When he felt himself giving in to the seductive promise of the cabin, he dug his fingernails into his palms and reminded himself to be strong.

Ricky flung open a cabinet door.

"Hey, look here. Real food! Beanie Weenies. SpaghettiOs. Canned chili. Lemon drops." He popped the top off a can of SpaghettiOs, upended it, and poured so much into his mouth that the food spilled over onto his chest.

The others scrambled to grab cans, but Chet stood his ground. Then belatedly, Ricky's words registered. Lemon drops. His mouth watered for the tangy sweetness of the candy, and images of his father flooded his mind.

*Lemon drops!*

Arms outstretched, he started to push his way through the knot of fellow travelers, then stopped abruptly.

*What the hell am I doing?*

Lemon drops. Bob knew he'd be here. Knew the one treat in

203

the entire world that would entice Chet back to the fold.

"It's a set-up," Chet cried. "A trap."

The others turned and gaped at him, open cans clutched in grubby hands. Bunched together as they were, open mouths full of partially masticated food, they looked like nestlings at feeding time. For just a second, he considered keeping the truth from them. Despite all they'd gone through, they were still children who couldn't quite grasp the enormity of their new world.

"What kind of trap?" Tisha asked.

Don't listen to him," Lance said. "He doesn't know what he's talking about. From the beginning, he's done nothing buy try to undermine your authority."

"Be honest." Chet held Tisha's gaze. "What have you been craving the most?"

She chewed slowly and swallowed with an audible gulp.

"Beanie Weanies."

Chet nodded at Ricky.

"What about you?"

Ricky held up the empty can of SpaghettiOs and wiggled it, smirking.

Chet turned to Lance.

"And you?"

Lance threw a punch in the air like a triumphant fighter.

"Pop tarts! Do you see any Pop Tarts?"

"Hey, Lance," Barney called. "Catch."

He lobbed a small box at Lance, who caught it with his upraised hand.

Lance looked from the box to Chet.

"Pop Tarts. So what?"

"So…" Chet let his voice trail off.

He could feel the trap but could not see the point of it. Bob could have stopped them any time. Why now? Were they nearing their destination, whatever that might be, and Bob decided to hurl one more test their way? But a test for what? Their worthiness to proceed? But that would mean the whole escape had been part of

Bob's plan from the beginning. Maybe it wasn't just Chet that Bob was trying to train, but all of them.

"What a jerk." Lance ripped open the box of Pop Tarts, pulled out a packet, and pointed it at Chet. "In battle, he who hesitates loses."

"This isn't a battle." Chet realized the lie as he spoke the words. Their lives were a battle, a battle to the death, and only Bob would be the winner. "It's about Bob manipulating us. Again."

"Why would he do that?" Tisha demanded.

"I don't know. You people can do what you want. I'm sleeping outside."

He tossed one more longing look at the quilts, wrapped his arms around his bare middle, and marched toward the door.

"Chet?" Francie's voice stopped him mid-step.

He slowly set his raised foot on the ground and turned.

Francie clutched an as yet untasted chocolate bar.

"What have you been craving?"

If it had been anyone else doing the asking, he wouldn't have answered, but her direct look pulled the words from him.

"Lemon drops."

Silence accompanied Chet's final few steps through the doorway, but as soon as he crossed the threshold, the chatter started up again.

Chet rolled his head back and looked at the stars, so many the sky appeared to have been slathered with silver glitter. He knew he wasn't alone—sentient beings inhabited planets revolving around some of those stars—but he felt as if he were the only creature left in the universe.

"Chet?"

He thought he'd imagined Francie's soft query, but when he turned to look, there she stood, bathed in starlight. Without thinking, without even realizing what he was doing, he enfolded her in his arms and held her tightly.

It took him a moment to realize she was clinging to him with a desperation that matched his own.

After long minutes, they loosened their grasp, but did not move from the protective circle of each other's arms.

"Why?" Chet asked when he could find his voice.

"Why this?"

She kissed him softly on the corner of his mouth.

He chuckled.

"Well, that too. But I meant why come out here with me? Aren't you scared?"

The flirtatious glint faded from her eyes.

"I don't think there's any danger, my being with you. And I've noticed that you are often right. Remember that mountain you claimed was a monster and everyone laughed at you? I saw a cave...well, what I thought was a cave...and it winked at me. And you were right about those trees. They were afraid of us. I could feel their fear. But mostly, I remembered how gently you held Mara's baby, and I know you'd never purposely hurt anyone."

She drew in a ragged breath.

"I admit didn't like you at first. I thought you were a sniveling Mama's boy, but you...sorry. I'm babbling. I always talk too much when I'm nervous."

Chet felt his palms grow moist.

"Nervous? About what? Well, there's this whole re-creation thing, and we're on a journey to nowhere, wearing only these silly garments. Oh, and Bob, the Right Hand of God is playing games with us, but other than that, what is there to be nervous about?"

Francie's arms tightened around him once more, and she whispered in his ear, "This."

He breathed in the sweet candle-scent of her hair, the natural odor of an unsoaped, unperfumed human body, and felt something deep within himself relax.

"You feel so good," he murmured.

"So do you."

The smell of lemon wafted toward him, but it held no temptation. What need had he of artificial comforts when he had the real thing right here? But Francie brought him so much more than comfort. Tension of a different kind rose in him, and he moved his lower body away from hers so she wouldn't feel his erection.

She slid her hands down his body to his buttocks, and brought him close again.

"Are you sure?" he asked.

She kissed the hollow of his neck beneath his ears.

"Shhh."

He drew in a ragged breath, turned his head. Their lips met. He'd never tasted anything as luscious as her kiss. If he did nothing the rest of his life but stand here, Francie in his arms, lips gentling each other, he'd count his life well lived.

Their kisses deepened, breath quickened. The magnetism between them grew so strong they didn't loosen their grasp when they sank to the ground. They lay on their sides, bodies entwined, lips greedy. He wanted to kiss all of her, taste her, explore her delectable folds, but he didn't move, didn't want to break the spell. Didn't want to give Bob a chance to take her from him.

His erection found its way out of the protection of the loincloth. Francie shifted her body. And as easily as that, he found himself deep within her.

He rocked her slowly, needing to make sure their union was as perfect for her as it was for him. He could feel himself growing even bigger inside her, and soft moans escaped from her lips and into his mouth.

Her inner muscles tightened around him, caressing, and his urgency grew. He slowed his rocking, holding Francie tight, barely moving. Wetness touched his cheek. Her tears or his? He didn't know. For long moments, he couldn't tell where he left off and she began, where their breaths ended and the air started. He could feel them pulsing together, and an answering pulse deep within the earth.

Francie writhed in his arms.

"Now," she said in a strangled voice.

Chet rolled onto his back, Francie on top of him. He rested his hands on her hips and let her set the pace. She rode him slowly at first, perhaps afraid that he'd slide out of her, but he'd grown so big and hard and she held him so tightly within her there was no chance of a slip. He smoothed his hands down to her buttocks, feeling the bunching and releasing of her muscles as she moved.

The delicious pain, the agonizing sweetness grew until it seemed to encompass not just their bodies but the whole universe. Francie must have felt that same intensity because she arched her back, raised her face to the sky, and screamed.

He exploded into her with such force he felt as if he'd been turned inside out. She collapsed on top of him, sobbing. He held her tightly, afraid they'd lose each other in the vast loneliness of space. After long moments, he became aware of the hard ground beneath his back, the lemon-scented air above them. He let out a long sigh.

She lifted her starlit face and smiled down at him.

"Where did we go?"

"I don't know. Some place else. You were magnificent." He touched her cheek with the back of his hand. "You *are* magnificent."

Her eyes widened and her lips parted. She stared at him.

"What's wrong?" he asked. Then he felt it. He'd been so focused on her he hadn't realized he'd become hard again.

"I don't know if I have the strength to do that again," Francie said.

"We don't have to."

Chet tried to ease out of her, but she held him tightly.

"No. Don't go."

"If you're tired, wouldn't you rather be on the bottom so I have to do all the work?"

"This is perfect."

She lay on top of him, rocking her hips, sucking his tongue. He thought of all that happened to bring him to this place, to Francie. The deletion. The re-creation. The enclosure. The escape. The cabin. Then the ecstasy of the moment swept over him, obliterating any semblance of rational thought.

Chet woke in Francie's arms. The sky seemed blindingly blue, the air unbearably sweet, and she…he could think of no words to describe the total wonder of her.

She opened her eyes and smiled at him.

"What happened?"

"I slept with you."

She laughed. "Uh...yeah."

"No. I mean I *slept* with you." He kissed her, a delicate kiss, no more than the brush of his lips on hers. "I've never been able to fall sleep with any woman before. I never could relax enough to doze off."

Francie stretched.

"I'm relaxed now. I feel boneless. Like a cat in front of a fireplace. But I sure wasn't relaxed last night. What did you do to me?"

His pulse quickened.

"What did I do to you? It's more like what did *you* do to *me*? I'm still hard. Or hard again."

"I want you, but I'm afraid I'm too sore."

She gazed at him, and he could see the longing in her eyes.

"Just lay still," he whispered. "I'll take care of you."

He kissed the corners of her lips, her jaw line, her throat. Gently suckled first one breast then the other. Kissed his way past her waist, down her belly. The scent of her nectar grew stronger as he neared the flower that had given him so much pleasure during the night. He slid his hands beneath her buttocks and raised her to his lips. He kissed her swollen petals, then dipped his tongue inside and lost himself in her tart muskiness. He licked her tenderly and soothed her. When she bucked wildly beneath him, he kissed his way up to her lips. He paused before touching his lips to hers, wondering if she'd be disgusted by the taste of herself on him, but she pulled his face down to hers and kissed him deeply.

He slipped inside of her body and held himself above her, wanting to see her desire change to fulfillment when she came. His own orgasm gripped him with such strength, he couldn't see anything but a diffused brightness through his eyelids, but afterward, she smiled up at him with the sleepy look of a woman who'd been well filled.

I wish we could stay like this forever," she murmured. "You in me. Right now, nothing else matters. Not the re-creation. Not the uncertainty of our future. Just this—you and me together."

He brushed a strand of damp hair away from her face. "Before I got lost in making love to you, I thought about everything that happened to bring us to this moment. It almost seems as if Bob recreated the world simply so we could meet."

She caught his hand. "Would we have met in the real world?"

"Perhaps. I did see you once right after the deletions began. You were running down the street as if the world were coming to an end. Oh, wait! It did come to an end."

"Yet here we are—beginning."

He traced her lips with his right forefinger, marveling at their perfect form.

"We're part of the re-creation. We can recreate ourselves any way we wish."

"Just you and me and—oh, my God!"

She pushed him, and he rolled off her.

He picked himself up.

"What happened?"

"The others. They'll be waking up soon. What if they saw us?"

He helped her to her feet. "Is that a problem, their knowing we're a couple?"

"No, but…what if they think I'm…"

She didn't finish the thought, but he understood what she didn't want to put into words. If the other men saw her with him, they'd take her—by force, if necessary. She'd been safe as long as she'd played den mother, but now his love had put her in jeopardy.

"I'm sorry," he said, his voice breaking. "I shouldn't have—"

She put two fingers on his lips to seal them, "I wanted you. I still do. We just have to be circumspect."

She picked up her discarded dress and handed him his loincloth. He couldn't remember when they'd shed their clothes—their coming together had been graceful and without a single moment of fumbling or awkwardness.

He wanted nothing more that to keep her close, but to ensure her safety, he'd have to stay as far from her as possible. He stepped away from her, and the look of pain that contorted her face told him she felt the wrench as much as he did.

She pivoted slowly.

"Where's the cabin?"

He pointed to a patch of bushes.

"I thought it was over there."

She took off running in the opposite direction. He loped after her, following her to the top of a rocky knoll that gave them a panoramic view of the area. Scrubland stretched as far as he could see.

"There!" Francie pointed to the only thing big enough to be the cabin

Chet shaded his eyes and peered at the mass, trying to get a better look, and saw that it was only a rock formation.

No cabin.

"We should look for them," Francie said. "Maybe they're wandering around here some place. Maybe they're lost."

Chet could tell she didn't believe her words, but the truth—that only the two of them remained in their world—did not bear thinking about. Last night it had been a romantic conceit that they only needed each other. And now here they stood. Alone.

Francie's dry eyes looked hard and implacable.

"We killed them."

"We didn't kill them. They killed themselves because they couldn't handle the responsibility of being free."

"We should have known it was a trap."

"I told them it was a trap." Chet said softly. "They didn't want to listen. You're the only one who believed me."

"You should have made them believe you."

She raised her fists as if to pummel him, but instead dropped her hands to her side.

"How was I supposed to do that?" He tried to keep his voice

mild, but all the frustrations of the past months made his tone steely. "From the moment we embarked on this journey—no, from the moment I entered the enclosure—they designated me the scapegoat. Everything they couldn't face about their lives and themselves, they heaped on me."

Francie glowered at him.

"I know, but still, you could have stopped them."

"You know as well as I do that once group roles have been assigned, it's impossible to break out of them. As long as the group existed, no matter what I did, I'd be the scapegoat."

"You let them define you?"

"You defined me, too. Remember? At the oasis? And anyway, my role didn't define me. I accepted it. Every group needs a scapegoat. If it weren't me, it could have been anyone. Like you. Or Barney. Someone not able to handle it as well."

She put her hands on her hips. She looked like a warrior standing against the stark setting, her hair turned to flame by the sun.

"Are you calling me weak?"

"Never. It's just that you have a tender heart."

Her rigid stance softened.

"So what was my group role?"

"You were our heart. Our den mother. You tended to everyone's needs. You never got angry. You kept us on track, reminding us of our goal to find a new home. You kept us human."

She tilted her head and studied him, as if trying to find the truth in his eyes.

"Is that really how you see me?"

"It's how you are."

She shook her head.

"I'm not at all like that. I got resentful at times because I didn't think I was highly valued, and I was jealous of those who were valued. I'm as competitive as some of the others, but I felt I needed to hide my aggressiveness so I didn't cause more problems. And I got angry a lot, but I hid that, too."

"Those feelings don't take away the truth of you." Chet smiled at her. "I wish you could see yourself the way I do. You'd never again think you weren't highly valued."

"You're not just saying that?"

"I mean it. If I had my preference of any person in the entire world to be with right now, I'd choose you."

Francie laughed.

"Good choice since besides you, I *am* the only person in the entire world."

# **Chapter 25**

THEY STOOD IN the middle of the scrubland where the cabin had been, weary from their futile search.

"We can't stay here," Chet said.

Although Chet had known they wouldn't find any sign of the others—not a footprint, a candy wrapper, a crumb of food—he'd gone along with Francie's insistence they comb the area, but now there was no place left to look.

"We have to stay." Francie planted her hands on her hips. "What if they come back?"

"They won't."

"You don't know that."

"Has Bob brought anyone back?" Chet asked softly.

Francie stared at him for a moment, a hint of her old dislike in her eyes, then she dropped her chin to her chest, and shook her head.

Chet held out a hand to comfort her, but drew it back.

"I'm sorry."

Francie must have seen the gesture out of the corner of her eyes, because she caught his hand and held it tightly.

"Where are we going to go?"

"We'll find a place." He tried to sound reassuring, though he had no expectations of finding a location with water, food, and shelter. Even if they did find such a place, chances were Bob would recreate it again, though at some point, shouldn't the re-creation be finished? God had left the earth to its own devices for eons. Surely, he'd get bored with his plaything and focus his attention elsewhere? Unless...no, even a landlord God wouldn't be so cruel as to make the re-creation a permanent fixture. The world had always been in a state of flux, but the changes had happened so slowly, they'd only been discernible in retrospect.

Chet put the thoughts out of his mind. There was no way he could fathom the workings of God, even an area supervisor God. And he certainly could not fathom the workings of Bob, the right hand of the area supervisor God.

*Why had Bob kept those people alive all this time only to delete them in the end?*

But it wasn't the end, and wouldn't be the end as long as someone survived to witness the re-creation. If there is no one around to experience the recreated world, does it mean the re-creation never happened? But there'd always be someone—or something—to experience it.

*I'm going nuts.*

He put the useless thoughts out of his head and concentrated on the realities. For all practical purposes, he and Francie were alone in the world, and they'd have to find their own way. No fantastic city of gold would pop up on the horizon to afford them protection.

"Can't we stay another night?" Francie asked, brown eyes magnified by unshed tears. "I don't want to leave."

"Another night shouldn't hurt," Chet said, grateful for an excuse not to have to leave right away.

By leaving, he would be admitting they were alone, and though their being alone was a romantic notion, it was a hard truth to deal with.

The next morning, though, safe in Francie's arms, the thought of leaving didn't seem so terrifying. They wouldn't be alone; they would be together.

"We really can't stay here," Chet said.

"I know." Francie snuggled closer. Then suddenly, she popped into a sitting position. "No. I don't know. Why can't we stay here?"

"Bob brought us to this place."

Francie looked around the empty land and held out her palms. "So? Maybe that means we should stay."

"I don't want to do something just because Bob wants me to do it." Hearing a harshness in his tone, Chet softened his voice. "I don't think Bob has our best interests at heart."

"But this looks as good a place as any we've seen." She gave a short, unamused laugh. "And better than some."

"For now. But it's almost too cold at night already. If we didn't have each other for warmth..." Chet felt himself blushing. He'd lost track of how many times they had warmed each other, and he still wasn't used to their wanton ways. "And," he added, lowering his voice even further, "I don't want the constant reminder of this final deletion. We'll always be wondering if we're next."

She lay down with her head on his chest. "I wish..."

"Me too."

Chet rubbed her back with slow circular movements, feeling as if he wanted to cry. He wished the world was back the way it had been. With all of its problems, humans had muddled along for tens of thousands of years. He wished he could keep Francie safe, and he feared he wouldn't be able to. He wished they could find a place where they could make a life for themselves, but he feared such a place would always elude them. He wished...

Suddenly Francie laughed, dispelling the sense of shared melancholy.

"I wish I'd kept that chocolate. Sure would taste good round about now."

Chet inhaled the lemony scent still lingering in the air and refused to think of the lemon drops he'd left in the log cabin.

"We'll be fine," he said. "I promise to take care of you."

She lifted her head and smiled down at him.

"And I promise to take care of you."


The first step away from the area where the others had been deleted was the hardest, but hours later, even when a backward glance showed that the place had receded from view, Chet still felt the tug.

*Could Bob and his mysterious training be pulling at him, or could it simply be they were moving away from the last of their own kind?*

They walked in a silence that seemed both companionable and melancholic, and Chet surmised that Francie also felt, if not a pull to the place, then the wrench of leaving. That night, Chet and Francie grabbed each other and didn't let go. Their wild couplings alternated with gentle cuddles, and though they didn't sleep much, it didn't matter—they desperately needed the comfort of being together in the vast and lonely world.

As the days—and nights—passed, the silence gradually became filled with talk of the journey, such as which way to go, when to stop to eat the nuts and seeds they'd gathered, how to find water, and where to spend the nights. They even talked a bit of their previous lives, though mostly, it was Francie asking questions and Chet answering.

They'd stopped to soak their aching feet in a brook, and after talking about his pet shop and his dream of a refuge for abandoned animals, Chet asked, "Where were you when it happened?"

Francie laughed.

"Are we going to start doing the where-were-you like we did when we were inside?"

"*Inside.*" Chet shivered melodramatically, to cover up a very real tremor of distaste. "Makes it sound like a prison."

Francie cocked her head and stared into the middle distance with blank eyes.

"It was, though, wasn't it? Much more than a refuge."

Chet nodded.

"Very much of a prison except that we were able to walk out."

"Not all of us." She fluttered her feet in the water. "I wonder how Trip is doing? He was the one who talked us all into escaping."

"That was Trip?"

For no reason Chet could fathom, his question made Francie go rigid.

She spoke in a voice as stiff as her posture.

"Why is that a surprise? Who did you think instigated it?"

"Bob."

"Couldn't have been Bob."

He spoke simply, striving to sound non-confrontational.

"Why not?"

Francie glared at him, then her expression changed, and she let out a sudden lighthearted laugh.

"Are we having our first argument?"

Chet didn't laugh with her.

"Not an argument. I really want to know what you think."

"What I think?" Francie looked at him as if she were a teacher facing a not-so-bright student who had made a surprising remark. "There's no real reason why I think it couldn't have been Bob who instigated the escape except that he wasn't there. Why do you think it could have been him?"

"Just a feeling I had when I saw all of you planning the escape." Chet felt tension rising at the memory, and he forced himself to relax. "I mean, I didn't really know very many people in the refuge, but every one of the people I knew was in on the escape. It seemed...too coincidental."

She leaned back on her hands.

"But why would Bob have wanted us to escape?"

Chet shrugged, not wanting to talk about or even think about Bob training him.

"Could Trip have been some sort of agent provocateur?" Francie asked. "Or a...*spy*?"

"It's possible. We have no way of knowing if the humans in that place were truly human." Chet slanted a glance a Francie. "Wait a minute. You don't care about this. You're just trying to keep from having to answer my question about where you were when it happened."

Francie scowled at him.

"What's the big deal? I never noticed you having much interest in the where-were-you when we were inside."

Chet laid a gentle touch on her knee.

218

"But I am interested in you."

"Oh." Again that assessing look as if he'd taken her by surprise. "I never told anyone. It was too personal. And made me seem pathetic."

"I can't imagine you ever being pathetic." Seeing a wrinkle form between her brows, he added quickly, "You don't have to tell me. I don't mean to pry."

"No, it's okay. It's kind of a long story, though."

Chet spread out his hands. "I've got nothing better to do."

Francie's lips twitched.

"Me neither." A long pause. "I'm sure you've heard the story a dozen times. Young nurse falls in love with a doctor she works for. The doctor wines and dines her, focuses his attention on her and makes her feel so special she quits her job and moves into his luxury condo to be with him. Suddenly he has no more time for her. Gets angry when she says she wants to spend time together. Gets even angrier when she wants to go back to work. Then he becomes…not abusive exactly, but very cold. The sex turns violent. But the stupid girl is still in love with him. Can't figure out what she did to make him turn on her, so she tries even harder to be whatever he wants, and ends up reclusive and feeling dreadfully dull and unloved."

Chet wanted to wrap her in his arms, but he wasn't sure she would welcome his embrace right then, so he gripped his thighs until his fingers ached and waited for her to continue.

"Then I got pregnant." She cradled her belly and swayed as if she were rocking the baby. "I was so happy. I told myself he'd be glad when he got used to the idea, but he was so unpredictable, I was afraid to tell him. He figured it out when I was about two months along, and he…" Her eyes grew glassy with tears and her lower lip trembled. "He told me I had to get an abortion, and when I refused, he tried to beat the baby out of me. I bled, but I never ejected the fetus. When the bruises healed, I went to my obstetrician for an ultrasound. I saw her—a perfect little girl. She seemed so happy and serene floating inside me, and I worried what her life would be like. Then, as we watched, the technician and I, my baby faded and disappeared. The technician thought it was the machinery, and had someone bring in a portable machine. But we got the same results. No baby."

Her breathing grew ragged.

"It was just too much. The loss of a chance to love and be loved, the beating, the baby disappearing. So I ran. I was wearing a suit and heels, but I didn't care. I just ran and ran. As I ran, it felt as if the whole world were falling apart. It wasn't until I was almost at our high rise near Cheesman Park that I realized I wasn't having some sort of breakdown, but that the whole world really was falling apart."

Chet nodded, and she took that very moment to turn her head toward him. She glowered.

"What?"

"I saw you on Easter. It didn't dawn on me you lived close to the park, though it should have. You came back so quickly with your bags.

Her shoulders slumped.

"Lot of good that did me. I thought I was being so smart."

"You were smart. Are smart. None of the rest of us thought to bring anything." Chet flexed his aching fingers. "What happened to your boyfriend?"

She smiled, a not very nice smile.

"I don't know. I never saw him again. I think about that poor baby sometimes. What did I do that was so terrible Bob took my unborn girl from me?"

"I don't think it had anything to do with you," Chet said. "It was probably something she was going to do."

Francie scooted away from him.

"How can you say that? She was an innocent baby."

Chet drew his water-wrinkled feet out of the brook, and folded them beneath him.

"According to Bob, the past, present, and future all exist at once, so even though the girl wasn't born yet, she had already had done whatever she had done to get deleted."

She picked up a rock and flung it into the water.

"Bob. Always Bob."

"I'm sorry you lost your baby," Chet said quietly. "But you didn't lose your chance to be loved."

She looked at him with a hint of reproof.

"What are you talking about?"

"I love you," he said.

Tears sprang to her eyes.

"You don't have to say it."

He leaned over and brushed a soft kiss on her lips.

"But I mean it. I love you."

"And I...and I love you."

Wonder tinged her voice as if she had just that moment realized the truth.

Clutching each other, they rose and, hand in hand, moved away from the brook. They lay in a field of wildflowers and made love until they fell asleep.

The sound of Francie's voice woke him.

"Chet. Chet. Look!"

Eyes still closed, he reached for her, but felt only the ground where she had lain. He opened his eyes to find her standing, out held arms forming a bow, turning from side to side like a radar detector.

"What?" he said.

And then he saw. The ground was covered with twinkling stars and the blossoms that used to be in the field were strewn across the heavens.

"Isn't this fabulous?" A frown replaced the look of wonder on her face. "But I don't feel the creative bubble."

"Creative bubble?"

He felt a stirring between his legs, but he didn't think that was the sort of creativity she meant.

"When a pocket of reconstruction was going on before I went into the enclosure, I could feel the energy the recreators were using." She moved to a different spot and continued her swaying. "But I can't feel any energy."

Chet tried to remember what it felt like when the city turned into an ocean and the volcano erupted into being and the river cracked open the earth. He thought he recalled a sensation like the electricity before a storm, but he also thought he might be reacting to the power of suggestion.

He sat up and watched her naked body moving in the starlight.

"If there isn't any energy, maybe this isn't part of the re-creation."

"Then what is it?"

She stopped gyrating, and put her hands on her hips. He felt his heart leap into his throat. The loveliness of the stars on the ground and the flowers in the sky paled beside her beauty.

He plucked a star from the ground and held up a yellow violet. "An illusion."

Francie plopped down beside him.

"Well, that's disappointing."

He smiled at her.

"Stars on the ground and flowers in the sky are disappointing?" She peered into his face.

"Are you laughing at me?"

"No. Not laughing." He gave her what he hoped was an earnest look. "I love the way you look at things is all."

"Oh." She picked a star and shook her head at the primrose between her fingers. "An illusion. Sheesh."

"Maybe it's all an illusion. Or some sort of dream."

He reached up and tried to pull a flower from the sky, but all he grabbed was air. She tucked the primrose behind her ear.

"Are you saying we're going to wake up from this?"

He gently tucked the violet behind her ear next to the primrose and was rewarded first with a smile and then a cocked eyebrow as if to say she knew he was stalling.

"I don't think it's that kind of dream," he said finally. "But maybe what we call reality is as malleable as a dream. Or maybe reality is what we're trained to think it is.

She nodded slowly.

"You might be right. How else could an area supervisor God

recreate the world that the real God created in the first place? If we think the world back to the way it was, will everything return to normal?"

"No." He took her hand in his. "And even if we could, I'm not sure I would, because then I'd lose you."

Tears came to her eyes.

"I think you mean that."

"I do." He kissed the back of her hand. "I told you. I love you."

"But why all of this?" She swept her free hand out to indicate the flowers and the stars. "If it's all an illusion anyway, why create an illusion in the illusion?"

He gently settled her hand on her knee and leaned back on his elbows.

"Why? To mess with us. That seems to be Bob's specialty. He's not a nice person or being or entity or whatever he is."

"I'm going to phrase this delicately," she said. "You're not freaking nuts, are you?"

He laughed.

"That's delicate? But no, not nuts." He considered telling her about Bob playing with his senses, about the conversation concerning his training, even about his bizarre thought that the tangerine cat was the God Bob was the Right Hand of, but then she truly would think he was nuts. "No, not nuts," he repeated to reassure himself as well as her.

"Look," she exclaimed.

The sky lightened and the sun rose with unseemly rapidity. The flowers fell from the sky, the stars faded from underfoot, and a new day began.

Despite Chet's claim that the flowers and stars changing position was merely an illusion, he couldn't help feeling lighthearted as he and Francie continued their trek.

*After all, wasn't this why he'd left the enclosure—not just to try to recreate himself and his life, but to experience this second creation in all it's glory?*

And glory there was.

The butterflies flitting from wildflower to wildflower, the red fox daintily picking its way across their path, the angular birds riding air currents high above, the balmy air smelling of rich loam and all the rest of the small miracles might have been leftovers from the original creation or newly formed for the new creation, but they were lovely either way. Chet kept sneaking peeks at Francie whenever he saw something special, and always she returned his glance, telling him she shared his joy.

And so, time passed. Weeks, maybe months.

One morning, they woke to clear skies and the sound of thunder. As the thunder grew closer, the ground trembled.

"Earthquake?" Francie asked.

"I don't know."

Chet clambered to his feet and trotted to a small rise. In the distance undulated a brown, fog-banked river, maybe five miles wide and endlessly long. His jaw dropped when he realized that it wasn't a river he was seeing but a galloping herd of bison kicking up dust. Once, millions of the creatures had roamed the plains of America; all had been slaughtered except for a tiny herd in Yellowstone National Park. And now here bison were, back where they belonged.

"Buffalo." Francie said, her voice tinged with awe. "There's so many."

They watched for more than an hour as the herd galloped past, leaving behind a vast swathe of churned soil.

When the last straggler moved out of sight, Francie blew out a breath.

"That was awesome."

Chet put a hand to his chest over his rapidly beating heart.

"Seeing those bison was almost worth the price of admission."

Francie bristled.

"How can you say that? Billions of people are gone, cities deleted, civilizations destroyed, for what? A herd of buffalo?"

"Don't you love the irony?" Chet said. "Humans destroyed more than sixty million bison in a mere twenty-five years. Now humans are gone, and the bison are back."

Francie looked at him as if she'd never seen him before.

"Would you really exchange all those people for *buffalo?*"

"Not buffalo. Bison." Realizing how sharply he had spoken, Chet softened his tone. "And maybe I would. Humans don't own the earth. Other creatures have as much right to be here as we do. And anyway, it wasn't my choice. I didn't have anything to do with the deletions or creations or reconstructions. I'm like you. Trying to make the best of a bizarre situation."

Francie's tenseness dissipated, but she still looked at him as if she didn't recognize him.

"I'm sorry," Chet said. "I shouldn't have corrected you."

"What? Oh. That's okay. I didn't know there was a difference. I just..."

Chet waited, but she didn't finish her sentence.

When the silence dragged on too long, he asked, "Are you ready to go?"

She turned to him.

"Go? Go where?"

He gestured toward the south, but before he could get a word out of his mouth, she held up a finger to stop him.

"And then what? Keep going?" A tear gathered at the corner of one eye, and she scrubbed it away with a fist. "There is no city, is there?"

"There might be."

Chet wanted to comfort her, but when he raised his arms to hug her, she backed away and jutted out her chin.

"Where?"

"I don't know." Chet kept his hands dangling helplessly by his side. "I got the impression from Bob there was a city, but not the city of gold the others were looking for."

Again, she gave him that same considering stare as if he were a stranger.

"Why do you keep looking at me like that?" he asked. "What did I do?"

A brief smile hitched up one side of her mouth.

"It's what we both did." She stepped closer and peered into his eyes. "I keep trying to see the father in there."

"Father?" His knees buckled. "Are you saying...?"

She stood, unflinching, though the hesitation in her voice told him she expected censure.

"We're going to have a baby."

"How?"

She let out a little laugh.

"The usual way."

He took her in his arms, and this time she let him hold her. They clung together for a long time. Finally, he let her go.

"You're going to be a wonderful mother."

She held his hand tightly.

"What are we going to do?"

"What we need to." He smiled, a wobbly little thing. "Whatever that is."

"I figure I'm three months along. We can keep going for a while, maybe even for a few more months, but then..."

"I always intended to find somewhere to settle down. A place that's not too hot in the day, not too cold at night, and plenty of food for the taking."

She shivered.

"Sounds like the refuge we escaped from."

"I've been looking for an Eden," Chet said, "but maybe the refuge was Eden."

She laughed.

"At least we didn't have to deal with snakes offering us apples."

"Actually, there was a snake, a peppermint snake," Chet said. "If that place was anything like the original Eden, I can see why Adam and Eve left."

"Adam," Francie said with a sharp nod. "That's what we'll name him."

"Him?"

Francie swatted his arm.

"The baby, silly."

"I knew that. But what if it's a girl?"

She cradled her belly, and a secret smile appeared on her face, making her look luminous.

"It won't be."

"Do you want me to…" Chet swallowed hard. "…to try to contact Bob and ask about the city? Or a town? Or anywhere there might be people?"

She looked up eagerly.

"Do you think he'd respond?"

"Maybe. In some way." He winced. "But whatever, we can't trust him."

"Please?" She gently rubbed her belly in a circular motion. "For the baby?"

He opened his mouth to remind her of what had happened to her last baby, then pressed his lips together without saying anything and patted his pouch, hoping a phone had miraculously appeared, but all he felt were the nuts and wizened pears left from his last foraging efforts.

He strode a several yards from Francie, not wanting to yell in her ears, and shouted, "Bob! Bob, can you hear me? It's Chet. I'd like to talk to you."

He listened for a response. The world was utterly quiet. Not even the chirp of a cricket or the buzz of an insect or the call of a bird disturbed the perfect silence.

"Bob!" he yelled again, and when the faint echo of the word died out, he could hear a crackling from the ground beneath his feet.

Seemingly all at once in a single chaotic moment, the earth rose and fell like a storm-tossed sea, Chet flew into the air screaming Francie's name, and the world ended in pain and darkness.

# Chapter 26

BRIGHT WHITE LIGHT at the end of a tunnel. No, not a tunnel. A cave. Flickers of orange light playing on the dark walls. Fire?

*Where am I?*

Chet raised a hand and gingerly touched his aching head. A bump.

*What happened?*

He heaved himself to one knee, rested a moment, then struggled to his feet. He stood swaying, and wondered if he was off balance or if the earth was tilting. After a minute or two, the swaying stopped, and he staggered past the fire and out of the cave.

Nothing looked familiar except Francie, facing a stand of trees and posing like an archer, one hand out, one at her cheek. She looked fierce, fabulous, totally free. And focused. After a couple of seconds, something whizzed from her raised hand, and he realized she had let loose a rock from a slingshot. From the woods came the tiny thud of the rock hitting its target, and a big grin appeared on Francie's face. She ran into the trees and came out holding a limp rabbit by the ears.

"What's going on?" Chet asked.

Francie stopped short, as if hitting a wall.

"Me and Adam were craving meat." She held up the slingshot, and her cheeks turned pink. "You mean this? The night after Grady died, I snuck back and got his flint and slingshot. I didn't tell anyone because I didn't want to start a fight. And after they were gone, I didn't know how to tell you."

"Oh." Chet swayed. "That's not what I meant."

Francie peered at him.

"Are you okay?"

"No." He held out his arms out to the side to try to stop the earth from tilting. "Where are we? How did we get here?"

Francie dropped the rabbit.

"Don't you remember?"

"I remember the buffalo, and then...darkness."

She ran to him and studied his eyes.

"Your pupils are even, so that's a good sign. What do you see in your peripheral vision?"

"It's distorted. The light seems strange."

"You better go back inside and lie down. I think you have a concussion."

She took his arm and tried to steer him into the cave.

He shook her off.

"Please? How did we come here?"

She laughed.

"We didn't come here. 'Here' came to us." She must have caught his confusion, because she added, "After you called out for Bob, the ground...lifted. And folded. What was a plain seems to have become some sort of mountain top. You don't remember any of this?"

Chet shook his head, and when he felt his brain jostling, he wished he hadn't.

Francie gave him a concerned look, but kept her distance.

"You got caught in a swell and were thrown into the air and came down hard. You seemed to be okay, even found this cave to protect us from the boulders that were flying around. When things settled down, you went to sleep."

"How long did I sleep?"

His voice sounded harsh to his ears, but she didn't seem to notice his tone.

"Just the night." She put her arms around herself and shivered theatrically. "It got so cold, I had to start a fire to keep us from freezing."

Chet looked around, trying to compare the trees and terrain, the plants and boulders with what he remembered of the place, and it still seemed familiar.

"A concussion can cause amnesia?"

Francie nodded.

"But the amnesia is specific, centered around the cause of the concussion. I wish we could get your brain scanned to make sure there isn't any bleeding or cracks, but..."

He felt a frisson of fear, but tamped it down.

*Best not to think of all that could be wrong, all that could go wrong.*

"So now what?"

"You rest. Take it easy. You could feel the effects, like a headache and disorientation, for a month. Maybe longer."

Chet put his hands to either side of his head as if that would clear the fog from his brain.

"What about you?"

"Me?" She laughed. "Me and Adam are fine. The place I was standing rose as gently as a cloud. I think the kid liked it. I was feeling sick to my stomach before it happened, and now the nausea is gone."

He wobbled, and this time when she came to him, he leaned on her as she led him into the cave.

"What now?" he asked, huddled near the fire.

She put her hands on her hips, her face radiant in the flickering light.

"We live. You're not going anywhere for a while, and I don't want to take a chance on something happening to Adam if we were to experience another upheaval like this one. We're safe here." She laughed again. "As long as you don't try to get Bob's attention again."

Chet marveled at how happy she seemed. He hadn't heard her laugh so lightheartedly in all the time he'd known her. Maybe this place would be good for her. And for Adam. And for him.

"Believe me," he said drowsily, "the last thing I want is any more of Bob's interference.

The cold nights reminded them that winter would be particularly hard without any of the accoutrements of civilization to protect them from the elements, so Chet spend his time near the cave, gathering nuts and fruits, roots and mushrooms, even some shoots and leaves. A couple of times when he tasted something he thought might be good to eat, he got sick, but he always pretended the nausea was a side effect of the concussion. He didn't want Francie to worry about his experimentation, but he knew no other way of testing what foods were edible than to eat a small bit.

Francie continued to bloom, both in her pregnancy and in the enjoyment of her days. She took to hunting as if she'd been born for this life, and when she wasn't hunting, she was drying the meat. She was always respectful of his views on eating meat, but she claimed meat of any kind was the only thing Adam wanted her to eat.

The nights, spent in each others arms, were warm and cozy when they weren't hot and frantic for each other.

And so time passed. After Adam was born in the forest glade pool, a miraculously easy process, or so Francie claimed though Chet thought it unbearably long, they donated their scant garments for the child's well-being. The loin cloth became a swaddling cloth, and the dress became a sling so Francie could keep Adam with her wherever she went.

"There's only one thing that would make this place perfect," Francie said one lovely spring day when all three were out enjoying the warming rays of the sun.

"Clothes?" Chet said idly, his attention on Adam, watching to make sure the naked toddler didn't get too close to the light-splashed pond.

"No."

He shot a glance at Francie.

"Really? You don't mind not having clothes? Me neither. I admit clothes would be practical, at least in winter, but it would be a shame not to be able to enjoy your beauty whenever I wish."

She giggled.

"Beauty? This?" She cradled her swelling belly, the dark

striations from her first pregnancy still apparent.

Chet stroked his beard and nodded.

"That. And the rest of you."

"I'd miss seeing you, too," she said, with a leer that promised a wonderful time later that night.

"Then what would you want to make this perfect? Blankets? Toilet paper? Leaves get a bit rough."

She laughed.

"Both of those would be nice, but I would really like a pot. Something we could use to boil water for tea or make stew or...oh, so many things."

He answered her laugh with a chuckle of his own.

"I'll keep my eyes open in case one is lying around somewhere." Then, in a more serious tone, he added, "There's a spot not far from here where the soil seemed to be mostly clay. I wonder if we could get the fire hot enough to make some sort of pottery."

"That would be wonderful." She slipped a hand into his. Together, they watched Adam toddling after butterflies. "But truly, even without a pot, is anything more perfect than this?"

Looking at the two of them, his child and his woman, he had to agree. All his dreams, even the dream of the animal refuge seemed to pale in light of this reality, and all the hardships of his life seemed scant payment for this moment.

A faint whirring sound brought his attention back to the present. He shot to his feet.

"Do you hear that?"

"No. Yes!" Francie yanked the slingshot from around her neck. "What is it?"

He scooped up Adam and held the child close.

"I don't know, but I'm afraid..."

"Me, too," Francie whispered, stepping close to Chet and Adam. "That's not a natural sound."

Chet caught a glint of silver above the trees, and a saucer-shaped vehicle appeared overhead, blocking out the sun.

Various creatures, among them a sheeple, a peppermint snake, and the grinning orange cat peered down at them through the oval windows.

With a sinking feeling in his stomach, Chet gathered his small family close and tried to protect them as best as he could, but nothing could protect them from the words Bob spoke.

"Of all the domesticated Earth creatures," Bob intoned, "humans were the most difficult to reintroduce into the wild, but we finally succeeded. If you look down and to the right, you will see a typical family unit. One day we hope to have a whole herd of humans running free."